BEDLAM AT THE BRICKYARD

15 Stories of Bedlam, Bafflement and Bewilderment at the Brickyard 400

Speed City Indiana Sisters in Crime

Brenda Robertson Stewart

Edited by:
Brenda Robertson Stewart and Wanda Lou Willis

Wanda Lou Willis

Fact Insert Sheets Edited by: M. B. Dabney
Compiled by: Mark Zacharias

Blue River Press
Indianapolis

Cover designed by Phil Velikan
Proofread by Dorothy Chambers
Packaged by Wish Publishing

Printed in the United States of America
10 9 8 7 6 5 4 3 2 1

Distributed in the United States by
Cardinal Publishers Group
www.cardinalpub.com

"The mission of Sisters in Crime is to promote the professional development and advancement of women crime writers to achieve equality in the industry."

Bedlam at the Brickyard is a collection of 16 short stories revolving around the Brickyard 400 at the Indianapolis Motor Speedway. All the stories are written by members of the Speed City Indiana Chapter of Sisters in Crime.

ACKNOWLEDGEMENTS

The editors would like to thank the members of the Speed City Indiana Chapter of Sisters in Crime for their support in the planning and development of this project. In particular, we would like to thank the editors, Brenda Robertson Stewart and Wanda Lou Willis; Michael Dabney for collecting and editing the fact insert sheets; Mark Zacharias for the big job of compiling the book; the authors who contributed fact sheets used between the fiction stories; James Alexander Thom for his generosity in writing the foreword; and Adriane and Tom Doherty from Cardinal Publishers Group for their support. Most of all, we would like to thank the authors for their stories involving bedlam, bedevilment and battery for the sake of justice.

TABLE OF CONTENTS

FOREWORD
by James Alexander Thom

To a storyteller, a racing event is like a battle: a huge, noisy gathering of people for an event that is dramatic in itself, but is also a spectacular backdrop against which any of thousands of individual stories can be played out. Like a battle, the race is a contest whose outcome will be important to all individuals involved. Like a battle, the race is too big to be seen in its entirety by any individual within it. What anyone sees of it will be a small section of the panorama, limited by the senses of the individual and colored by the individual's self-interest.

In this collection of stories, the self-interest of many of the individuals is crime. An advantage of committing a crime at a racing event is the possibility of getting away with it in the greater confusion, while the authorities and the witnesses are distracted.

The writers in this book have explored that possibility in many ingenious ways. Their culprits and heroes are colorful and complex. Some are connected with racing, some are mere spectators. Some stories confirm the adage that "revenge is a dish best served cold." Some of the stories are built on the simmering antipathies of stock-car versus open-wheel racing fans. Some plots deal with sabotage in the garage, some with ancient grudges going back to the shine-running days in Appalachia. Other stories are as up to date as women race-driving champs. Several of the stories evoke old racing traditions and superstitions.

This compilation of wistful and diabolical short stories proves that women not only challenge men as race drivers today, but as auto racing storytellers, too. They really know their way around the oval and across the keyboard.

9

WINNERS OF THE BRICKYARD 400
by Michael Dabney

The first Brickyard 400 was held on August 6, 1994, to a capacity crowd. The Speedway never releases crowd figures but estimates put the crowd at between 250,000 to 300,000 people. Since the Speedway reportedly has the greatest seating capacity of any race track in the world, it was the largest crowd ever to witness a NASCAR race.

Rick Mast won the pole position, but it was the local crowd's favorite, Jeff Gordon, who won the race. Pittsboro, a small town 15 miles west of Speedway where Gordon spent some of his youth, claims Gordon as a hometown hero.

Gordon was in his sophomore year in NASCAR competition in 1994, and he took the lead late in the race when Ernie Irvan suffered a flat tire. Gordon's average winning speed was 131.932 miles per hour and he won $613,000 for the victory. He also was – and remains – the youngest winner of the race at 23 years, nine months and 27 days.

Past winners and winners' purses (through 2008) are:
- 1994, Jeff Gordon, $613,000
- 1995, Dale Earnhardt, Sr., $565,600
- 1996, Dale Jarrett, $564,035
- 1997, Ricky Rudd, $571,000
- 1998, Jeff Gordon, $1,637,625*
- 1999, Dale Jarrett, $712,240
- 2000, Bobby Labonte, $831,225
- 2001, Jeff Gordon, $428,452
- 2002, Bill Elliott, $449,056
- 2003, Kevin Harvick, $418,253
- 2004, Jeff Gordon, $518,053
- 2005, Tony Stewart, $554,661
- 2006, Jimmie Johnson, $452,861

- 2007, Tony Stewart, $463,111**
- 2008, Jimmie Johnson, $509,236
- 2009, Jimmie Johnson, $448,001

Four drivers have won the race more than once and account for 10 out of 15 races held. Jeff Gordon has won four times, the most of any driver (1994, 1998, 2001, 2004), while Dale Jarrett (1996 and 1999) and Tony Stewart (2005 and 2007) have won twice. Jimmie Johnson (2006, 2008, 2009) has won three times.

---

* *Includes Winston No Bull bonus of $1 million which Gordon was eligible to win.*
** *Includes $25,000 subtracted from Stewart's purse for the use of an obscenity on ESPN during a post-race interview.*

THE BALLAD OF THE MIDNIGHT TRAVELER
by S. M. Harding

S. M. Harding has published short crime fiction in Detective Mystery Stories, Great Mystery and Suspense *magazine,* Crime and Suspense *magazine, and* Mysterical-E, *and the anthologies* Racing Can Be Murder, Medium of Murder, *and* Dying In a Winter Wonderland. *She has completed,* The Shadow of Truth, *the first in a series of Sam Wolfe mysteries. Sam appears in "Whatever Happened to Marilyn?" in the September/October 2008 issue of* Crime and Suspense.

"Hey, Dad, I ran into Billy Fowler today," Sheriff Sarah Barrow Pitt said, walking into the kitchen.

"Hope you didn't hurt the old fool," Micah said, looking up from the newspaper.

"I think he's trying to mend bridges," she said with a sigh. "He's got a couple of tickets to the Brickyard 400, wants to know if you want them."

Micah folded up his paper, took off his glasses and stared at Sarah.

"For free."

"Why in the good Lord's name would I want tickets to go watch a passel of pretty boys with three-day beards chase each other round an oval that was built for open-wheel racing?" He tucked the glasses in his shirt pocket, crossed his arms. "Them 'stock cars' they got now, nothin' but gussied-up tarts. Cost a king's ransom and need a whole crew to keep 'em runnin'. Not like the old days."

Sarah took off her duty belt, hung it on the peg by the door with her cap atop it. She sat across from her father, tried to figure out if Micah was ticked at Billy Fowler, the Indianapolis Speedway, or NASCAR. "What old days?"

"Don't you get sassy." He leaned back in the chair, looked out the window. "When I was a kid, county fair used to feature stock car races. Beat up old jalopies, mostly Ford and Chevy coupes, sliced and diced and souped up. Used the horse track. Good ole boys driving, doing the circuit, one mechanic with 'em. Smell of candy corn and spun sugar cones, hogs and sawdust. Crowds rootin' for local guys."

"Sounds like NASCAR to me. Except for the hogs."

Micah snorted. "And then, there was the story my daddy told 'bout the Fogarty brothers and the Midnight Traveler."

"Sounds like a country-and-western song."

"You want to hear this or not? I got plenty a things I gotta do other than settin' here, chewin' on a old rag."

"Sorry, Dad. I'm waiting with bated breath."

"Well, Sarah Anne, you're gonna hear the whole darn thing." He looked at the ceiling, recalling the story his daddy had told him one cold winter day during World War II when the radio had been on the fritz. "Reckon them Fogarty brothers came to McCrumb County from Georgia 'bout 1925. Bought a small farm twixt two ridges down 'round Canaan. Paid cash-money for it. Drove a Model A coupe into Greenglen, nothin' special 'bout it. But after six, eight months, word got around them boys was producin' a different kind of crop. High-grade whiskey, even some apple brandy. Sellin' it to some of the roadhouses. Used to be fair number of them places, out in the country on high-use roads. Prohibition 'bout put them outta business, 'ceptin' them that got their liquor from bootleggers."

"So the Fogarty brothers were bootleggers?"

"Sit back, Sarah Anne, an' let me tell the story.

"Now by law, there was other moonshiners 'round southern Indiana. All those German farmers, upright folk if there ever was any, but with a serious taste for beer. For the most part, them who brewed it kept it in the community. But some of the younger guys figured they could make a little extra, put it back for a rainy day."

"More like a drought."

"So, some of them was sellin' to the roadhouses, too. Sheriff knowed about it, but he had a taste for beer, too. Things was pretty quiet, not like Chicago with all them hoodlums and mobsters. Was a young guy, Willy Hesse, brewin' beer for outside the Germans, heard 'bout the Fogarty brothers. Went an' hooked up with them. Thought with whiskey, brandy, and beer, maybe they could supply some of the speakeasies up in Indianapolis. Which they did."

"Spring of 1928 come, Willy comes home with a new truck, a Chevy pickup with the spare tire mounted 'round the back window. Little later, Jerry Fogarty drives into Greenglen in a 1928 Studebaker Commander. Low-slung, it was for them times. Good engine, plenty of room."

"An' that's when your granddaddy Ezekiel entered the picture."

"Was he a deputy then?"

"Didn't join the department till he married your grand-mother. In 1928, he was still sowin' his wild oats—not with the ladies, don't get me wrong. But with automobiles. Reckon he weren't but a year or two outta high school and workin' for a garage down the road a bit from Crawford's Steakhouse an' Grill. He saw the Studebaker parked outside one day an' that was it for him. He was in love."

"With a car?"

"With a very fine automobile."

"I never in my life seen such a fine automobile," Ezekiel Barrow said. "'Cept for that Stutz Model 695 convertible drove through one day. How fast can this baby go?"

The man standing by the car looked him over, from old boots to the grimy coveralls. "You know about cars?"

"Yessir, work at Chatham's Garage." He wiped his hands on the rear side of his coveralls, stuck out a hand. "Name's Zeke Barrow."

"Jerry Fogarty," the man said, shaking hands. "You a good mechanic?"

"Yessir, an' gettin' better ever day."

"You do any work on the side, so to speak?"

Zeke ran a hand through his hair. "Don't rightly know what you mean, but I'd sell my soul to work on that baby."

Jerry laughed. "Don't have to sell your soul, leastways, I hope not. Come down to my farm, work on it there? Got some ideas on how we can put some more speed in the engine. Maybe do a little bit to tighten the suspension, make it corner better. Interested?"

"Yessir, it would be a fair dream, it would."

Saturday morning, Zeke showed up at the farm early when the morning mist was still rising from the tilled fields. A two-story, clapboard house looked like a gray kerosene wick box set on the only level place. When no one answered his knock, he wondered if he'd gotten the directions wrong. He knocked harder and was rewarded with the clatter of shoes coming down the stairs inside.

Jerry Fogarty opened the door, bleary-eyed and unshaven. "Good God, man. Talk about the early bird. Ain't got no worms, but if you know how to make coffee, the kitchen's back there."

By the time the percolator was bloop-blipping, Jerry came in smelling of soap, his black hair plastered to his head. "My brother, Mick," he said as he pulled another man into the room and slapped him on the back.

"You guys twins?"

"This here's my baby brother by eleven months," Jerry said.

"Mama always wanted a girl, kept trying," Mick said. "But all she got was six boys. Poor Mama."

"Somebody said you was from Georgia," Zeke said.

"Yep," Jerry said. "Country lots like this, only with mountains."

"With mean, wicked roads," Mick said, pouring coffee into an enamel mug. "Twisty with switchbacks you wouldn't believe. I remember one time–"

"Zeke ain't here to listen to your brag. Finish your coffee and let's get to work. We got us a real mechanic, best not to waste his time."

"So, he started workin' with 'em ever weekend," Micah said.

"Didn't he realize what they were doing?" Sarah asked. "How dangerous it was?"

"Told you, he was in love. Besides, Elliot Ness and all them guys was busy in Chicago." He ignored Sarah's snort. "Spent ever weekend workin' on that car. When it was done, they christened that Studebaker with some fine apple brandy."

"Christened it?"

"Named it the Midnight Traveler."

"I never knew Granddad was a dim bulb."

"He was doin' what he loved, Sarah Anne. But then, when they started workin' on Willy's Chevy pickup and got a phone installed on the farm, he started gettin' a whiff of dead possum."

"About time."

"Barely in time. In late May 1929, Granddad had put enough money aside to ask Muriel Palmer to marry him. And though he didn't know it, things in Indianapolis was beginnin' to get rough. Chicago mob saw a business opportunity with lots less risk. Started movin' in on them speakeasies. Got nasty."

❖❖❖

Hot for May, Zeke thought, wiping his forehead with his arm. Working on this truck sure wasn't as much fun as working on the Midnight Traveler. Harder, too, with lowering the roof. He'd been real careful with the paint job, a pretty greenish blue color with red wheels, and then they'd gone and painted the whole thing black. Taken off all the chrome. Taken the head lamps off and put them below the bumper.

He put the wrench on the workbench, walked to the house for a drink of water. Good well, sweet cold water. He stopped at the kitchen door, his hand on the latch.

"Truck's not quite ready, and that's too many cases for the Midnight Traveler unless we make two runs," Jerry said into the phone on the kitchen wall. "Look, you got hoodlums muscling in, we're going to have to quit dealing. Mob means T-men, and we don't need that kind of trouble. Got us enough business down here to keep us busy." He nodded, lit a cigarette. "I'll see if we can get the truck up to speed by Thursday. If not, what we can fit into Midnight's going to be it. And it'll be our last run."

Zeke backed away from the door. Federal agents from the Treasury Department could only mean bootlegging. He returned to the barn, sweating from fear as much as the heat. He had a couple of days' work to finish the truck, take a road run, fine tune it. If he stayed and worked tonight, maybe he could be finished of this thing when he left Sunday.

When Jerry wandered in later, he asked Zeke how close he was to winding up.

"I been thinkin' 'bout that. My girlfriend's gettin' on my case 'bout workin' all the time. If I stay and work tonight, should be able to get the road test in by tomorrow afternoon. "

Jerry whistled. "That'd be swell. Really appreciate the effort."

"'Course Muriel ain't gonna like me breakin' a date tonight."

"You do it, and we'll give you enough of a bonus to keep your girlfriend happy for a couple of months. As long as you spend it on her."

"Got nothin' else to spend it on."

Zeke felt relief when the road test went without a hitch. The truck hugged the road, and they must have been doing a hundred on a straight stretch. Like flying without wings. He hooped and hollered along with Jerry because of the speed—and because his work here was done.

Jerry slapped him on the back and went up to the house to get his pay. Mick brought out a Mason jar full of a deep amber liquid and three tin cups. "Since you all finished up, thought we'd toast to a job well done. This here is the really good stuff. Aged in hickory."

"You make it?"

"Sure enough did," Mick said, pouring generous measures. "Old family recipe, we been making it over a hundred years. Best in Chattahoochee County. Only the government had its hands in our pockets the whole time. Got worse with that personal income tax, take your earnings coming and going."

"Mick, you talk too much," Jerry said, handing Zeke a roll of bills. "Truth is, one poor Georgia farm can't provide for six brothers. Being the youngest, Mick and I took our skills and hit the road with the family recipes. And I'll be damned if I pay one penny to a government that says after a hard day of labor, a man can't enjoy a drink of good whiskey he can afford."

The brothers raised their cups and drank. Jerry looked at Zeke. "And if you want to take your girl someplace nice, say for a honeymoon, just tell the manager at West Baden Springs, Jerry Fogarty sent you."

"Well now," Micah said, leaning forward and putting his elbows on the table, "your Granddad thought he'd got outta that situation clean as a leg bone been given to a pack of coon dogs. Bothered him, but he figured the Fogarty brothers had a point about taxation. An' buttin' into people's druthers. An' all he'd done was do what he did ever day. Fix automobiles."

"He was an accessory."

"They was different times, Sarah Anne. Country was tryin' to figure out where it was goin'. Lotta corruption in government, not that there ain't none now. Did you know that before the income tax, 'bout a third of the national budget was paid for by tax on liquor?"

"No, I didn't. Nor did I realize people drank so much back then."

"Don't know it had so much to do with people drinkin' as it did the size of the national debt."

"And what does Granddad's close scrape with the law have to do with not wanting tickets to the Brickyard?"

"I ain't finished the story yet. Good Lord, you've become an impatient woman. You want some iced tea? Made a batch this mornin', should be chilled good now."

"Sure, Dad, just finish the story."

Micah came back to the table, put a glass of iced tea in front of Sarah and resumed his tale. "Remember I said it was ungodly hot that spring? What comes after a hot spell in spring?"

"Twisters."

"Bad storms that year, and one doozie of a storm. Highest recorded gusts in the history of the state. One hundred eleven miles an hour. That was on a Thursday night. But before that storm, your Granddad found out some very bad news."

Zeke read the headlines of the *Greenglen Sentinel* Wednesday morning with mounting feelings of dread and disbelief. Willy Hesse had been shot to death in Indianapolis on south Meridian Street. Body riddled with bullets. Police weren't commenting, but the reporter wrote that it looked like a Mob hit. The editorial went on and on about the rising crime rate and how the violence in Chicago was spreading. And how the federal government was looking into this most recent murder.

"T-men. Oh, good Lord," he muttered. He scanned all the pages in search of a mention of a black Chevy pickup that had been worked on– by someone who knew what he was doing. A mechanic. In McCrumb County. Nothing. "Oh, good Lord, thank you."

Tucking the paper under his arm, he paid for his coffee at the counter, quick-stepped down Main toward work. He heard a car pull up to the curb and turned to see Jerry's beautiful Studebaker level with him. "Give you a ride to work, get in."

"Thanks, but I'm almost there."

"I need to talk to you. Please."

Zeke didn't want to, but walking down the street with a car like that following him would get more notice. He checked the street and got in.

"Guess you saw the news," Jerry said.

"What happened?"

"I wasn't there, but Mick was. He was driving, caught a bullet, but made it home."

"Is he all right?"

"Hit in the arm, lost some blood." Jerry pulled up to the garage. "Willy talked him into the run. Getting greedy, I guess. Leastways, used poor judgment because he'd never delivered to that place before. Order came out of the blue and it was a setup the whole way. Mick said Willy walked into the place and they opened up. Thank the good Lord Mick was still in the truck."

"It was the guys from Chicago? The Mob?" Zeke hated to even say the word. The paper had been full of the running battle between cops and Mob, sometimes Mob and Mob, for years. Always bodies left behind.

Jerry turned to look at him. "Look, I need a favor. A big one. I've got one more order going to Indianapolis, a big one. Mick can't drive."

"Oh, no. I'm no bootlegger."

Jerry hit the steering wheel. "You just help them when there's no risk for you. Dammit, Zeke. I've been dealing with this guy since I started up business. He runs a restaurant, not a speakeasy, and wants to get in a good supply in case a Mob war starts. We take the pickup and Midnight tomorrow night, quick in, quick out. The restaurant's closed on Thursdays. Nobody'll be there."

"Bet that's what Willy said, 'One more trip.'"

"Look, greed has nothing to do with it. I promised this guy. I gave my word. If I have to make two runs by myself, I'll do it. But that would make it twice as dangerous." He looked at Zeke. "I need your help and I'll pay real good for it."

"I don't break the law."

"Because you might get caught?"

"No. Because it's wrong. I gotta get to work."

Jerry sighed. "Just think on it. I'll be here when you get off."

Zeke didn't have much time to think. It was a busy day, full of taking care of customers whose cars had broken down over the weekend. Every time he left the interior of the garage, the sky was darker. The storm broke about 3:30 with torrents of rain and howling wind. Boss told him to go on home before it got worse.

"It's gonna get worse?"

The old man nodded. "Feel it in my bones."

Zeke grabbed an old slicker from the pile of lost and found, even though he thought he'd be soaked by the time he walked home. He hadn't taken more than four steps when the wind whipped back the hood and he saw the Studebaker pull up. "Any haven in a storm."

"I gotta get home, Jerry. My dad's out in the upper forty today and that crik can come up real fast."

"Be glad to take you out to check," Jerry said, throwing the car into gear. "Have you thought about my proposal?"

"You're not goin' on a night like this? They're sayin' it's gonna get worse."

"Best cover in the world." He shifted gears smoothly and the car purred forward. "Look, I wouldn't even ask if it weren't real important."

"What about Willy's brothers?" As soon as the words were out, Zeke realized how awful the suggestion was. "Forget I said that. But there's gotta be someone else. Didn't you guys get to know your neighbors?"

"Not many neighbors out our way. Besides, you already know what's going on. You finished the truck knowing what was going on." He glanced at Zeke. "I saw you walking away from the kitchen door when I hung up."

"I'm not an outlaw."

"Well, if they'd change the damn laws, I wouldn't be either. You have to understand, the Fogarty name is as good as the Bible for swearing on. People know that, then they treat you with respect. My pappy always said mutual respect is the foundation for any business."

"Bootlegging is not a business."

"Of course it is. As soon as they repeal the Eighteenth Amendment, I'll be called a distiller."

Zeke shook his head. He didn't like the guilt or the sense of responsibility he was feeling. They pulled into the farmyard, and he saw his dad walking toward the house, leaning against the wind. He didn't open the door, just rolled down the window. "Dad, I'm goin' to help a friend. Probably ride out the storm at his place, go to work from there."

His dad waved, and Zeke rolled up the window. He turned to Jerry. "I'm not doing this outta a sense a business, but because you been a friend to me."

The trip into the city wasn't easy with the wind buffeting them especially hard on the ridges, though it wasn't much better when they hit the flatlands. "Don't know why you wanted fast cars when we crawled all the way up here," Zeke said when they'd pulled up to a loading dock lit by a single bulb. Jerry knocked on the door while Zeke started unloading. They'd finished when a man came from the restaurant, whispered to Jerry.

Jerry jumped off the dock, ran to Zeke. "We're going to get visitors any minute. Let's go. Stick on my bumper as much as you can. Two flashes of your lights if you think someone's following. If you're losing it, get off the road, hide the truck, and get out of there as quick as you can."

"Visitors?"

"Gun-toting ones." He ran over to the Midnight Traveler, pulled away.

Zeke was on his tail as quick as he could catch up. Just as he was turning onto the street, he saw headlights turn into the other end of the alley. He flashed the headlights and stepped on it. They zig-zagged around the city, running lights where they could. When Zeke saw the sign for Highway 421, he relaxed his grip on the wheel as much as the weather would permit.

The hood of the car separated the scrim of rain so he could see the taillights ahead. Every few minutes, strong gusts drove the rain horizontal and Zeke felt like he was driving through a hurricane, the car skittering and bucking on the slick road.

No lights in the rearview mirror. Not until they got within 20 miles of Jerry's farm. Zeke saw them coming up rapidly, two big ones mounted on the fender, two smaller running lights below. The same kind of lights he'd seen entering the alley. He flashed his lights. Instead of speeding up, Jerry waved him ahead. He passed Jerry, wondering what was up.

He speeded up as much as he could, easing his way around turns in the road by slightly accelerating and riding the center line. It was tricky with the wind. He took it on faith no one else would be on the road on a night like this.

He saw Jerry start moving into the left lane and wondered if he should slow down. But then Jerry moved back in line behind him. Another gust shimmied the truck across the center line and Zeke struggled to hold the wheel steady. Maybe just the wind. He was worried about the run on the ridge. Wind must be fierce there, and that last turn before the descent to the valley was rough on a clear day. And the ridge was coming up soon.

As soon as he topped the ridge, his worse nightmare came true. He fought the road and the rain and the wind for control. He saw the big car pull out to pass, but Jerry blocked the way again. And again. They were almost at the bad turn. The big car pulled out again and this time Jerry let it pass. So did Zeke, but as he glanced at it, he saw what looked like a rifle barrel tipping out the back window.

The big car began the turn, brake lights flashed, and the car spun sideways in the road. Zeke downshifted quickly, applied his own brakes gently. A gust of wind from the devil himself grabbed the front end of the big car and flipped it off the road. For a moment, it teetered on the brink. Then the devil let go and the car plunged over the edge and down. The rear end exited from sight first, headlights shining into the sky until the explosion.

Sarah found herself holding her breath. "They made it back to the farm OK?"

Micah nodded. "Not a scratch on 'em or their faithful steeds."

"I never knew Granddad had an adventure like that."

"Excitin', wasn't it? Even in the tellin'."

"And that's why you don't like NASCAR? Not exciting enough?"

Micah rubbed his chin. "Not exactly. See, they was doin' a road race that night under really awful conditions. With a car and a truck they'd modified out in the barn. Somethin' to be proud of."

Sarah finished her tea. "You think that's why Granddad went into law enforcement?"

"That's what he said. 'The bad guys almost won that night, Micah. If there wasn't no police, them bad guys'd always win and the world'd be a sorry place.' Plus, Muriel worked for a lawyer, and while Dad was debatin', she put her firm hand on his back and pushed."

Sarah laughed. She could indeed see the small woman doing exactly that. The Barrow women were always smart, steely, and just a tad bit pushy. "What happened to the Fogarty brothers?"

Micah shrugged. "When they got back to the farm, Jerry turned the truck over to your granddad, told him to use mineral spirits to take the black paint off. When Dad went back a couple of weeks later to show him how good it'd cleaned up, they was gone. Note on the door said, "Renamed the car Hurricane Runner. A good life to you, Friend."

Two days later, Sarah walked into the kitchen with an old book, found her dad in his easy chair in the living room. "I found the Fogarty brothers." She opened the book to the bookmarked page.

Micah fumbled for his glasses, read the section she pointed to. "Well, I'll be danged. Did the southern race circuit. Jerry Fogarty, driver; Mick Fogarty, mechanic." He read on. "Won the big race in Daytona Beach in 1939. Well, I'll be."

Sarah handed the bookmark to him. "Your ticket to the Brickyard 400. Suite in the pavilion. You can sit there and entertain the folk with your story of the Midnight Traveler and ignore that passel of pretty boys."

A FITTING MERGER
by S. M. Harding

In 1895, the first auto race in the United States took 10 hours and 23 minutes to cover 55 miles. The winner of the Vanderbilt Cup, Frank Duryea, beat three gas engine racers and two electric cars. By the time of the first race at the Indianapolis Speedway on a gravel track in 1909, the top lap speed had dramatically increased, and after the track had been paved with bricks, drivers broke the 100 mph mark in 1919. But these race cars were built from scratch for racing at maximum speed and cost a lot of money to design and build. "Open-wheel" racing was considered a rich man's game.

With the advent of Ford's assembly line, automobiles became affordable for the majority of Americans, especially those with a need for speed. Prohibition lasted from 1919 to its repeal in 1933. In the meantime, bootleggers with loads of white lightning raced away from revenuers through the mountains of Appalachia in the 1920s. They began to get together to both boost their speed and work on the suspension of their cars for better handling on mountain roads. Black Ghost, Grey Ghost, and Midnight Traveler were some of the cars that inspired folk legends and songs.

What could be more natural than beginning to race among themselves? Country roads provided the first races, then cow pastures, then dirt tracks normally used for horse racing. The term "stock car" referred to the fact that cars were off-the-assembly-line variety and then modified. The first organized stock-car race was held in Stockbridge, Georgia, in 1937. Many county and state fairgrounds hosted stock-car races, especially in the South. During the late '30s and early '40s, stock-car racing spread all over the country. Drivers like Fonty Flock, Buddy Shuman and Junior Johnson became early legends.

Daytona Beach hosted races in 1936 and 1937, using the hard-packed sand of the beach for part of the course, but didn't see the financial boon they'd hoped for. For the 1938 race, they approached "Big Bill" France Sr., to organize the race. When he took over, admission to the '38 race was 50 cents; the next year, he raised it to one dollar. He also organized a set of basic rules and found local sponsors. Almost 45,000 fans viewed the '38 race and the success lasted until the war, when all auto racing was suspended.

After World War II, new paved tracks began opening. Norwood Arena Speedway in Massachusetts was built at a cost of $111,750 in 1948; in 1950 the first 500-mile stock car race took place in Darlington, South Carolina; in the early 1950s, racetracks like Brownstown Speedway and Paragon Speedway opened in Indiana; and places like Gardena Stadium in southern California hosted not only stock-car races, but jalopy, hotrod and midget racing.

Stock-car racing was becoming big business. However, drivers found great disparity in rules governing different tracks. Often they had to refit their cars to meet the specifications for each race. Enters "Big Bill" again, intent on forming a sanctioning body for stock-car racing in the United States that would standardize specifications and procedures. Early in 1947, France met with a group of drivers, mechanics and promoters. They formed a national sanctioning body, the National Championship Stock Car Circuit (NCSCC), which set up a point system and a prize fund. Not satisfied that the NCSCC was effective enough, he got together with 35 major racing people in December of '47 in the Streamline Hotel on Daytona's beachfront. The following year, NCSCC was incorporated as the National Association for Stock Car Auto Racing — NASCAR.

Open-wheel and stock-car racing met at the Indianapolis Speedway with the Brickyard 400 in 1994. A fitting merger.

ONE LAST RACE
by Sherita Saffer Campbell

Sherita Saffer Campbell is a great-grandmother, freelance mystery writer and poet. She has been published in Alfred Hitchcock's Mystery Magazine, Fate *magazine,* Branches, Sagewoman, Humpback Barn Festival, Country Feedback, *and* Racing Can Be Murder. *She facilitates a poetry workshop, a Just Journaling writing group, and a fiction critique group in Muncie, Indiana where she lives.*

The new Chevrolet entered the race personnel gate of the Indianapolis Motor Speedway. The car stopped by a uniformed guard who checked the credentials handed to him by the chauffeur. They nodded to each other. The chauffeur in jeans and a baseball-like cap that said Hanerford Cars Inc. smiled. In small letters underneath the company name, "Little Jim Young" was written in script.

"Still driving an American car, Mrs. Hanerford?"

She gave him a long look. "This is an American track, made so by American men and women who risked their lives driving from the revenuers. Paul, you're damn straight I drive, buy, and use American."

"I know; just checking." He laughed and motioned them through.

They drove into a montage of country music, laughter, cussing and mechanical noises, mixed together like an old recipe for speed's success. No one stopped the car. Mrs. Hanerford had paid for most of the drivers and cars at some point through the crews' working lives.

There was a pause in the activities. Hats were taken off as Mrs. Everett Young Hanerford moved with a practiced step that let the spectators know not only a woman of age, but a woman of command, was in their midst. She extended her hand and a younger driver took it and smiled.

"Grandma, I didn't expect you here. I'll win without you coming down here. We're just doing practice laps." But he smiled. She kissed his cheek. He was as tall as she had been. She was still tall enough to be regal, not bent as she should have been for her 75 years.

"One last race. I had to see my grandson win."

"Or my own grandson, Faye Anne Young Hanerford," said a shorter, chubby man, puffing as he walked toward her.

"Why, Harold Lee Clifford, as I live and breathe, imagine seeing another old codger here." She bent to kiss his cheek. Then whispered. "We are going to beat the pants off you to-day." She poked him in the stomach. "You look like the Pillsbury Doughboy, and you best watch your weight. Too much biscuits and ham. Come see me when this is over and I'll brew you up some healing herbs."

"Brew that grandson of mine some. You know he's a Democrat? Heard me talkin' about shine once. He's not going to race NASCARs anymore. Joined the Indy Racing League. A grandson of mine. He told me he can't stand me." He shook his head.

They walked to a small cart that was waiting to take them to the seats. Front row seats, close to the track. Both liked the smell of fuel, the engine roars, the crowd. No elevator, no closed-in fancy spaces for either of them. The rest of their families and corporations could sit with the rich and mighty. They were still hill folks that knew how to drive in their day and how to brew the sauce that started the whole thing.

When she was seated, she looked at her opposition owner and smiled. She thought, *This war between us ends today. I'm going to win.* She watched the track and thought of how this love of racing began. Back when she lived with Grammy and Grandpa while Daddy was in prison.

Faye Ann Young walked out of the log cabin onto the porch. The birds had just begun to chirp, and one was even singing.

She heard the screen door squeak just a little. *It was almost as if it was answering the bird calls*, she thought as she turned. Grandpa was standing behind her looking at the door hinge. She knew he'd squirted oil on it last night before all the men sat down to eat with them. A door was not allowed to squeak. Not on delivery day.

"Door's a mite noisy," he whispered.

She nodded. Then smiled. You didn't talk out loud either.

He put his hand on her shoulder, bent down until his lips were close to her ear. "Your smile is like the sunshine, baby girl," he whispered. He pressed hard with one hand while he pointed to the sun coming up with his other hand. She saw the first red and orange streaks across the top ridge of King's Mountain. Not quite a bloody birth as her Grammy said sometimes. But almost. Gram didn't like a sunrise with a bloody birth on shine delivery day. "A bad sign," she always said.

Grandpa was looking toward the mountain road. No cars. He turned his head from side to side, tried to see through the trees, watched the buildings as the shadows disappeared into the coming light. The dogs lay quiet. They raised their heads when he came out the door. Faye Anne knew he had given them the hand sign not to bark or growl. But they were watching the countryside and road as careful as Grandpa.

Bub and Sam, his house dogs, had followed him out the door, their toenails not even touching the wood floor of the porch to make a sound. She saw their necks quiver like a sound was there. They looked up at Grandpa. He gave the hand sign. They never made a whimper.

Everyone was waiting, watching the roads. Listening for sounds. Sounds that should have meant company coming for breakfast.

Delivery day was tricky. The product was all out in the big shed, covered with stacks of hay and straw. One by one the cars would pull in running fast and silent into the shed. Cecil Ray would fill their tanks from the hose. Then they pulled out like a gray ghost that never existed. Sometimes.

One by one her big brothers and uncles would slip out of their cabins on King's Mountain. They would shinny up trees, creep around the sheds, walk silently to the tops of the mountains and watch and wait. Watch for those damn revenuers. Cecil Ray would stand by the barn door. If he saw a signal from one of his brothers that the revenuers were coming, he'd trip the trap door to the big cave and all their hard work of making the product, the corn and sugar they grew, would slide down into the cold cave to flow underground to Dawson Creek 30 miles away. The creek fed into the big river, and Grandpa said with a laugh that "when the government men came by, everybody went fishing to catch and eat the drunk fish from Jason County."

She held her breath. All was still.

"It's too quiet, baby girl." This time he wasn't whispering. Just talking real quiet like. "Go inside now. I'll ring the dinner bell. Help your grandma cook breakfast." She nodded and slipped into the house as the dinner bell began to ring.

Her Grammy put the bacon in the hot skillet and shoved the bread into the oven. Faye Anne got the eggs and began to count them. "I need to gather more eggs ..."

"No, child," Grammy spoke sharp, but quiet. "I'll scramble them; we've got the porridge. Don't go out. Not now, stay close by me, right by the cellar door."

She looked up at her grandma and carefully, with shaking hands, broke the eggs into the big bowl. Her hands were shaking so bad she didn't think she'd have to stir the eggs one bit.

Soon another dinner bell began to ring at the next cabin down the mountain. She counted the rings as she broke eggs, each one farther down the mountain, all the way to the holler.

The room filled with the smell of food. Grandpa was sitting on the porch whittling, the shotgun by his side.

The boys started milking, feeding the hogs. She could hear them grunt. Cecil Ray would have pushed the trap and all the shine was headed down to the cave.

She looked at her grandma as they finished cooking. She was watching the window, her body tensed as she listened to every sound outside. Faye Anne listened also. For the sound of tires, gunshots.

Two of her brothers drifted from the barn. They walked slowly across the barnyard. Faye Ann started to run to the door. Gram reached with one hand and grabbed her shoulder and pulled her back to the egg bowl.

Faye Anne nodded and continued stirring eggs. Gram smiled, kept frying the side meat.

"Breakfast 'bout ready?" asked the older of her two brothers. "I'm sure hungry." He talked a little loud. Not too loud, but Faye Anne knew it was so everyone would know. Know what? That he was coming in and not driving out because those awful revenuers were about? What did they look like? Revenuers? Faye Ann wondered.

There was a different footstep on the porch.

"Hey there, Big Jim, I'll join you for a cup of coffee, unless ..."

"Why, sheriff, there's coffee and more if you have time. Grandma's 'bout got breakfast ready."

Gram took the egg bowl from Faye Anne's shaking hands and smiled. "Thank you, Faye Anne." Then she started pouring the eggs into the hot skillet. "Set another place, darlin', for the good sheriff."

"Come and sit with us and eat breakfast, there's a plenty," she said, loud enough for the sheriff to hear, but in her sweet, slow, company voice.

Then just as fast she switched back to stirring the eggs in the hot skillet and winked at Faye Anne, who went to set another place at the table.

"Ready to make hay, Big Jim? Up a mite early." She heard the sheriff speak to Grandpa.

"Yup." She heard the rocking chair stop with a thud. She pictured him laying down his whittling, shutting up his knife, slowly slipping it in a top pocket. She'd seen him do this many times while she sat on the porch with him waiting for "them damn revenuers." He would shove the gun into his arm, break it open, then slowly walk with the sheriff into the house, hitting the door with his other hand. The sheriff would nonchalantly have his hand close to the gun in his holster.

"Get the butter out of the box, child."

"Yes'um."

She glanced at her grandpa as she went to get the butter, his gray eyes like the old wolf he'd hunted last week. The sheriff was still watching outside. Cecil Ray and Harold, the neighbor boy, came up the porch steps, watching behind them as they scratched the dog's ear. Faye Anne knew that as sure as if she could see it.

When all the men came in and sat around the table, Faye Anne watched as she and Grammy set the food on the table. Grammy poured the coffee. She set the cream and sugar down and watched the eyes of every man and boy as she did this. She felt a funny twitch in her stomach when she looked across the table. *That one*, she thought. She wasn't sure what those words meant to her. They were just there swimming in her mind like the minnows in the pond. Around and around. The run was over.

Later that night the house was quiet.

"Grammy, you look awful tired," Faye Anne said to her as she watched her darn socks and rock beside the fire.

"I am, child. Not to worry. It's been a long day."

Grammy's tired look began to appear more and more often, and the delivery days became harder and harder to come by. Sometimes three in a row were stopped.

"Grandma," said her grandpa one night. "We have a tattler somewhere. A tattle tale in our midst."

Grandma nodded. Times were hard that winter. Her two older uncles went to jail. Money scarce, Grandma sick. One day Grammy was gathering herbs. "Come, child, you need to know about my garden herbs."

Faye Anne watched her Grandma for days after the sheriff had been to their cabin. She had these strange thoughts. It was about that day. Something wrong with someone that day. The sheriff, was he warning them? She didn't know, but there was a look on someone's face, a mood she couldn't catch. Someone in the valley was talking too much? That's what Grandpa said when things went wrong. Someone talked too much. She couldn't figure it out.

Grammy walked around with a worried expression. She began putting in more time on the beautiful quilts she made, sending Faye Anne to the attic to bring down bits of material. They had bags all over the house. It was that year that her grandmother began to teach her about quilting.

"You must sew perfect, child." Then she would smile. "You do everything perfect; this is as important as the delivery day. This can bring in money from the folks who come to fish and hunt. It's tax time."

That's the change in Grammy, she thought. *Tax time.* She didn't understand the word much. She knew it was a worry for everyone in the valley. Tax time meant money somehow because widow Hanerford had almost lost her farm like Dude Hall had. To the damn revenuers. Only this time, the whole valley did an extra run and got money that Faye Anne and Grandpa delivered to Mrs. Hanerford. Just by dropping by for coffee and leaving it on the table under the cookie jar. She remembered that because she and Grammy got a new dress made by Ms. Hanerford every Easter, and she got a warm coat every year for school.

"You have to be careful how you help folks, child. Folks can't be takin' charity."

They also got homemade bread and pies until the widow died. Her son, Everett, came over bringing coal to them in a bad winter, when Grandpa was real sick. They had a long talk. Everett was in junior high and began to work with the valley men on delivery day.

Grammy began to feel poorly when Faye Anne was in junior high and began to take her to the barn to learn how to make the Recipe For Delivery. Grandpa looked pale when Grandma began to teach her this.

The first day after that he began to refine her driving skills. She'd been driving tractors and old cars since she was five. This driving was different. "You have to watch every minute you're in the car, girl. Like we watch and listen on delivery day. Watch your back and every side road you pass."

Grammy brought out a picnic lunch and climbed in the car. "It's time to visit your dad," she said. They went once a year on his birthday, driving the 100 miles there. Going into the big prison for a couple of hours to visit, then driving home. Stopping beside the road and at friends' houses to sleep as they drove back home.

"You like that Everett Hanerford, child?"

"Yes, um." She blushed.

When she was 14, she began driving the run on delivery day. No one liked it.

"Big Jim, you can't let that little girl drive."

"There's no one else to drive. No one. They're all off fighting the war or in jail. We've got to have money."

"Tax time," said Faye Anne as she got in the car. She had known now about the smug look that someone had when he came to visit. She knew her grandpa knew by the way he watched that young man. But no one talked about it. She knew that when she got big she'd have to do something about it. She began to plan.

She'd driven just out of the lane. It was a dark night. Cloudy, not a waning moon. You start money-making projects on a waxing moon. Dark moon is for getting rid of things. A new moon is OK. A waxing moon is better even if there is cloud cover. This was a dark moon, and Grammy did the hill spell for dark moon protection.

Faye Anne's stomach was reeling the same way it had that long-ago day when the sheriff and her granddad acted so funny on the porch.

She glanced in the mirror. Nothing behind. Her younger brother was 20 minutes back. Still out of sight.

The wind was blowing and the trees were almost bent double when she was driving. They bent low to the road, and the wind whistling through them seemed to whisper her name. She watched the speedometer. The secret was not to speed, not to run stop lights; just be easy on the road.

Grandpa was worried that a young woman driving alone would cause talk. Grammy spread the word they were going for coffee. Everyone knew Grammy got headaches if she didn't have coffee.

She never got stopped. Everett was her spotter in the front. He drew the maps, told her where to pull in when the sheriff came calling. Harold offered. She and Grandpa said no. No one could read his writing.

"Faye Anne," her grammy said the day before she started her run. "I want to have all folks invited to a chicken-and-dumplin' supper Sunday."

"But, we were thinkin' of a run that night."

"No, I had this dream. We won't have a run."

Everyone looked at Grammy.

"Not that night. But we'll talk about it. So everyone else will think we run."

That worked for a couple of runs. Things got tricky again. The sheriff was on her trail.

That summer she watched her grandmother carefully. She was breathing hard, and she labored hard as they planted the tobacco crop.

The next delivery and the next were the same. She walked around the table the same way, watching her grandfather, watching the eyes of the men sitting around the table.

On her rare trips to town when she saw the men that made the deliveries, she watched where they went. Made notes in a little notebook she kept close by.

She woke one time to a pounding on the door. Grammy was patching pants and opened the door first. Liege, her oldest uncle, fell inside the door to the floor.

"Get Grandpa, child, and towels." But Grandpa came running, holding his shotgun.

"Liege."

"Don't touch him." The sheriff walked in. "Caught him runnin' shine. Tried to outrun me. If he had stopped ..."

The sheriff and his deputy reached down to grab him.

"Don't you touch him like that, sheriff, or you won't have time to worry about Big Jim's shotgun." Faye Anne's eyes got big. Her grammy pulled a small Derringer out of her pocket. It was Grammy's great-grandpa's gun from the Civil War.

"This might blow up in my face when I shoot it, but you'll be dead."

"Now ... you can't stop me from arresting him, Mrs. Young."

"I'm not about to. I'm a law-abiding woman. I intend to patch him up as best I can and see that he's give a decent ride to jail, or to the cemetery, if you don't back off."

The sheriff helped carry Liege to the daybed, and Grandma began to work. "Fetch me the herb box, child. Scissors, Big Jim. Hot water, sheriff; there's a kettle on the stove."

Faye Anne held that scene in her mind for a long time. It was the last time she saw Liege. He died in prison.

"They beat him to death with a whip." The sheriff delivered the news in person. He was angry.

"He wouldn't talk," said her grandpa. The sheriff just looked at him.

"You can claim the body." Then he left. Faye Anne remembered he never came back for coffee after that. It was always the deputies that came to do the arrests or just nib around.

Grammy and Grandpa watched as first one boy, then another, got hurt, killed or arrested.

There were fun days also. They would pack a picnic, and all the hill families would drive to the sand beach and race those cars that carried the shine north. Only this was just for fun. Fun and games. They used the same shine to race that they sold.

"You could brew up a batch of that stuff," Grandpa said, "fill the tank with it, then drink it when you drained the tank after the run." Grandpa had a name. For his racing on the dunes in Daytona Sand, and for his shine.

The boys raced, too, the time trials, the speed runs. Then the tracks. They even had a system. Faye Anne watched them practice in the field. Her older uncle held back, way back, at the end of the pack, her other uncle took the lead and blocked all the other stock cars. Then bam! the uncle in back floorboarded it and passed all the other stock cars and won. Then the next time they'd switch.

"You guys look like a sling shot," Faye Anne laughed. That became their secret name for their trick.

They drank shine and raced. That was their lives. Cecil got so he didn't want to run shine, but Grandpa made him. And he got caught once before a big race and had to do time.

"Grammy, Uncle Cecil spends a lot of time in that jail." They were eating pinto beans, cornbread, potatoes and apple dumplings for dessert. Cecil's favorite meal.

"I know, and this time best be the last. We don't need to spend time and money on shine. We need to do what Cecil says and buy race cars."

"I tell you, woman, there's no sense ..."

"I tell you, I saw it in my dreams, Big Jim." There was a silence. Faye Anne knew that they would run no more shine. Sure enough, Grandpa and Cecil, when he got out, began to buy cars. Everett and she, engaged by then, went along and helped drive.

Those stock cars made their money and led them to big-time tracks. Though it was exciting to be in the big time, it lacked the thrill of the sand beaches and barnyard fields.

Grammy and Grandpa didn't get to see NASCAR racing, as it was now called, in the Yankee land. It made lots of money there. No one knew Faye Anne was one of the biggest owners and backers of those NASCARS. Stock cars to her, and she bet she could still outdrive any of them youngsters today.

Faye Anne Young Hanerford blinked her eyes. Brought her mind back to the Indiana 500 track. Smiled at Harold.

"We've had a good run. It took me a long time to figure out how the sheriff and the revenuers knew we were running shine. I watched, oh, how I watched everyone. Listened. Spied on y'all."

There was a long breath from Harold. "Now, it wasn't nothing personal. We needed the money," they both said at the same time.

"Well my grandson found out what I did," Harold tried to explain. "When I was drunk. That's why he quit NASCAR. That's why he hates me. I told him it was for the money. We needed it."

"Well, now you have money and so do I. Between us, we own or sponsor enough NASCAR. I wanted you to lose more than money. I wanted you to lose everything. You know how Grammy did the recipe for the shine? How she was the granny woman that did the herbs? She taught me all she knew. So I stopped off and saw your grandson in the Al Pete Special, red, white and blue. I gave him a special ring for luck that I marinated. I like that word, marinated, in herbs. I slipped it on his finger, tight."

She looked away from Harold toward the track. "Notice how he's slowing down as he rounds the track. He's almost stopped now. I didn't think it would work that fast."

Harold jumped up and ran to the fence that enclosed the race track. "Bernie Ray," he cried. Then he slumped toward the fence and slid down to the cement, his right hand clutching his heart.

Mrs. Hanerford got up.

She touched the alarm meter on her watch that had been her birthday present from her children. "In case you have any trouble, Mom," they had said.

Pit crews came running.

"Oh my Lord, help; Harold has had a heart attack or something."

"Get an ambulance."

"I'll do CPR."

'There's no heartbeat."

"Oh, my God."

"What happened?" asked the track official.

"I don't know, we were just talking about old times. We've known each other since we were kids, Harold Lee and I. Our families ran shi … raced together." She stopped. Smiled. "I was just getting ready to tell him what a horrible liar I always was. How I could tell the most awful stories. Then he ran off." She pulled a handkerchief out of her pocket. "My grammy's," she said. And wiped the tears away.

Later, when Bernie Ray arrived on the scene from the track, Faye Anne said, "Bernie Ray, your grandpa. I'm so sorry. His heart." She watched the grandson walk down to his grandfather. She turned as Cecil Ray, her uncle, walked up beside her.

"You finally did it. 'Bout time."

"Yes. It's over now. My last race."

"His, too. I'll get your car."

A FAMILY DYNASTY
by S. Ashley Couts

Bill France had a simple dream in 1936 – follow the sun, tinker on cars, and race. As legend goes, France, his wife and his kid headed south from Washington, D.C. He had 25 bucks in his pocket and his old car broke down in Daytona Beach.

And it was there on the sandy beach that France, a racer and gasoline jockey, planted the dream that one day grew into the multi-billion-dollar auto racing empire known as NASCAR. And along the way, his family became racing royalty.

After running a course at Daytona for more than a decade, France called together a group of racers and promoters in December 1947 and founded in February 1948 the organization whose official name is the National Association of Stock Car Auto Racing. Its first "strictly stock" car race was in June 1949.

France's son, sometimes called Bill Jr. or Little Bill, although he wasn't actually a junior, spent his teenage years at Daytona Beach hawking tickets and concessions. During Speed Week in February, he was assigned to Beach Patrol, which meant waking campers and alerting them to an impending beach race. After college at the University of Florida, Bill Jr. joined the Navy, spending two years in service. After he returned, Bill Jr. learned every aspect of stock-car racing from flagman to scorer, and from race steward to vice president of the overall business.

With the business on a firm foundation and looking to expand, Bill Jr. stepped into his father's huge footsteps in 1972 as NASCAR president. He piloted the industry into a new age. He recognized the importance of marketing to big business and to television and aggressively courted both. When cigarette and tobacco ads were no longer allowed on television, he landed R.J. Reynolds Tobacco Company as a title sponsor in 1971 and changed the name of the top-tier series to the Winston Cup series.

Though most races still remain in the South, Winston Cup racing expanded into the North, Midwest and West Coast, with nearly three dozen points-paying races over a season that started with the Daytona 500 in mid-February and lasted until November. By the mid-1990s, when open-wheel racing underwent a split, NASCAR was the most popular and recognizable form of motor sports in America. By 2001, when Bill Jr. was named chairman of NASCAR, the family's International Speedway Corporation had grown from a two-speedway company into a 12-track conglomerate.

Bill Jr. died of cancer in June 2004, and several thousand mourners packed an auditorium to remember the man and his contribution to motor sports. They recalled his love of hot dogs, fishing and stock-car racing. And in true NASCAR style, teams placed tribute decals on their cars.

Like his big brother Bill Jr., James France grew up in the family business. As a teenager, he liked motorcycles and go-kart racing. In college he studied business and after two years in the Army, he returned home to resume his place as the second prince. In 1999 he founded the Grand American Road Racing Association and served as co-vice chairman of the board at NASCAR with his brother at the time of Bill Jr.'s death.

In 1999 Bill Jr. handed the day-to-day operation of NASCAR to Mike Helton, and in 2003 he passed his titles as CEO and board chair over to his son, Brian France.

The third generation of France children inherited a multibillion dollar business. By 2007 Forbes magazine listed Jim's estimated worth at $1.5 billion, and he was listed as the third wealthiest person in American motorsports.

Brian France and his sister, Lesa France Kennedy, are both heavily involved in the family business. In fact, France family members hold four of the five seats on the NASCAR board of directors. And Lesa, as president of the family company that owns 12 race tracks, was named one of the Most Influential Women in Sports Business.

NASCAR is the top spectator sport in the country. Annually it generates more than $2 billion in sales.

A DANGEROUS HABIT
by Jaci Muzamel

The daughter of a Navy photographer, Jaci learned at an early age the power of recording life's events using a camera. Being an avid race fan, combining a NASCAR race and a camera was inevitable. Her story, "Killer Traditions," appears in Racing Can Be Murder, *and she also has a short story, "My Little Marine," in* Pets Across America, *a book benefiting shelter animals in every state.*

"Oh good God, how could you lose someone? It's not like you can misplace a person." Brian imagined Tammi's words in his head. He was getting concerned as he squeezed through the crowds milling around the vendors and looked for Bates. He'd been right there beside them but was now out of sight. The race would be starting any minute, and Brian knew Tammi would be livid if they didn't get to the suite in time for her favorite part, "Gentlemen, Start Your Engines." She was already testy. Brian wished he could start the day over. Dealing with Tammi's moods and Bates' selfishness was beginning to make him wish he were home watching the race on the TV. Alone.

It had started as soon as they'd gotten to the track. There's not a married man alive who hasn't been on the receiving end of the "look." Each one will inwardly cringe and do whatever it takes to escape that withering gaze. Brian had been a recipient as soon as they'd stopped the car and Tammi and Bates had gotten out.

"I can't help that we're late," he whispered. "Bates should have gotten up earlier and not bugged Ted quite so much for freebies. What am I supposed to do?"

Brian leaned over the console of the stopped car and looked out the open window at Tammi. Her hands were on her hips in a defiant posture. He sighed, knowing the day was off to an iffy start. He did his best to get out of trouble, "I'll let you out here so you don't have to walk so far, sweetie. How 'bout if I go park the car and meet you guys inside?" He picked up her bags and tried to hand them to her.

Tammi snatched her purse and camera bag out of his hand, "That's not going to work. Bates wants to go look for a stupid hat. It's hot already and it's still early. You know as well as I do he'll go from place to place trying to get the best deal. God, that's annoying. He hates being late but hates spending money even more. He'll be upset when we're not on time but won't even consider it's his fault." They weren't late yet, but Race Day festivities started early, and the track was filling fast. They'd be cutting it close if Bates didn't hurry.

Brian smiled and shook his head. He watched as his wife straightened and flashed an everything's-OK, be-with-you-in-a-minute smile in Bates' direction. He knew she was right but it was too late to make a difference, so they might as well try to have fun. Tickets to watch the race from the President's Suite didn't just drop from the sky.

Bates was oblivious to their heated exchange and smiled back. He gave her a slight wave of his hand, and without waiting for Tammi, headed toward the vendors. *It's August in Indiana, America's sauna. Only an idiot wouldn't have brought a hat with him anyway,* Brian thought.

James Edison Bates. He preferred to be called JEB — as in Jeb Stuart, southern officer and gentleman, he frequently pointed out— but most people called him Bates, or often be-hind his back more derogatory names, and laughed at his at-tempt at southern gentry since he was born and raised in the Midwest. He had an annoying habit of thinking only of him-self and expecting everything and everyone to fall into place–his place. A retired military man, he was now a professor. He'd spent his life with protégés, as he called them, doing as they were told.

They'd gotten to the track in plenty of time, but Bates had spent so much time in Ted Moffit's office they might be late for the start of the race. What more could Bates have expected he'd get for free?

Now Tammi was anxious, something she didn't cope with gracefully.

"It's not funny," Tammi said as she turned back to Brian catching him unable to snap the smile off his face.

"Come on honey, it'll be OK. The race isn't for a while, and being upset isn't going to help. Once you get him away from the trinkets, we'll meet at the suite and get something to drink. Let me get out of the middle of the road before people get mad."

Tammi's mouth twitched in annoyance as she checked out the traffic stopped behind their car. "Fine. I'm just so pissed. He's such a pain in the butt when he wants something. I could just smack him when he starts in on his usual what's-in-it-for-me nonsense. It was so nice of Ted to give us these VIP passes; I wish just once Bates would be grateful and say thanks. Period." She backed away from the car. "We have our tickets; I guess we'll meet you at the suite."

As Brian inched closer to the gate, he thought being in Ted Moffit's suite for the race certainly had its advantages. The gate and parking area were directly behind the suites on the infield just steps away from the track. They'd been to the speedway before but had never been in a suite, let alone the track president's personal suite. They'd have a great view of the race. Brian couldn't help his excitement. He was sure they'd gotten the tickets from Moffit only because Bates had badgered the poor guy. Ted had been Bates' student before he graduated and moved on to manage some of the biggest race tracks in the United States. Bates assumed he'd be treated like the royalty he considered himself whenever he wanted to see a race in person. Brian knew Bates had seen a lot of sold-out races from the luxury of Ted's suites. This time he'd wanted to bring them along as guests. Brian had to agree with Tammi, Bates could be extremely annoying when he wanted something. They always did what he wanted, and while most of the time they enjoyed his visits, it really was like having a child—a spoiled child.

Brian hoped he'd be able to wander around the exclusive area once he got beyond the gate. He was anxious to get to the suite and knew Tammi and Bates would be awhile. The last time they'd been to the track had ended in a fiasco with the death of a spectator they'd talked to during the afternoon. Brian had found the guy dead in the men's room, and they'd been held for questioning. Tammi's cameras had been confiscated so the police could review her pictures. She never tired of telling people that those photos had helped 'capture a murderer." She didn't bother to mention that she'd been scared to death.

Brian was jarred from his thoughts when he heard a loud whump on the car. Tammi, out of breath and red faced, tossed her bags on the seat next to him and said, "Change of plans. I'm tired of babysitting Bates. I'll park the car and go up to the suite. Fair's fair. I've spent all week with him; it's your turn."

Brian knew arguing wouldn't change her mind, so he held the door as they exchanged places. He watched her hand the VIP parking pass to the security guard. When she'd driven out of sight, he turned and headed toward the vendor stands, shading his eyes from the sun as he looked for Bates.

When Brian didn't see Bates at any of the stands along the street, he fought his way against the flow of spectators headed toward the gate to continue to look for him in a fenced area of stands across from the Main Gate. He moved around the tables as fast as he could, considering the crowd packed in to buy the junk. He was distracted by the sound of deafening rap music. He figured country music would be a staple at a NASCAR race. It didn't matter, they both annoyed him.

His discomfort grew when he heard the National Anthem echoing from the track. He knew the race would start soon. Where the heck was Bates? Once the race started, the vendors would close until it was over and people spilled, or more likely staggered, through the gates to head home. Money poured from drunken fans for anything displaying the race winner's name or car number. Beer was great for business.

Brian felt sweat roll down his back as the midday heat intensified. He was hot and getting angry. He could tell from the sound that the cars had been started and were headed off Pit Row to begin the race. There wasn't any way Bates could have gotten past him; he'd kept an eye on the entrance.

As he looked around Brain realized he was alone with the vendors. They ignored him and watched the race on small TVs or grabbed something to eat. Not only was he missing the race, but he was hungry. His annoyance grew as he contemplated calling Tammi on her cell phone to see if somehow Bates was in the suite. The problem was that by now she'd be glued to the rail yelling at Jimmie Johnson in the 48 car—she just knew he could hear her—and taking pictures as fast as she could press the shutter release. He hoped she'd taken her phone outside with her, but wondered if she'd thought of it. Of course, even if she had, the sound from the track would make it almost impossible to hear the silly ring tone she insisted on using.

He stood momentarily paralyzed as he tried to decide what to do next. His relief was replaced with dread as his cell phone chirped and he saw it was Tammi calling.

"Where on earth are you two?" He jerked the phone away from his ear but could still hear her even with it inches from his face. He tried to keep up with her rapid-fire comments, but his mind drifted to a vision of his sister's old Chatty Cathy doll, her string broken off in the ON position. "The race has already started, had its first yellow, and you guys have missed it. I waited to go outside by the rail, but when you didn't show up and they got ready to start, I went on out. You know Jimmie's on the pole and Tony started in fourth. What's the problem? Ted was here. Even the mayor showed up. Bates wanted to suck up to Ted a bit more, but it's too late now, he's already gone back to his office. I guess he'll be back later. I don't know. Where are you guys?"

Brian felt better knowing Bates was not with her, and then realized neither of them knew where he was. Despite the heat, his hands were cold and clammy. He started to scrub them down the front of his jeans but realized he was wearing dress slacks. Tammi had insisted he dress nicely—no jeans or cowboy boots—since they were going to watch the race from the Presidential Suite. He pulled his handkerchief out of his back pocket and wiped his hands on it instead.

"Tammi, listen to me." He thought of what to say as he folded his handkerchief and returned it to his pocket. The sound of the race surrounded him through the muffled background noise of her cell phone.

"I was, but you haven't said anything."

"Bates isn't with me. Is he with you?"

"What? Of course he's not with me. Where is he?"

It was hard for Brian not to sigh out loud. If he knew, they wouldn't be having this conversation. "I don't know, honey. I never saw him after he walked away from the car."

"You lost him?" The unspoken *you idiot* was crystal clear.

"I didn't lose anybody." He felt his face flush. She'd implied the same words of criticism he'd thought to himself earlier. They were more alike at times than he liked to admit.

"I'm coming over. Just stay where you are. God, I can't believe this. We should have stayed together."

Brian leaned against a tree and found some relief from the stifling heat in its shade. It didn't take long to spot her as she marched through the gate, camera bag slung over her shoulder. Her eyes darted from side to side until she spotted him. He steeled himself.

"Where is he?" she demanded. "This is just so typical. What a friggin' nightmare. It's always all about him. If he's watching from someplace else, I'm going to kill him. Why would he wander away? Does he have his cell phone so we can call him?"

"I tried already, and it went straight to voice mail. That's why I thought he might be with you."

"God," she sighed, "Ted was in the suite asking about him. He left after the start of the race. I wonder if he ran into Bates and they're watching from Ted's office."

"You can't see the track from his office, remember?" Brian considered their options. "I don't think waiting for him here is a good idea. I wonder if one of us should go back to the suite and the other walk over to Ted's office. I don't know what else to do."

"Nope, I'm not splitting up again. That didn't work so well the last time, did it?"

While they walked the length of the track to Ted's office, Tammi chattered on about the race; the start, the first caution, the free souvenirs, the who's-who list of guests, the fantastic spread of food—which made Brian's empty stomach growl—and Ted being there to greet everybody. "He was very gracious. He asked about Bates. I think he likes Bates, but, well, I don't know, it just seems like there's something between them; like he can't get rid of Bates fast enough."

Brian agreed. "If you had Bates up the yin-yang everywhere you worked, you'd be tired of him, too. I'm amazed that Bates thinks nothing of asking Ted for so much. I feel guilty about the tickets he gave us. I wouldn't turn them down, of course, but still …"

"Yeah," Tammi said, "it was hard not to laugh when he described Bates to the mayor. He was dead on, saying that Bates was always there, a yapping puppy you wish you hadn't bought your kids. He commented on how the students felt about Bates and what they said behind his back. He even made fun of that stupid hat he was wearing. I guess it was pretty mean when you think about it. He didn't stay long. I was kind of surprised when he said he had work to do. I figured he'd watch the race from the suite."

There was no traffic as they made their way to the main entrance. A security guard waved them to the elevators when he saw their VIP passes. They weren't surprised to find the outer office empty; everyone, including the employees, was probably watching the race.

They stepped through the doorway into Ted's office and called his name.

"Doesn't look like he's here. Maybe we should go back and ask the guard to find him. I hate to bother him, but what else should we do?" Brian saw the thoughtful look on Tammi's face. "What? Do you have another idea?"

Her hesitant "no" faded to nothing when they heard a door close and saw Ted walk down the hall and come into his office. He didn't see them and let out a yelp when he heard Tammi say, "Oh, thank God. We're so glad to see you. Have you seen Bates?"

"No. Not since you were here earlier for the tickets. Why?"

Brian and Tammi talked over each other as they tried to tell Ted what had happened. His face took on a look of concern as he listened. "He doesn't have a car so he's got to be on the track someplace. I'm at a loss for what to tell you. I can alert security. If he's still on the Speedway property they'll find him. Why don't you go back to the suite and at least see some of the race. When they find him I'll get word to you. OK?" Ted walked to the elevator and pushed the down button." Let's get his description out right now."

Tammi reached for Brian's hand, a relieved grin spreading across her face. "Thanks, that's great."

They listened as Ted gave the head of security a detailed description of Bates, and then they left the building. "I feel guilty about leaving it all up to Ted, but I think it's best if we go to the suite. Don't you?" Brian said as they walked down the sidewalk toward the VIP gate. "I'm hungry, and there's no reason for us to miss the entire race. I'm worried, but Bates has our cell phone numbers, and he knows where he can find us."

They were silent for a few steps, giving Brian time to appreciate the sound of the cars downshifting as they went into turn one. His about-face was so unexpected, he almost knocked Tammi over.

"Ouch." The impact jarred the camera bag from her shoulder and she scrambled to keep it from falling. "Watch it."

Brian caught the bag before it hit the ground. "Tammi, tell me again what Ted said about Bates before the race started."

"Why?"

"Just tell me."

"But, why?"

"Tell me. I'll explain in a minute."

Tammi rolled her eyes skyward as if asking for divine intervention. "Oh good grief, I don't know what it has to do with anything, but he talked about the students' attitude toward Bates."

"What else? Didn't you say he described Bates?"

"Well, yeah, I guess he did, so what?"

"You said he made fun of the hat."

Brian nodded as his implication dawned on Tammi. "Oh my God, Brian, he made fun of Bates' hat. And he mentioned the hat when he described Bates to security. How could he have known about it? Bates didn't have one before the race, and Ted couldn't have known he was going to buy one. That was a last-minute decision. He asked where Bates was like he hadn't seen him, but if he knew about a hat, he had to have seen him after we left the office this morning. Why would he lie?"

"I don't know, but I think we'd better go back and ask him. Something's not right." Tammi jogged to keep up with Brian's determined stride as he retraced their steps to the office.

They'd just gotten to the corner of the building when they saw Bates stumble through the door, his hands pulled together behind his back and wrapped with duct tape. Ted Moffit was right beside him, his arm around Bates, propelling him toward last year's pace car, an obvious perk of the job Ted routinely drove. Brian threw his arm up to stop Tammi's forward motion and raised a finger to his pursed lips in warning. They watched in stunned silence. After a short hesitation, Brian moved his hand in a circular motion and pointed to the right of the line of parked cars. Then he held his other hand up and shoved his palm at Tammi's face in a classic gesture to stop. He could only hope she would understand and stay where she was. He doubted she would.

Brian squatted and crab walked to remain out of sight. He wondered what was going on, but more than that, he questioned what he would do when he got to them. If he and Tammi hadn't seen the tape around Bates' hands, it would have appeared Ted was supporting him as if Bates were sick. Brian kept his eyes on the two as he maneuvered around the cars. A jolt of pain shot through his right ankle when his leather shoe met a beer can and his foot shot out from beneath him. He reached toward the nearest car to steady himself and swore silently as the only thing he could grab, the car's antenna, slipped through his grip and snapped from side to side, making a sound like a cracking bull whip before it settled into a noisy vibration.

Ted dragged Bates to a stop, and his eyes swept across the parking lot. He spotted Brian and shoved Bates into the car. Brian knew he couldn't move fast enough to stop him from driving off to do God knows what. He watched in alarm as Tammi sprinted from her hiding place raising her camera bag over her head, her face contorted like an insane Black Friday shopper racing to buy her prized acquisitions and victoriously claim them forever as her own. Afraid to alert Ted to her approach, he didn't yell out to stop her, but that didn't matter. She was screaming as she lunged the short distance forward. Brian almost felt sorry for the guy as he turned and was rewarded with the full force of her loaded camera bag against his head. He dropped to his knees, and her forward momentum drove his face into the side of the car.

Tammi was panting when Brian got to her side. "I didn't kill him, did I? Tell me I didn't." He smiled at her belated conscience. He leaned into the car and saw Bates had a stunned expression but was otherwise OK. He pulled his cell phone off his belt and dialed 911.

Ted groaned and reached for his head as he tried to sit up. Brian lowered himself to one knee beside him and whispered, "I have no idea what is going on here, but you'd better just sit tight. I've called the police and they can straighten this out when they get here. Besides, honestly, Ted, you don't look so good." He winked at Tammi as he stood up. "That's quite a wallop you pack there, kiddo. How's your camera equipment?"

The look on Tammi's face was priceless. It appeared she hadn't thought about her cameras when she'd hit Ted with the only thing she had in her hands. She jerked the bag open and rummaged through it. "I can't believe I did that. It doesn't look like anything is broken," she said with a worried frown, "but I guess I won't know until I use them."

The lot filled with track officials and police. Ted's right eye looked like a kid's marble, wonderful shades of blue, green and yellow, and he massaged the side of his head while he accused a for-once speechless Tammi of assaulting him. Brian could tell from her arched eyebrow and reddening face that she was rapidly recovering from the surprise of Ted's accusations. She started to respond when Ted's eyes locked onto something over her shoulder and he started wailing, "Noooo more." A police officer had helped Bates from the car and was cutting through the tape at his wrists. Ted lunged past Tammi, grabbed Bates, and shook him hard. Bates' freed hands flailed in the air as he tried to maintain his balance against Ted's rage. His head bobbed back and forth like a dashboard Chihuahua, and his hat flew off and skittered under the car. They stared in disbelief as two county sheriffs handcuffed Ted Moffit and dragged him to a nearby cruiser.

"What on earth is going on?" Tammi asked as Bates got down on his hands and knees and retrieved his hat.

"I believe he meant to kill me," Bates found his voice, replaced the hat on his head, and cocked the brim forward. Ted's howls of denial pierced through the air.

"Yeah," Tammi said with a note of sarcasm, "I'd say that's pretty obvious, but why? And how'd you get over here to his office?"

"He approached me on the street while I shopped for a hat and told me he'd forgotten to give me something. I followed him back to his office and waited. He was OK for a moment and then seemed to lapse into insanity. He started accusing me of vile wrongdoings and threatened me. When I turned to leave, he attacked me. I am sure had the police not arrived he would have carried out his murderous plan."

With tiresome talk like that Brian could see why. People often teased him about being stiff—they should hear this guy when he got wound up. He was half aware of Bates' continued explanation as he contemplated the truth of it. Ted had seemed rational and in control when they got to his office earlier in the morning. Of course nothing had appeared out of the ordinary when he and Tammi had returned to ask about Bates, and he'd had Bates someplace in his office the entire time, calmly acting as if he'd known nothing. Something didn't fit.

As Bates continued to talk at length, like he was on a stage before an adoring audience, Brian stepped away and approached Ted who was now quiet, his head resting against the car's back seat. When Brian said his name he looked up, focused, and shrugged his shoulders.

"Hey, Brian," he shook his head in resignation, "I don't know what came over me." He took a deep breath and continued, "I was headed to the suite for the start of the race when I saw Bates shopping the vendors. I thought we could walk over to the suite together. I'd only been with him a moment when he demanded tickets for the Formula One race we're hosting. I told him I doubted I could get them. Formula One races draw crowds from around the world and this is the first time we've had one at the speedway. We're expecting record crowds and comp tickets will be tight. The ones I have will be used for major sponsors. He became belligerent and threatened me. Honest to God, I don't know what I was going to do. I don't think I would have killed him, but I'm not sure."

"Couldn't you have just said no?" Brian asked, marveling at Bates' audacity.

Ted looked at his hands and didn't reply. "I can't," he finally said. "Bates knows I plagiarized my book in grad school. Because of that book being published, Max Freed hired me at the Charleston Motor Speedway. Building that track from the ground up and making it the number-one motor sports destination in the United States launched my career. I can't afford the negative publicity it would cause to have a scandal like this get out."

"All this is over a book?" Brian knew his face registered his disbelief. "What do you think will happen to you now? It's not like you can keep a kidnapping and possible attempt on someone's life a secret, Ted."

"Look at him." Brian followed Ted's gaze as he watched Bates who was in a heated discussion with Tammi. "Pompous old fool. He's ruined me."

"No," Brian said as he turned to walk away, "you did that to yourself, Ted."

Brian listened to Tammi and Bates argue as he watched the police car pull out with Ted Moffit in the back seat. Bates had made a big mistake since he enjoyed the sound of his own voice. He'd given Tammi the needed break in his monologue to allow her to take over the conversation. What a pair.

"Brian is the one who called the police, Bates. Did you think they appeared in a cloud of magic dust?"

"Magic dust?" Brian thought. He knew she was getting excited as her story took shape

"But I am the one …" *Uh-oh.* Brian thought, *here it comes.* "who saved you. If I hadn't hit Ted with my camera bag, God only knows what he would have done."

And there it was, the magic camera bag. Once again her cameras had saved the day. He knew she'd be beside herself to get home and email her friends. Pretty soon they'd have to bronze those cameras and place them in the speedway's museum.

Brian's laugh made them both stop and stare at him. "Come on, you two. The police have Ted in their custody. We'll probably have to go give statements later, and Bates, you'll more than likely have to stay in Indy until they get this cleared up, one way or the other. But right now there's no point in arguing; let's see if we can at least watch part of the race."

Bates seemed perplexed. "Why would I have to stay?"

"Do you even realize what you've done?" Brian asked. "You blackmailed Ted. You got tickets and other freebies from him at every major track by using something you know about him."

"But it's not like I've done anything wrong. I merely asked for things and he gave them to me."

"I think the police will have a different view," Tammi said as they reached the gate.

"And I think you'll be surprised. Ted Moffit won't face a criminal trial, because I won't press charges. The papers might run a small article about the disturbance, but I doubt it. Ted won't say or do anything because that would mean he'd have to admit what he's done and risk losing his career. When you think about it, this is a win-win for both of us."

"He tried to kill you," Brian said in amazement. "Doesn't that mean anything?"

"I doubt he would have followed through. I think he was under so much stress today that he got a tad angry with me. It happens. And that's what I will tell the police," Bates said.

Brian couldn't decide if he was more annoyed or amazed at Bates' blasé attitude, and wondered if there were other poor slobs under his influence. He didn't want to know, but he made a mental note to be very cautious around Bates in the future. He'd also be sure their always-open guest room was otherwise occupied the next time he came to visit.

Brian leaned closer to Tammi as they waited for the elevator to go to the suite. "I don't know about you, but I'm beginning to wonder if it wouldn't be safer to watch the races at home. We don't seem to have the best of luck at this track."

"Oh, you're no fun. Twice we've been here, and both times we've caught a criminal. Don't you think that's exciting? I will say, however, that next time I'd prefer to do it on our own, without interference."

"Interference?" Brian couldn't wait to hear her spin on this idea.

"Yeah," she said as they walked through the door of the suite. "We didn't really need the police; I nailed Ted with my cameras and stopped the whole thing."

She adapted to any situation, good or bad, with a speed that amazed Brian. Her unique way of looking at things made him smile as he thought the old saying about life never being dull must have been written with her in mind.

The interior of the suite was empty. Everyone except the staff was outside by the rail, some cheering or slapping each other on the back, others looking as if they'd lost a major bet. Bates scoured the suite for any leftover souvenirs as Tammi pushed her way to the front of the crowd. She waved at Brian, gesturing for him to join her. He was exhausted and hungry. He knew his enthusiastic wife would rehash the day's events over and over, and over, so he grabbed what was left of the food—a plate of cold and half-eaten nachos—cringed at the thought of eating them, and looked at the TV monitors. Tony Stewart, hometown boy, had just won the race for the first time in his career and was out of his car, scaling the fence by the finish line and waving to the fans.

Brian bit into cold cheese and beans on mushy tortilla chips, shook his head, and started to laugh. If he'd stayed at home, he'd have had the same view on the TV, but at least his nachos would have been hot.

HOW NASCAR CAME TO INDY

by Andrea Smith

(Adapted from an ESPN.com article by Ed Hinton, July 21, 2008)

It started in summer 1992 when Tony George, in just his second year at the helm, agreed to allow a tire test for NASCAR Winston Cup cars at Indianapolis Motor Speedway. George had vowed to run Indy as a business and wanted to see if the big, bulky stock cars could negotiate the 2.5-mile oval track that, in recent years, had seen much smaller, lighter cars.

The naysayers were loud. Stock cars at Indy? Sacrilege. A wanton violation of Holy Ground. Even George had his doubts. He assumed fans might come to a NASCAR race at Indy out of curiosity. But NASCAR also races on many smaller ovals, thus allowing fans to see all the way around the track. That wasn't possible at Indy and George feared NASCAR fans might not come back.

But George ignored the naysayers and his own qualms.

After that test in 1992, racing teams were so elated to be at Indy they spontaneously created a new Indy tradition: They knelt together at the start/finish line and kissed the bricks, the one-yard remainder of the track's original pavement. The photo was seen worldwide, and the American public demanded the marriage of America's most popular form of motorsports to racing's most hallowed ground. Resistance from traditionalists was swept away.

On the day in 1993 when ticket sales began for the inaugural Brickyard 400 in August 1994, demand in the first few hours blew out the Speedway's computerized ticket system. When it was fixed, the race was sold out within 24 hours. And the fans come back every year.

Now the Allstate 400 remains NASCAR's best-attended race, garnering crowds of more than 250,000, even in off years.

A CROWD PLEASER
by Marianne Halbert

Marianne Halbert

Marianne Halbert is an attorney in Indianapolis and has published several short stories. If anyone walking under the stands of the Indianapolis Motor Speedway in the mid-70s saw a group of little girls tossing M&M's off the top row, it was not Marianne and her sisters. That's her story and she's sticking to it. "A Crowd Pleaser" is dedicated to Sarah, Kristen, and Susan. Can you pass the M&M's, please?

Skeeter Lawson felt a nudge at his arm and looked up from his newspaper.

"Hey, buddy, I said would you like a cold one?" The guy held out a silver can, droplets of water falling back into the red cooler wedged between his feet. Skeeter noticed the neck of a bottle of champagne poking out of the ice at the bottom of the cooler.

Skeeter removed the earphone from his ear and draped it around his neck. "I thought you couldn't bring those in here. Thought glass bottles were against the track rules. How'd you sneak that past the officials at the gate?"

"Oh, you'd be amazed what you can sneak in," the big guy said. "Just takes a little finesse and a properly timed distraction. So you want one?"

It was still early. And canned beer wasn't on the agenda today. "No, thanks." He heard the pop-whoosh as the guy opened the beer. Skeeter looked around the stands. People in all shapes and sizes milled about, walking up the steps, searching for their seats in the bleachers. The majority sported shirts and hats showcasing their favorite NASCAR drivers, creating a colorful sight. And Skeeter knew that as much as each fan loved a favorite driver, they loved to hate a select few. Some people were reading programs or newspapers, soaking up the early-morning July sun along with details about the Brickyard 400. The man next to him finished his beer, crushed the can with one sandaled foot, and kicked the can under the bleachers. After a few seconds Skeeter heard the dull metallic clink as it hit the rocky ground below. The guy held out his hand.

"Name's Walter."

"Skeeter." Walter's hand was ice cold, but Skeeter forced himself to complete the handshake. A girl in her 20s, about a dozen rows down from them, squealed as her boyfriend put an ice cube down her back. She tore off her T-shirt, revealing a leopard print bikini top.

Walter was looking at her, too. "You gotta love the track and all those fringe benefits. You a big race fan?"

Skeeter was just about to put his earphone back in his ear to listen to the pre-race coverage. "Big NASCAR fan. Actually used to work for one of the teams, as the jack man. This is my first time to Indy, though. How about you? You here for business or pleasure?"

"I guess you'd say business. I'm an Indy car man through and through. Been coming to the track every May since I was a kid; brought my own kids every May while they were growing up. This is my first time at the 400."

Lucky me. Skeeter replaced his earphone. A family of four was headed down their row. Skeeter stood up and squeezed back as far as he could to let them pass. Walter didn't move. After a few unsuccessful "excuse me's," the family climbed to the row behind them, passed by two middle-aged women seated there, then climbed back down farther on. Skeeter stifled the urge to say something and focused on the track.

Walter started rummaging through a backpack and pulled out a radio. No headset. He tuned it to some country music station and turned it up. Loud.

Skeeter took off his own earphone again. "Excuse me, Walter. Don't you think that's a little loud?"

"No, no it's fine. I don't really follow the race anyway." His chubby hand plunged into the backpack again and came out holding a bag of pork rinds. "Want some? They don't really agree with me later, but going down, there's nothing like 'em."

"No," Skeeter tried to keep the annoyance out of his voice. "But I *do* follow the race. I follow every NASCAR race, and I listen to the commentary on my own radio, which I can't hear with yours turned up so loud."

Walter looked genuinely hurt. "Fine," he said, turning down his radio. "So you think there'll be any crashes today? Any fatalities?"

"I doubt it," Skeeter said. "Even if they're trading paint out there today, stock-car racing is safer than ever. Between the HANS device, roll cages, fireproof clothing, safer rims around the track and all, not to mention fuel cells and the kill switch, there hasn't been a NASCAR driver killed in years."

Walter looked out over the track. His voice was low when he spoke. "Not on the track, anyhow."

An image tried to bubble to the surface of Skeeter's mind. A loose car tried to slingshot around Buddy and clipped him. Buddy's green car covered in sponsor stickers, flipping end over end, crossing the finish line. Flames and smoke, then a figure emerging through the window netting. The crowd cheered. There was nothing else in the world like that sound. Voices united, no discussion necessary, just a mob of emotion erupting spontaneously. The crowd was *thrilled*. Buddy not only survived, he was uninjured. He and Skeeter even celebrated his victory later that night. Really celebrated. The image wanted to keep moving forward, but Skeeter shoved it back down into the recesses of his mind.

The race wouldn't begin for several hours. While Skeeter tried to listen to the pre-race coverage, Walter sang along to a few of the country songs coming out of his radio and downed another can of beer. The July sun climbed higher, and Skeeter put his sunglasses on. Then he pulled out a pair of binoculars and tried to see the pits. He couldn't get a good look, but he could picture the crews in his mind. Men walking around, checking and double checking. Every task a crucial step to ensure a safe win. Then rolling the car into position on the track as the crowd cheered, hats waving. He pictured himself there, remembered the feel of working on the car on race day. Lifting one side with the jack so the others could change the tires, quick as lightning. The adrenaline rush. The pride.

"Hey, Skeeter, can I borrow your binoculars?" Walter asked.

Skeeter hesitated. "I'm using them right now," as though that weren't already obvious.

"I know, I know. Just for a second."

Reluctantly, Skeeter sighed and handed them over. He watched Walter shove them up to his round eyes, and a big grin spread across that sweaty face.

"Oh yeah. They are a definite possibility." Skeeter followed Walter's gaze and saw three pretty young things a few rows down. They were putting sun lotion on each other's backs. Two blonds and a brunette. All showing a lot of skin.

"Possibility?"

"To invite to my hospitality suite. My family got one, and I'm tryin' to decide which lucky lady I'm going to invite with me. Oh, that's my favorite song." He handed the binoculars back to Skeeter.

A hospitality suite? "If your family's got a suite, what're you doing out here?" *I'd give my eye teeth to be in a suite today.* "Does it have a good view of the pit crews?" *Hell, what am I saying, they all have a good view of the pits.*

"I suppose it does, but I prefer the stands. Brings back good times, hanging out with my kids when they were still actually kids."

"But you could make new good times. They're all in the suite, right?"

"All but one," Walter said softly. Skeeter raised the binoculars and found himself using them to study the trio of possibilities. He had to admit they were easy on the eyes, but they'd never appreciate being so close to the pits. The smell of the fuel, the sound of the engines so close it made your chest tremble. Suddenly the country crooning cut off. "Dammit," Walter said.

"What's the matter?" Skeeter asked, lowering the binoculars. Walter was fiddling with his radio.

"Batteries must be dead. Dammit all to hell. How'm I supposed to sit out here all day without my tunes?" Then he eyed Skeeter's radio.

"Oh, no you don't."

"Please, Skeeter, I'm desperate. I'm stuck out here all day, and I need my tunes. I'll give you all the beer in my cooler."

"I don't drink beer."

"I'll buy you a souvenir, whatever you want."

"Whatever I want?"

"You name it."

"I want to be your guest to the hospitality suite." Walter's jaw dropped, and he looked longingly toward the trio of ladies.

"You're kidding, right?" He looked at the middle-aged women in the row behind them. "He's kidding, right?"

"I hope not," one of them said.

"Thanks a lot. No help from the peanut gallery." He looked back and forth from his radio to the pretty young things, and then his shoulders drooped. "Oh, alright. But I get the radio for the rest of the day."

"That's a deal." And they shook on it. Skeeter had been grateful when a ticket for the race had shown up in the mail, no name on the return address, just the name of the team he used to work for scrawled across the envelope. At least one of his old buddies hadn't disowned him. And he hated to look a gift horse in the mouth, but the seat wasn't all that great. A suite, on the other hand, now that would make the whole trip to Indy worthwhile. They both loaded up their gear, Walter with his backpack and red cooler, Skeeter with a small knapsack and his newspaper. Walter plowed through the row of spectators, Skeeter following in his wake, until they made their way down the stairs and walked along behind the grandstands. Skeeter caught the whiff of frying tenderloins and his stomach growled. "There'll be food in the suite, right?"

"Yeah, if you call that fancy, smancy stuff food."

Behind the vendors on the outer rim of the track lay the golf course. Couples lounged on blankets, hanging out, making out, passing out. Walter led the way, and they walked through an underground tunnel and emerged near the suites. Skeeter could feel his heartbeat quicken. This is where the race was. Not up there on those skinny metal bleachers. But here. There was the buzz of people, the *in* crowd. Passes hanging around their necks. He felt himself smile for the first time that day. Before he knew it, they were entering the suite.

It was beautiful in its simplicity. A large rectangular room, windows covering the front wall with a perfect view to the pits and the track. A few dozen people sat at long tables, chatting, eating, drinking. The room could've held a few dozen more.

Walter took Skeeter's radio and headed to a table toward the back, where he set it up to play his country music. He used the earphone and sang along to a song. Skeeter walked toward one of the tables closest to the windows. He saw a redhead sitting alone, sipping a cocktail. He pulled up a chair across from her.

"You a fan?"

"A wife of one of the drivers."

"No kidding? Which one? I used to be on a pit crew, knew a bunch of 'em."

She looked at him. Really looked at him. He felt her emerald eyes studying him.

"I shouldn't tell you. I wouldn't want it to bias your opinion today."

He tossed his head back and chuckled. "And just how would that bias my opinion?"

She swirled her drink, slender fingers, blood red nails, playing with a little red sword piercing a cherry. She kept her eyes on her drink while she spoke, long dark lashes shielding her eyes. "Why did you stop working for the crew?" She took in a deep breath, her generous chest heaving as she waited for him to answer. When he didn't, she raised her eyes to meet his. She didn't look away.

"It's complicated," he said. He drummed his fingers on the white tablecloth.

He felt a hand on his shoulder then, and a shapely brunette pulled up the seat next to his. Her dark hair was pulled back in a short, loose ponytail. "Welcome to the party. I'm Wendi."

"Skeeter, I'm a friend of Walter's."

Wendi laughed and glanced toward the back of the suite. "I didn't think Walter had any friends. Are you hungry? Thirsty? We've got about anything you'd want here." She looked toward the redhead. "You don't mind if I steal him for a few minutes. After all, this is a hospitality suite."

She didn't wait for an answer, but took him by the hand. They walked to where the bar was set up. She wasn't kidding. Anything you'd want. Canned beer hadn't been on the agenda today. Neither had anything in the bottles lined up along the table. Well, he'd quit half a dozen times in the last week. He could quit again tomorrow. After all, agendas change. He feigned as though he were contemplating, but his eyes had caught the black label almost immediately, and after what he'd thought was a respectable pause, he said, "Oh, how about a Johnny Walker. Black label."

"You got it. Up or on the rocks?"

He'd already turned away, trying not to count how many bottles were there. *Casual, casual.* "Rocks. With a twist."

Two high school boys, twins, darted past him, their shaggy hair whipping around their heads. "Mush!" one of them yelled to the other. "Rooms!" came the reply. They sprinted away. Skeeter turned back toward the track. Listened to the bustle of the race crowd. He heard the clink, clink of the ice dropping into his glass. His glass. Focus on the crews, what were they doing now? He heard the gurgle of the scotch as it spilled over the ice. He closed his eyes.

"Here you go," he heard Wendi's sweet voice say. He turned and accepted the drink.

"Thanks." He waited until she was moving ahead of him to take a sip, and felt the cool against his lips, the warmth run down his throat. She turned with a tantalizing smile.

"Well, come on, the food's the best part."

He followed her to another table. Took another sip. There were hot dishes, breads, even a prime rib with a large carving knife. She was fixing a plate for him, pasta salad, deviled eggs, smoked salmon, fresh raspberries.

"Here, open up," she said, a beautiful smile playing across her face. She was really enjoying this. Catering to him. He obliged. She popped something into his mouth. "Mushroom caps." He tasted cream cheese and some spices he couldn't quite place. With a full mouth he smiled and nodded his head. "Let's go say hi to Walter," she said. "He looks lonely."

When they got to Walter's table, Wendi set Skeeter's plate down, and he began to eat. Walter had moved from canned beer onto the better, bottled variety available in the suite. He'd also donned a large plaid flannel shirt over his T-shirt now that they were in an air-conditioned room. His little red cooler sat near his feet. Skeeter heard a bittersweet twang coming from Walter's radio. Skeeter's small handheld lay neglected and silent on the table.

"Hey, I thought your batteries were dead," he said. Walter didn't acknowledge him.

An old lady ambled up to them, holding an empty champagne glass. She looked more like someone dressed for the derby than the Brickyard. Lime-green rhinestone earrings gripped her earlobes. Coarse white curls peeked out from below her bonnet. She addressed Walter.

"Is it time for the champagne?" she croaked.

Walter ignored her and stared out the windows at the front of the room.

"It's not time yet, Grammy," Wendi said gently. The old woman tottered away.

"Walter, come on buddy, lighten up," Skeeter said.

Walter looked at him. Looked at the plate of food. "Lighten up? My boy should be here today. Look around. All my other kids are here, cousins, friends. But my boy's gone."

Wendi sat down next to Walter and rubbed her hand gently across his back. Skeeter took another sip of his drink.

"What do you mean, gone?"

"Car accident. He used to love the track, loved everything about racing. But then one day ..." and he choked on his words, not able to finish the sentence. Wendi finished it for him. She looked at Skeeter and spoke in a respectful tone.

"Traumatic brain injury, the doctors called it. He was only 27, but there was too much bleeding in the brain, and it shut down."

Skeeter had been annoyed with Walter all morning, but now he felt pity for him. He wasn't good at knowing what to say in moments like this, especially to a virtual stranger. His hand gripped his glass, and he took another sip.

"Walter, I'm so sorry." Walter came out of his reverie and stared hard at him.

"Are you? Are you *so* sorry?" He shook his head, and disgust took over his face. "You know, he had a living will. No feeding tube, no respirator. Took nine days for his brain to die. Do you have any idea, any idea what that's like? To watch someone you love, someone who has been your responsibility since birth, die right in front of you? And not quick like in the movies, but real slow." It wasn't a rhetorical question. Walter was waiting for an answer.

"No, I don't." *What 27-year-old has a living will?*

"It's hell on earth." Through gritted teeth he said, "It haunts me." He looked at Skeeter's plate of food. "You see that food there? He couldn't eat. Do you understand? He starved to death. Couldn't swallow."

Wendi stood up. "Let's let him be, he gets like this sometimes." Skeeter wasn't going to argue. They walked back to the front table and sat down with the redhead. Her emerald eyes flashed at Wendi.

"Get me another drink, love," she purred.

"But you haven't finished ..."

The redhead drained her cup, kept the sword and the cherry, and handed her cup to Wendi.

What the hell. Skeeter drained his, too. "Would you mind?" he said. Wendi smiled, and left to make their drinks.

The redhead tucked a long curl behind one ear. "You never answered my question. Why did you stop working for the crew?" She opened her lips, and the cherry disappeared. She withdrew the sword, and it seemed to point toward him.

Skeeter's head was buzzing. The scotch was stronger than what he was used to, and he'd downed it too quickly. He was feeling strangely introspective. Her eyes looked even greener than before, her hair a more brilliant red. And her lips, how could he not have noticed her lips before?

"Something went wrong. The car was in good shape. Buddy won the race, flying end over end across the finish line. We went out to celebrate that night. But when he left the bar, he got hit by a car in the parking lot. He didn't make it."

She paused. Or did she? Time was swimming. The waves of her hair were swirling, like a current in a copper river. "And they blamed you?"

Another drink appeared in his hand. He downed half of it. "Rumor had it I was high at the time. Combination of alcohol and drugs. And it was my car that hit him. But they couldn't prove that I was behind the wheel." He seemed to have lost all inhibition. He never talked about Buddy's death with anyone. The words had just flowed out of him.

She had a full drink and raised it to her full lips. Like smiling in response to a smile, he raised his own drink to his lips. To his numb lips. *Why can't I feel my lips?* He looked back at

Walter, who seemed to have sobered up.

"Why would a 27-year-old have a living will?" Skeeter asked the redhead.

"I don't know. A high-risk job maybe. My husband had one. He'd seen a friend hooked up to life support. Said that wasn't for him."

He pushed his glass away. Something didn't feel, taste, smell, look right.

"Had?"

"Had. He died two years ago. It took him nine days to pass away. Rumor had it a guy on the pit crew was high that night and ran him down in a parking lot."

Skeeter turned and saw Wendi sitting next to him. There were tears trying to form in her eyes, but she blinked them back. She looked at the track and smiled.

"My brother was really brave. I always knew he was brave on the track. But he was really brave in the hospital. He couldn't tell us with his mouth, but he told us with his eyes. He knew what was happening."

Skeeter stood up, knocking his chair over. He glanced around the room. Everyone was looking at him. Their eyes were so cold. Happy, but so cold at the same time. His stomach lurched. *They've poisoned me*. He looked at Wendi and envisioned her hand moving toward his mouth. *Here, open up*. The redhead. *Open up, tell me everything*.

He stumbled and saw everyone in the suite was standing, statuesque, staring. At him. The redhead and Wendi stood shoulder to shoulder, graceful hands entwined.

A twin giggled, "Mu ..." and lifted his hand for a high five.

The other blurted, "Shrooms!" and simultaneously landed the high five.

Grammy was teetering toward him, her clip-on earrings digging into her lobes, her swollen feet pudging out of her high-heeled shoes, her hot pink lipstick smeared. Skeeter saw a smudge of it on her top front teeth as her lips pulled back in a full, desperate grin. "Is it time for the toast?" her wavering voice asked. Her head tremoring ever so slightly, she held out her empty champagne glass and looked around the room. "Is it time to celebrate?"

Enemies all around. Walter was walking toward him, something in his hand under his loose flannel shirt, the long, rounded end straining against the fabric, but not revealing itself. "You killed my son, you bastard." Walter had said he could sneak anything in here. *My God, he's got a gun. He's going to shoot me. Right here in front of all these people.* Skeeter sprinted and fell on one knee, pushed up, and lunged toward the food table. He turned and saw Wendi pull out her cell phone. She punched in three numbers quickly. He couldn't make out what she was saying at first, but then her voice rose, sounding full of fear, loud enough for him to hear.

"… weapon! We're at the track, in a suite. He's gone mad, he's going to kill him. Please hurry!"

Thank God, help was on the way. Walter continued to move toward him, and that bulge under his shirt looked more ominous by the second. Skeeter grabbed onto the food table. He saw the knife glimmering, shimmering. He grabbed it, triumph rushing through his veins. Walter took a step closer, and Skeeter raised the knife. Just then, officers burst through the door.

"Drop it or we'll shoot!"

Skeeter kept his eyes on Walter, whose hand was still clutching something under his shirt. *Why won't he drop it? Doesn't he know they'll shoot?* Walter advanced, and Skeeter swung the knife toward him. The sound of bullets rang out. Skeeter felt his legs go limp, and he dropped to the floor. He forced his eyes to focus on Walter, and he saw the bottle of champagne emerge from underneath his shirt. A smile danced briefly across Walter's face.

He could hear the police telling people to stay back. Colors were no longer bright. They were fading. Walter knelt beside him and whispered in his ear. "I thought this would be all business today, but I have to say, it's been a pleasure after all."

In the distance, Skeeter heard the roar of the fans as the race was about to begin. The pain faded and he couldn't feel anything. The room faded, and his eyes no longer saw. But for a moment, he could still hear the crowd cheering in a rush of emotion. And he knew they were pleased.

SPONSORSHIPS
by S. Ashley Couts

Believe it or not, fancy marketing and advertising firms are busy scrutinizing, studying, and tabulating the demographics of all 70 million NASCAR fans.

Their statistics show NASCAR fans are college-educated, middle-class, middle-aged folks who own homes. Some 40 percent are women who might swoon over the brawny dude. The guys are patriotic, tend to vote Republican, are against anti-gun laws, and drink Budweiser and shop Home Depot.

Before the recession, a primary sponsorship, which got the sponsor's name in big letters across the hood and prominently along the sides of cars that race by at close to 200 miles per hour, would cost around $6 million. Their sponsorship money, which generally comes from consumers in the first place, covers most of the race team's annual expenses. George W. Bush was, in 2004, a primary sponsor for Kirk Shelmerdine.

Associate sponsorships for race teams pay for what the major sponsor doesn't pick up. At the Sprint Cup level, the price tag isn't counted in pennies. It can range from $500,000 to as much as $5 million. Even so, you might have to squint to see the brand.

That is just sponsorship of individual cars. Sprint is a title sponsor of the series, just like Nextel and the Winston brand were title sponsors before it. That is why it is called the NASCAR Sprint Cup series.

Some sponsors, like Budweiser, are official sponsors of NASCAR, which means they pay for exclusivity over products sold or used at the track.

BONEYARD BUSTED
by Diana Catt

Diana Catt is married to Barry, and they have three kids, a cat and a GS Pointer. She is an adjunct research faculty and instructor at the Indiana University School of Dentistry in Indianapolis. She is also the owner/operator of a private microbiology lab for testing water and indoor air quality. Diana enjoys writing, reading, racquetball, birding and hiking.

"It had to be sabotage," Lonnie said, looking from the lug nut to the open garage door, then back to me.

I didn't share my older brother's opinion. "No way, Lonnie. Someone was in the garage at all times. I made sure."

"Hell, Gage, what about early this morning? When you made the little visit to the Northe garage? Who'd you leave here then?"

I wiped my greasy hands on a shop towel, remembering my 3 a.m. sojourn. "No one," I admitted. "And you know why. I was just following your orders."

I glanced over at the rest of the crew. They were all busy making adjustments, checking computer chips, verifying all was in order. I didn't think anyone was listening.

"Damn right you were. And did you ever think that you got into Northe's garage so easy because maybe her people were over here? Check every bolt. Every connection. We can't take a chance there's another loose wheel or anything else."

I nodded and watched Lonnie storm out. My brother believes he's the greatest NASCAR driver in history. I guess it could be true, but his record doesn't show it. A streak of bad luck, like this loose lug nut today, has plagued our team for the last few years and has become his excuse. Bad luck or sabotage, take your pick. Lonnie's convinced someone wants to keep him out of play and will go to any length to ensure that the Team Sullivan car won't finish first, or maybe won't finish at all. But I'm not convinced.

I spotted Dakota Northe making a beeline toward Lonnie, looking like a hurricane bearing down on Louisiana. A beautiful dark-eyed hurricane, packaged into a tiny frame. Two storms were about to converge, and I wanted to watch.

"Lonnie Sullivan." His name sounded like a poisonous concoction that she was spitting onto the ground. He flashed his camera-ready smile, always able to disarm with charm. "You no-good SOB."

I smiled then. His charm must be off today.

"If it isn't sweet Dakota Northe," he said. "The fastest woman this side of Vegas. Have you come to borrow my chief mechanic? He's almost finished undoing all the help your boys gave us during the night."

"My boys? You're crazy, Sullivan. It was your boys that messed up my car."

"Now, hold your horses, Ms. Northe. That's fighting talk."

"OK, then, let's fight. I can take you."

"For God's sake, Northe, bring it down a notch. Why don't you just prance a few laps around the Alley, wagging that cute little behind of yours, and quit throwing out accusations that won't stand up in a strong wind."

She let out a sound like an engine that wouldn't quite turn over. "You arrogant … I can't wait to take you down. You'll be watching my behind all right, ahead of you at every turn."

"Look, sweet thing, I wouldn't waste my time playing dirty tricks on your sorry-ass team." He leaned toward her, raised an eyebrow and deepened his voice a notch. "But, let's talk about my lug nuts."

She stared at him in disgust, then turned and marched off toward her garage, Lonnie's laughter trailing behind.

I stepped out of Team Sullivan's garage and joined Lonnie, who continued to watch the lovely Ms. Northe's departure.

"Just what did you ever see in her, little brother?" he asked.

I shrugged. "Hard to explain, I guess." I didn't think I could make Lonnie understand the intricacies of Dakota I found fascinating. He couldn't see beyond the competition. She couldn't

74

see beyond my grease-monkey job.

Lonnie didn't waste time speculating on my love life. "She can't beat me with that clunker of hers," he said. "You checked out its specs?"

I nodded. The car was in sad shape. "Unless her crew performs some miracle, she won't be any problem," I said.

Lonnie grinned and slapped my back. "That's what I like to hear, little bro." His smile faded away as he looked over my shoulder at his car. "Just make sure you've found everything. I want to do a test lap this afternoon."

"Don't worry," I said. "You've got the best crew in the place."

"I'll be back in an hour," he said and headed out in the opposite direction of Northe.

Before I returned to my inspection of the car, I glanced toward Dakota's garage. I caught a glimpse of our sponsor's representative, Brent Willoughby, dressed in his trademark white one-button sports jacket and jeans. He cast a furtive glance around and then slipped through the entrance.

My heart sank. Rumor had it that Zipper Automotive, our sponsor, was going to add a new car to their current fleet of one. Dakota obviously wanted to be their driver. She was a pro at manipulating men, and it looked like Willoughby might have succumbed to her wiles. I feared that if Lonnie didn't finish well in the Brickyard, Willoughby might persuade the big boss to get a new driver, instead of a second car. Lonnie'd lose his ride; I'd lose my position as chief mechanic.

I was lying on the creeper, checking all the fittings under the car when I heard Sheila's laughter. I loved my sister-in-law, but she should know better than to disturb me this close to race day.

"Gage?" she called.

I slid out head first. "Go away, Sheila. I'm busy."

She squatted down beside me and planted a kiss on my forehead. There were hoots from the crew.

"You'll get dirty doing that," I said.

She did it again.

"Don't care," she said. "No one's going to look at me unless Lonnie should win, and we both know that's not going to happen."

"It won't if I keep getting interrupted," I said. "Now get out of here."

"What's going on?" Sheila asked, ignoring my demand. "This place is hopping."

"Just doing the final inspection, then Lonnie wants a practice run."

Sheila sighed. "Don't you get tired of this, Gage? You're still young enough to make a career change."

I didn't answer, just rolled back under the car. Sheila never understood why the Sullivan boys needed to be involved in the race; the thrill from the roaring motor, the smells of ethanol and tires burning, the challenge. We couldn't leave it alone.

"Well, I'd be tired of it," she said, "if I was you."

I contemplated her feet from my prone position under the car. Her pink-and-orange toenails had little 32s on them, painted to match Team Sullivan colors; toes a toasty brown. She'd purchased those sandals the last time I drove her to the mall. Cost more than I make in a week. Surely she wasn't tired of that.

"If you're just going to stand around," I said, "make yourself useful. I need a screwdriver. Third drawer down."

Her expensive feet trotted over to the tool box, and I heard the drawer open. "Which one?"

"Phillip's head, any size. Red handle."

"Hey, here's that Tequila we didn't finish the other night," she said. "Want a hit?"

"After the race, Sheila," I said. "I promise." The bottle dropped back into the drawer.

"OK. Here you go."

The red handle appeared at my side.

"Thanks."

"Anything else?"

"Nope. Just get in your seat before Lonnie gets in the car."

"Yes, sir." She pattered toward the garage door, then stopped as a pair of black cowboy boots decked out with silver toe tips and heel rands came into view. It could only be Brent Willoughby.

"Good morning, Mr. Willoughby," Sheila said.

"Mrs. Sullivan, great day to be at the track, hey? Where's that ace driver I'm paying for?"

"Why, Mr. Willoughby, I hadn't heard about you getting a stake in our team. Welcome aboard. I hope your employer, Zipper Automotive, doesn't mind."

I sighed. Sheila wasn't going to help our cause much. I rolled out from under the car. The crew had momentarily stopped working to watch the encounter.

"Morning, Willoughby," I said, hoping to diffuse the moment. I hopped up off the creeper and placed the screwdriver by my keys on top of the toolbox and shook his hand. "Lonnie's going out for a practice run here in a bit. Want to watch?"

"Don't mind if I do," he said. "His times looked good at practice yesterday."

"Should be a bit better today. Track conditions are favorable."

Sheila walked up to him and brushed something off the collar of his white jacket. "Looks like Dakota's shade," she said. "Better get that jacket cleaned before the wifey joins you."

Willoughby looked alarmed and glanced down at his jacket front.

"Thanks, Sheila," I said. "You'd better run along now."

"Care to join me, Mr. Willoughby?" she asked sweetly.

"No, um, thank you, Mrs. Sullivan. I'm going to visit with these boys for a bit. You run along."

We all watched Sheila stroll out the door.

"Don't let me hold you up," Willoughby said. "I'll only stay a few minutes, and then I've got to make a quick pit stop of my own before Lonnie takes the track."

I rolled back under the car and finished checking all the connections. Nothing else was loose; we were ready to rock and roll.

I radioed Lonnie to meet us trackside. Most of the crew headed for the pit area while the rest of us pushed the car from Gasoline Alley through the crowd to the track entrance. We positioned the car so Lonnie could easily get it into line. Fans were encroaching on the roped-off area, and I looked for Lonnie in the crowd. Fifteen minutes must have passed before I spotted him making his way along the last row of garages toward me. At the same moment, I saw Sheila heading toward the bleachers. She was rushing down the alley in front of a parallel row of garages. She could see me but not Lonnie.

I hoped she made the turn toward the bleachers before Lonnie reached the end of his row and spotted her. He'd be upset and distracted if Sheila wasn't in her seat to wave at him as he climbed into his car. One of my brother's inexplicable superstitions.

By the time Lonnie donned his helmet and got strapped into the car, Sheila was in place. She waved. He waved. He drove out onto the track. I glanced back up at Sheila, and she was watching me with a strange look on her face. Then I spotted the bottle of Tequila in her hand. Damn. She'd gone back to the garage and fished it out of the tool box. Well, I couldn't deal with that now. I fervently prayed she didn't make a scene and get caught on camera.

During his first lap around the track, we discovered our communication system was acting up. We could only hear about every other word Lonnie said, and it was obvious he was hearing nothing out of us. He pulled into the pit area and we swapped out the electronics in his helmet. He also reported the steering column seemed loose, so the crew checked that out as well. I had checked the steering column earlier and knew it was OK. As I expected, nothing was wrong. I couldn't help remembering Lonnie's certainty about sabotage. I knew my brother. He was superstitious and could dwell on things. He needed to get past this sabotage fear to be at top performance.

Thirty minutes later, I was sprinting toward the Team Sullivan garage, asking myself if this day could possibly get any worse. Lonnie had wiped out on turn three, smashing our number 32 car into the wall. Fortunately, he wasn't injured, but it would take my crew all night to get the car ready for tomorrow's race. If it was even possible at all. On top of that, Sheila had apparently already finished off the Tequila and was making a spectacle of herself.

I halted my run outside the side entrance to the garage and fumbled in my pocket for the key. No key. Where the hell had I left it? I looked around for George, my assistant crew chief, but knew he'd be on his way to meet Lonnie and the wrecked car at the Boneyard. I slammed my fist into the door, and it slowly creaked open.

I smiled. My luck had turned. I could grab the laptop and high tail it on the four-wheeler out to the Boneyard, download the diagnostics from the track's analysis equipment, and haul the car back here in no time.

I stepped into the darkened space and then paused uneasily. This door should have been locked. With a sense of dread, I flipped on the overheads. Our tools, extra parts, computer systems, all seemed to be there. Nothing was missing, but something had been moved. A canvas tarpaulin that usually covered a stack of spare tires was on the floor in the corner, curled up into a roll. My day went from bad to worse when I spotted the shoes poking out from the center of the rolled tarp.

Speedway police officer Lauren Sprinkle obviously didn't like racing and didn't seem to appreciate my problem.

"But I need my tools," I said again.

"Nothing leaves the crime scene, Mr. Sullivan. Nothing in, nothing out, until we release it."

"Call me Gage," I said, flashing my famously successful smile.

"Save it, Sullivan," Sprinkle said. "How well did you know the victim?"

Victim. Dakota Northe was the last person I would expect to be referred to as a victim.

"I knew her," I admitted. "She drives number 87. Drove, I mean. God, this is difficult for me to grasp. We've traveled the same circuit for about four years. You get to know everyone pretty well doing that."

"Did you like her?"

I wasn't sure how to answer. Last year I thought I was in love with Dakota. I shrugged. "She was OK, I guess. Yeah, I liked her."

"Did she have any enemies, Mr. Sullivan?"

Now that was a loaded question. We all have something at stake, competing not only for the big win but for points. It can get intense and tempers will flare. Then again, rivals on the track will just as likely turn around and share a few beers and laughs. Hard to say who might be holding a grudge.

"Maybe you should be asking her crew," I said. "I don't know any."

"I will, Mr. Sullivan, you can be sure. But you found the body and it's in your garage." She looked around the small space. "Who has access?"

"Me, Lonnie, the rest of the crew. About 10 people, I suppose."

"Do you usually leave the garage unlocked when your car is out on the track?" she asked.

"Never. I'm sure I locked up when we pulled the car out," I said. "The whole crew was with me. We were busy from the time we left the garage until I found the body." I could vouch for all of them. "And we all need to be getting back to work," I added. "The race won't wait."

She ignored my protestation. "When did you last see Ms. Northe alive?"

I'd been giving that some thought while I waited for the police to arrive. I hadn't decided how much I should say about this morning. That little confrontation probably wouldn't look too good for Lonnie. "I last saw her going into her garage," I said, truthfully, "and Brent Willoughby was right behind her."

She wrote the name in her notebook.

One of the police officers walked up to Officer Sprinkle carrying a red-handled screwdriver, holding it carefully with a shop towel. "Looks like we might have the murder weapon," he said. "Matches the wound in her neck."

My mouth went dry. It was the screwdriver I'd been using just before we took the car out for the practice run. The one Sheila had handed me. Both our fingerprints were on the murder weapon. "That's mine, Officer," I said. "I was using it today and left it on the toolbox over there." Then I remembered my keys had been sitting there, too. Had I picked them up? Had someone else picked them up? "I usually put my tools away," I continued, "but we were in a hurry."

I was jabbering. I needed to stay calm. Officer Sprinkle was staring at me in a way I couldn't interpret. She might even think I'm guilty.

"Well, I found it in a pan of oil," the policeman said. "Still might get prints, though."

"Were you in too big of a hurry to make sure you locked up?" Officer Sprinkle asked.

"I suppose that's possible," I said, "but I always lock up." I needed to get to the Boneyard and speak to Sheila. She'd gotten that bottle of Tequila from my toolbox in the garage after we'd pulled the car out. Had she borrowed my key? Had she decided to make sure Dakota wouldn't put Lonnie and crew out of a job?

"We'll need your fingerprints for comparison," the policeman said, pulling out his kit. I supplied my hand.

"Is that all?" I asked, eager to get to the Boneyard.

"For now. Don't leave town."

I pushed through the crowd that had gathered around the garage, ignoring the questions that came my way. I had to get to Sheila before the police questioned her. When she's snockered, she'll tell everything, and I wanted to make sure she told me, not the authorities. I found her next to Lonnie and the wreckage of number 32.

"I think we can get her going," George was saying. "Body's shot, of course, but doesn't look like the frame's bent anywhere."

"We need to find another garage." I explained the situation. All the crew members present looked shocked. Sheila started to cry and flew into my arms. Lonnie didn't meet my eyes.

"We need to talk, Sheila," I said, steering her away from the crew.

"Why, why, why did you do it?" she sobbed into my ear.

I stopped and held her by the shoulders, looking into her tear-stained face.

"What are you talking about?" I asked.

"Why did you kill Dakota?" she asked, swaying a bit from side to side. "I mean, I know she was a bitch and broke your heart, but you stabbed her in the neck. God, Gage, that's so violent. I never knew you to be so violent."

"It wasn't me," I said.

"But I saw the screwdriver. You know, the one I handed you."

"I didn't kill her. Did you? You can tell me, Sheila. I'll help you if I can."

"Me? God, no. Gage, I can't believe you'd think it was me."

"Did you put the screwdriver in the oil pan?"

"Well, yes. I did that. Only to protect you, though. I figured your prints were all over the thing, so I pulled it out of her neck ..." She started to cry again.

"Hey, hey, it's OK. I didn't kill her. You didn't kill her. We've got nothing to worry about. Don't cry." I patted her head. "How'd you get into the garage, anyway?"

"Well, that's just it. The door was open, and I found your keys on the toolbox." She reached into her pocket and pulled out my keys. "Here." She fumbled and dropped them while trying to hand them over. "I thought you must still be there somewhere, but the place was empty except for … ," her voice faded away, "...her," she said, barely above a whisper.

Sheila needed to go back to the motel and sleep it off. I called George over and instructed him to get her out of there before the police showed up to question everyone.

"She just looked so frail, lying there on the floor like that, in all that blood," Sheila said as George took her arm.

"Wait a second," I said. "Dakota was just lying on the floor?"

Sheila nodded. George gave me a questioning look. I pointed my head toward the parking area and he led her away.

Why would the killer come back to our garage and roll Dakota's body up in a tarp? I couldn't think of any good reason. But I could think of a very good reason for someone who wasn't the killer to hide the body. He was trying to protect his wife. I looked at Lonnie. He was watching George and Sheila disappear into the crowd. Lonnie must have stopped back by the garage before meeting us at the track entrance to get into his car. He had time. He could have witnessed Sheila extracting the screwdriver and dropping it into the pan of oil. No wonder he was off his driving game. But, wrapping up the body in a tarp? What had he planned to do with it?

I walked over to my brother. "She didn't do it," I said.

He jumped like I'd delivered a sucker punch. "Of course not," he said. "Why'd you even suggest something that stupid? Just get the damn car back together and let me worry about my wife."

"Damn it, Lonnie. Dakota was murdered in our garage. This won't just go away. I can alibi the crew, but not you and not Sheila. You need to talk to me about what happened."

"No, Gage, I don't. Now get back to work."

I wanted to pound some sense into him. Instead, I turned back to the car. The track officials were unhooking their analysis equipment. The crew was puttering around trying to look busy, but casting surreptitious glances in our direction. I checked the readout from the computer: no evidence of equipment failure. Their conclusion — driver error. Great. I sensed someone reading over my shoulder. I turned and came face to face with Brent Willoughby. He'd ditched the swanky white jacket because of the heat, or maybe the lipstick smear, and looked a little more approachable.

"Our boy used to have nerves of steel," Willoughby said. "I hope we're not witnessing the end of a career."

So I was wrong again. His casual appearance didn't improve his personality one bit.

"He'll be fine tomorrow," I said. "Took a wild spin's all. Happens to everyone."

"Maybe his mind was somewhere else? Like taking out his competition?"

"And what's that supposed to mean?" I asked.

Willoughby didn't answer, just walked away with a smirk on his face.

"Oh, yeah?" I yelled after him. "You, of all people, had better not be implying anything about Dakota."

Willoughby stopped and whirled back toward me. I don't know what I'd intended to add, but it died in my throat. His glare was menacing, and as he closed the space between us, I realized how much he towered above me.

"I hope that wasn't intended to be a threat," he said.

I shook my head, unable think of a response that wouldn't get me hurt.

He glared a few seconds longer, then abruptly turned and moved away. I wondered about his violent reaction. I wanted to talk to Lonnie about it, but he was still acting weird. Then police officer Sprinkle showed up at the Boneyard to interview Lonnie and the crew. By the time she was finished, I'd convinced myself that Willoughby's reaction was important enough to mention. So I told her about Dakota's flirtation with Willoughby and the lipstick on the jacket and his reaction to my mentioning her name.

"Describe the jacket," Sprinkle said.

When I did, she walked me over to her squad car and pointed to a bag lying on the back seat. Inside was a white jacket covered in blood.

"Found that in a dumpster behind your garage. Willoughby's?" she asked.

I nodded. There was no mistaking the man's signature style.

"This was in the pocket." She held up a key in an evidence bag. "It fits your garage." Sprinkle radioed for an arrest warrant to bring in Brent Willoughby.

I never knew Willoughby had been issued a key. He knew our garage would be empty during the practice run and would make the perfect place for a private assignation amid the racing crowd. Or a confrontation.

Poor Dakota. A tiny whirlwind of ambition, competition and misguided determination. Even after witnessing Brent Willoughby's temper, I was still shocked that he would stab Dakota. What had set him off? Did Sheila's comments about Willoughby's wife finding Dakota's lipstick on his jacket send him over the edge? Or had Dakota made more specific threats, like threatening to tell all to the wife if she wasn't given a sponsorship? I could see her doing that. Well, I'd let the police sort out the motive. I had work to do on number 32.

NASCAR GOES TO THE MOVIES
by Diana Catt

Hollywood has always recognized the magnetic attraction of speed, danger and romance. NASCAR provides all these elements and more. Whether a documentary, biography, or spoof, if you love NASCAR, you should look for these:

- *Ride of Their Lives* (2008) – A documentary narrated by Kevin Costner, with interviews of Richard Petty, Dale Earnhardt Jr., Jeff Gordon, Bobby Allison, Darrell Waltrip and others. Available from Paramount Home Entertainment.

- *NASCAR 3D: The IMAX Experience* (2004) – A documentary directed by Simon Wincer and narrated by Kiefer Sutherland, that charts the rise of NASCAR and features "rare behind-the-scenes glimpses, as well as gripping footage of the un-predictable action on the track."

- *The Last American Hero* (1973) – Re-released as *Hard Driver*. Loosely biographical film about moonshine runner and NASCAR driver Junior Johnson. Directed by Lamont Johnson, starring Jeff Bridges, Valerie Perrine, Geraldine Fitzgerald, Ned Beatty and Gary Busey.

- *Greased Lightning* (1977) – A biographical film directed by Michael Schultz, starring Richard Pryor, Beau Bridges and Pam Grier. Based on the true life story of Wendell Scott, the first black stock-car racing champion in America.

- *43: The Richard Petty Story* (1974) – A biographical movie directed by Edward J. Lakso, starring Richard Petty as himself and Darren McGavin as Lee Petty, Richard's father.

- *3: The Dale Earnhardt Story* (2004) – A biographical movie directed by Russell Mulcahy, starring Barry Pepper as Dale Earnhardt.

- *Days of Thunder* (1990) – Action and romance packed into a film directed by Tony Scott, starring Tom Cruise, Robert Duvall and Nicole Kidman.

- *Viva Las Vegas* (1969) – A musical comedy directed by George Sidney, starring Elvis Presley and Ann-Margaret.

- *Speedway* (1968) – Another Elvis musical comedy, directed by Norman Taurog and co-starring Nancy Sinatra.

- *Six Pack* (1982) – A comedy directed by Daniel Petrie, starring Kenny Rogers, Diane Lane, Erin Gray and Anthony Michael Hall.

- *Stroker Ace* (1983) – A comedy directed by Hal Needham, starring Burt Reynolds, Ned Beatty and Jim Nabors.

- *Herbie - Fully Loaded* (2005) – A comedy directed by Angela Robinson, starring Lindsay Lohan, Michael Keaton and Matt Dillon.

- *Talladega Nights: The Ballad of Ricky Bobby* (2006) – A comedy directed by Adam McKay, starring Will Farrell, Gary Cole, Jane Lynch and Jason Davis.

Joan Bruce

I LOVE YOU, JEFF GORDON
by Joan Bruce

Joan Bruce is the pseudonym of D. B. Reddick.

"Jeff Gordon!" the voice bellowed so loudly it practically shook the ground under my feet.

I turned to see who'd swallowed the megaphone and spotted this little guy in a neon orange Tony Stewart T-shirt that barely stretched across his gut. His blue jean shorts hung just above his knees. And he had a death grip on his can of beer. Two dorks in matching outfits stood behind Mr. Pumpkin Man.

"What'd you say?"

"I said I hate Jeff Gordon," the guy barked louder than before.

Several racing fans had formed a wide circle around us. No doubt they were hoping pudgy and I would start wrestling with each other in front of the Indianapolis Motor Speedway.

"What's your problem, mister?" I asked.

"You deaf? I hate Jeff Gordon," he replied before taking a healthy swig of beer and wiping his mouth off with the back of his arm. "Gordon's a wuss, and anybody who loves him is a wuss, too."

It was all I could do to keep from kicking the guy where it would hurt, but I didn't. I was wearing flip flops. Instead, I just glared at him and said, "Get a life, fatso."

As I turned back to my friend Mandy Malone, she grabbed me by the arm.

"Look out, Candi!" she yelled.

Without looking up, I did a quick two-step as Mr. Roly-Poly tripped over his shoelaces and fell flat on his face beside me.

"Now, look at what you've done," Fatso said as he tried picking himself up. "You've made me spill my beer. You owe me a drink."

"In your dreams, buster."

I grabbed Mandy's arm and steered her toward the gate that would take us to our seats in the grandstands.

"What was Fatso's problem?" I asked her as we sat down in our seats.

"I think it was your T-shirt."

"What's wrong with it?"

"Oh, I don't know," Mandy said as she squirted suntan lotion on her arms. "Maybe it's Jeff Gordon's picture on the front or the 'I Love You, Jeff Gordon' lettering on the back."

"Isn't it great?" I said, pulling my shirt out in front of me so I could get a better look at Jeff's gorgeous face. "I won it last week on WYMN. Besides these seats, I also got two pit passes to meet Jeff afterward. Just for telling Martha Rae Folger's listeners in 30 seconds or less why I love Jeff Gordon."

"Why didn't you bring Bobby?" Mandy asked. "Isn't he a big NASCAR fan?"

"Bobby's a huge fan, but he's mad at me because I won and he didn't. When Martha Rae asked him why he loved Jeff Gordon, Bobby choked up on air and nothing came out."

"Sounds like your marriage," Mandy said. "Oops, I didn't mean to say that. It just popped out."

"Don't worry," I replied. "Bobby's biggest problem was forgetting to come home at nights. He's history now, but you're gonna be hooked on NASCAR before this race is over."

"Don't count on it."

The Brickyard 400 was terrific. After a four-car pileup on the 14th lap, the race settled down to an exciting duel between Jeff Gordon and Tony Stewart. But on the final lap, Jeff's car was bumped from behind and Jimmie Johnson roared past him.

"OK," Mandy said as she stood up in her seat. "I admit the race wasn't too bad after all. Ready to go?"

"We're not going anywhere," I quickly reminded her. "Don't you remember, I won pit passes to meet Jeff in person."

"Do we have to?" Mandy whined.

"Absolutely," I replied. "Jeff's going to pick the grand prize winner."

"And what's the winner get? A giant hug from your hero?"

"Don't I wish! No, it's an authentic red leather team jacket."

"Whoopee."

Mandy and I were about halfway to Jeff's garage in Gasoline Alley when I spotted a restroom just ahead of us.

"I need to go potty," I said, turning to Mandy. "Want to come?"

"No, I'll stay here and watch everyone else leave," she said.

I hurried into the restroom and quickly found an empty stall. As I sat there checking out the tiles at my feet, the woman in the next stall appeared to want to play a game of footsies. Part of her orange running shoe was sticking under the partition over on my side.

I coughed a few times, hoping she'd take the hint, but her shoe didn't move. I stood up, flushed the toilet, and quickly left the stall. I fully intended to wash my hands and quickly leave, but a tiny voice inside my head suddenly told me that I should check on the woman in the next stall. What if she wasn't one of those funny gals after all, and she was sick and had passed out on the floor? I walked over to her stall and tapped on the door.

"Is everything OK in there?" I asked politely.

No answer. I rapped a little harder. This time, the door slowly swung open. And sitting on the floor was Fatso in his neon orange T-shirt. A hot dog was sticking out of his mouth.

"What are you doing in here?" I shouted.

He didn't answer, so I quickly ran out of the restroom to find some help.

"What's the matter?" Mandy asked as I ran toward her. "You look like you've seen a ghost."

"Worse," I said, trying to catch my breath. "It's Fatso. He's lying dead inside."

"What?" Mandy exclaimed. "Why would he be in there?"

"Beats me, but he is. And it looks like he choked on a hot dog."

"Well, we can't just leave him there," Mandy said, reaching into her purse and pulling out her cell phone. "Women need to use that restroom. Let's call 911."

About 10 minutes later, a tall, good-looking guy walked up to us. The two dorks were in tow.

"I'm Detective Dan Parker of the Speedway Police Department," he said, flashing his police badge. "What's the problem?"

"In there," I said, pointing to the restroom.

The detective ran into the restroom with the dorks right behind him. They emerged a minute later.

"We need to talk, miss," Detective Parker said as he approached. "These two men just told me you confronted their friend earlier today and threatened him."

"So …?"

"That's him inside the restroom," the detective said. "These men have identified him. They haven't seen him since he went for some food more than an hour ago. They were worried that something happened to him. That's why they stopped me a while ago and asked if I could help them find their friend."

"And you did," I said. "Good police work on your part, Detective."

Detective Parker wasn't amused. He just glared at me.

"You've got some serious questions to answer about all of this," he said firmly. "But first I need to call for some help. Then I'm taking you to the police station."

A few minutes later, Detective Parker stuck Mandy and me in the backseat of a big black police cruiser. The air inside suddenly felt like we were stuck inside a meat locker. Mandy didn't say a word and refused to look at me.

When we arrived at the police station, Detective Parker put me and Mandy in separate interrogation rooms. I got stuck talking to a middle-aged detective with a cheap toupee.

"So, Ms. DeCarlo," Detective Hairpiece began, "what exactly did you say to Leonard Walton?"

"Who?"

"The deceased. I understand you threatened him before the race began?"

"I just called him Fatso. That's not a threat. It's a fact of life."

"Maybe so, but what were the two of you doing inside that restroom?" the detective asked as he glanced across the table at me.

"Not what you're thinking," I said, glaring at him. "I needed to go, and he was already in there. End of story."

As Detective Hairpiece stared at me, a uniformed officer wandered into the room and whispered something in the detective's ear. The cop must have brushed up against his toupee because it suddenly looked slightly off center. The two of them left, and I was left to wonder what would happen next.

About 15 minutes later, the detective returned. He told me Mandy had vouched for my whereabouts during the Brickyard 400 and had mentioned how I'd simply slipped into the restroom on our way to Jeff Gordon's garage.

Didn't I say that a half-hour ago?

"I'm going to drive you back to your vehicle now, Ms. DeCarlo," the detective said, "We still need to do an autopsy on Mr. Walton. But you're still a person of interest in my book."

Tips & Toes, where I work as a manicurist, is closed on Mondays so I usually spend the morning doing my laundry at *Sun & Suds*, Bartonville's combination laundromat and tanning parlor. I was sitting there on a red plastic chair, reading an old gossip magazine, when my cell phone rang.

"Is that you, Candi?" Martha Rae Fogler asked.

"What's up?"

"I just read a news story about an unidentified woman finding a guy lying dead inside a woman's restroom at the track yesterday," she said. "It reminded me of you and the Jeff Gordon contest. How'd you make out?"

"I won the booby prize," I replied. "I'm the one who found that guy."

"You're the one who found Lenny Walton? Is he still as chunky as ever?"

"You know him?"

"If he's the same one I knew while growing up on the eastside of Indy. I used to baby-sit a fat little kid by that name. I suppose it could be him."

"Did the story say anything else?" I asked.

"Only that the cops questioned the woman and later released her," Martha Rae said. "But a Detective Harrington is quoted as saying she remains a 'person of interest.' Candi, do the cops really think you killed Lenny?"

"That detective does, but I didn't do it."

"I believe you, sweetie. Is there anything I can do to help?"

"Yeah, give me Lenny's old address. Maybe one of his relatives still lives there, and they'll tell me how he ended up in the restroom with a hot dog stuck in his mouth."

After Martha Rae had given me Lenny's address, I started making plans for my trip to Indianapolis. A bunch of questions flooded my brain.

Like, if the cops still planned to do an autopsy on Lenny, maybe they didn't think the hot dog was to blame for his death. Could it have been something else? Did the cops think that somebody actually murdered him and used the hot dog to help cover up the crime? And why was Lenny in that restroom in the first place? He didn't seem like the drag queen type.

I left *Sun & Suds* with my laundry basket tucked under my arm and jumped in my Ford F150. It took me nearly an hour before I pulled up in front of a dilapidated two-story white house on East Washington Street in Indianapolis.

I walked up on the creaky porch and knocked on the front door. A moment later, a tiny, white-haired woman in a faded blue housecoat peered around the heavy brown door and snapped, "What do you want?"

So that's where Lenny got his winning personality.

I wasn't about to let this old lady slam the door in my face, so I quickly told her about meeting Lenny at the track and how sweet he seemed. I know. I lied. Sue me. I finished by asking her if Lenny had any friends or enemies.

"He used to hang around with the Shaw twins, Steve and Cleave," she replied. "And then there's his ex-girlfriend, Molly Pollock. She looks a little like you, only younger. Lenny lived with her until she wised up and threw his sorry butt out a couple months back. He begged me to let him live here. I'm sure Lenny had some enemies, but I don't know who they are."

"Where can I find Molly Pollock?" I asked.

"Hold on," the woman said. "I've got her address and phone number written down somewhere. I'll just be a minute."

After Granny stepped away from the doorway, I glanced at my Betty Boop watch. Not quite 2 o'clock. Once I had Molly's number, I'd call and talk to her for a few minutes before heading home. With any luck, I could still enjoy a 30-minute bake at *Sun & Suds* before dinner.

The old woman returned a minute later with Molly's information. I mentioned Lenny's winning personality again.

"Yeah, right," she replied with a look of disbelief. "My grandson was about as sweet as a rattlesnake."

Back in my truck, I quickly dialed Molly's number. No answer. Granny also had given me directions to Molly's apartment in Beech Grove, so I drove over there and left a note in her mailbox. I'd call her later. I had just turned south onto State Road 37 for my ride home when my cell went off.

"Where are you?" Mandy asked.

"On my way home from Indy," I replied. "What's up?"

"I just had a call from Mary Donavan at the Bartonsville Police Department. She didn't have your cell number. The Speedway cops are looking for you. They found some witnesses earlier today, and they want to do a police lineup. You'll need to bring your Jeff Gordon T-shirt with you."

"Looks like I'm not out of the woods yet, does it?" I sighed. "I'll head over there, but if you haven't heard from me in an hour, drive up here after you close your store, OK?"

"Great, that's how I want to spend my evening," Mandy said before hanging up.

It took me 20 minutes to reach the Speedway Police Department. After finding a parking spot, I rummaged through my laundry basket and found my Jeff Gordon T-shirt.

"Good, you're finally here," Detective Harrington said after greeting me in the station lobby. "We need to put you in a police lineup."

"But what if I don't want to?"

"Then we'll arrest you for obstruction," the female officer standing next to the detective said firmly. "So, do we have your cooperation?"

I shrugged.

"Good," the female officer said. "Follow me. You'll need to put on your T-shirt."

Once I finished changing in the woman's restroom, Melissa Peterson, the female officer, stuck me in a room with five other blonds. All were wearing Jeff Gordon T-shirts. A minute later, Detective Harrington ordered each of us to step forward and slowly turn around so the witnesses behind the one-way window in front of us could see the back of our T-shirts.

When the lineup ended, Officer Peterson stepped back into the room.

"You can all go except Ms. DeCarlo," she said. "You'll need to stay behind."

"What's going on?" I said, raising my voice. "I didn't kill Fatso."

"Calm down, ma'am," Peterson said. "One of the witnesses picked you out of the lineup, so we need to ask you some more questions. Let's find a smaller interrogation room."

As we stepped into the hallway, I looked up and spotted Mandy sitting on a wooden bench in the waiting room at the far end of the hall. I broke free of Officer Peterson's grip on my arm and ran toward Mandy.

"Tell this cop I didn't kill Lenny Walton," I said, bursting into tears.

Mandy put her arm around my shoulder and tried to console me as Office Peterson caught up to us.

"Do that again, Ms. DeCarlo, and I'll put you in hand-cuffs," Peterson said, giving me a look that could kill. "Now, let's go."

"But officer, I didn't kill Lenny Walton. You've gotta believe me. That witness is lying."

"Witness?" Mandy said.

"Yeah, somebody picked me out of a lineup a few minutes ago."

"Were two of them the dorks that we ran into at the track yesterday?" Mandy asked.

"I don't know," I said. "Why?"

"Cause I spotted them as I was walking into the station a few minutes ago. They were talking to some blond. From behind, she looked a lot like you."

"Molly Pollock," I said.

"Who's that?"

"Lenny's former girlfriend," I explained. "That's it. Lenny must have followed her into that restroom. And I'll bet you anything that she was wearing a T-shirt just like mine. Why else would he go after her?"

I turned to Officer Peterson, who now had a vise grip on my arm.

"Was Molly Pollock one of the witnesses?" I asked.

"I can't tell you that, but since your friend mentioned it, one of the witnesses did look a little like you," Peterson said.

"Let's put you and your friend in an interrogation room for a minute. I need to check on something."

Mandy and I sat on some uncomfortable metal chairs in an interrogation room for at least a half-hour before Officer Peterson returned.

"What's going on?" I asked.

"We contacted the witness that your friend saw, and she's agreed to return to the station. Tell me the name of Lenny Walton's girlfriend again?"

"Molly Pollock," I said. "She looks a little like me, only she's younger, according to Lenny's grandmother."

"Thanks," Officer Peterson said as she left the room. "I'll keep you posted."

"Think that witness was Molly Pollock?" Mandy asked after Peterson left.

"Absolutely," I replied. "What's the chance of those dorks knowing another woman at the track?"

"Good point."

An hour later, Peterson returned.

"Ms. DeCarlo, you and your friend can leave now."

"I'm no longer a person of interest?"

"That's right, you're not," Peterson said.

"What's happened?"

"We're still waiting on Mr. Walton's autopsy, but Ms. Pollock has admitted to owning a Jeff Gordon T-shirt like yours and to being at the track on Sunday."

"See, I told you it had to be her."

Officer Peterson just smiled and escorted us to the front door of the station.

Two days later, I'd just stuck Lonnie Sparks' nails in a soapy solution when my cell phone went off inside my handbag.

"Is this a bad time, Candi?"

I glanced across my nail station at Lonnie and whispered that Martha Rae Folger was on the line. Lonnie nodded approvingly before sticking an iPod earplug in her ear.

"I'm working on Lonnie Sparks right now, but she says it's OK to talk to you for a few minutes."

"Great. Tell Lonnie I said, 'hi.' What a great lady. I hope I'm as bright as her when I'm 80," Martha Rae said, before adding, "I just read a news story out of Indianapolis that says Lenny Walton's girlfriend has been charged with his death. Something about them pushing each other in the woman's stall and him hitting his head against the toilet bowl. Looks like you're finally off the hook. Can I get your reaction once this commercial ends in five ... four ... three ... two ... and one second.

"Welcome back, folks!" I heard Martha Rae tell her audience. "Candi DeCarlo is on the line. Best darn manicurist in town. So, if you need your nails done, give her a call at *Tips & Toes*. But that's not why we're talking to her today. You probably heard about the guy who was found lying dead inside a woman's restroom at the Brickyard 400. Well, turns out Candi found him. The cops thought she killed the guy and were all set to lock her up and throw away the key. That is, until his girlfriend was charged with his death today. Candi, is that an accurate account of what happened?"

"Pretty much, Martha Rae," I said. "But I've gotta tell you, I was really scared after I got picked out of the police lineup."

"This story says the police think Lenny Walton followed his former girlfriend into the restroom, but it doesn't say why. Got any ideas?"

"I heard they just broke up, but I think the real reason is that she must have been wearing a Jeff Gordon T-shirt just like mine."

"Why would anybody get mad about that?"

"Lenny was a huge Tony Stewart fan," I said. "And everybody knows Jeff and Tony don't always get along."

"Let me ask another question," Martha Rae said. "Is it true what they say here? Did Lenny have a hot dog stuffed in his mouth?"

"Yup," I said. "Only a little bit of it was sticking out."

"Wow," Martha Rae said. "I guess I'll let you get back to Lonnie. I'm glad you're no longer a person of interest. And I'm sorry that you missed the finals of the Jeff Gordon contest. But you're a winner in my book."

A commercial began playing in the background before Martha Rae came back on the line.

"Thanks for the interview, Candi," she said. "I appreciate you not letting on about me knowing Lenny. My listeners don't need to know I used to babysit that jerk."

On Friday night, I trudged up the outside stairs that led to my second-floor apartment. I was exhausted. It'd been a long week, but it still wasn't over. Judging from our appointment book, Saturday was going to be another busy day at *Tips & Toes*. All I wanted to do right now was take a warm bubble bath, munch on the Ho Ho's I'd just bought at the *Grab 'n Run*, and pour myself a diet Dr. Pepper.

As I neared the landing, I noticed a FedEx box leaning against my front door. What could that be?

I quickly unlocked the door and threw my groceries on the kitchen counter before retrieving the box. I then sat down on my couch and ripped open one end of it. A white envelope fell out. I picked it up off the floor and quickly opened it.

"Dear Candi," it began. "Your friend, Martha Rae Folger, told me how you ran into some trouble on your way to the finals of our contest. Sorry to hear that, but I understand everything's OK now. Hope you enjoy the little present inside. All the best. Jeff."

I reread the letter before glancing at the return address on the front of the box. Hendricks Racing Team. Charlotte, North Carolina.

"It's from Jeff Gordon," I screamed, as I tipped the box on its side. A red leather racing jacket fell out. I picked it up off the floor and quickly tried it on. It fit perfectly.

"I love you, Jeff Gordon," I shouted at the top of my lungs.

A HOOSIER IN NASCAR – TONY STEWART
by Diana Catt

Tony Stewart, a Columbus, Indiana, native, began his racing career at age 7 behind the wheel of a go-kart, with his father, Nelson, serving as car owner and crew chief. By 1989 Stewart began the transition from karts to higher-horsepower, open-wheel machines. He raced three-quarter midgets before turning his attention to the USAC ranks in 1991 where he was named Rookie of the Year.

Stewart had five wins in 22 starts in 1994 when he won the United States Automobile Club's National Midget championship but reached greater heights the following year with his famous Triple Crown triumph, winning USAC's Silver Crown, National Midget and Sprint Car championship in the same year.

His success allowed him to get a ride in an Indy Car. He won Rookie of the Year honors in the 1996 Indianapolis 500 and won the Indy Racing League championship in 1997.

Then Stewart jumped to NASCAR, where he was Sprint Cup Rookie of the Year in 1999.

While Stewart has never won the Indy 500, he has won at the Indianapolis Motor Speedway, claiming the Brickyard 400 in 2005 and 2007. And while he also has never won NASCAR's biggest race, the season-opening Daytona 500, he has won nearly everything else at the Daytona International Speedway. He is a three-time winner of the NASCAR Nationwide Series race at Daytona (2005, 2006 and 2008) and is a two-time winner of the famed Chili Bowl, an all-star Midget race at the Tulsa (Okla.) Expo Raceway (2002 and 2007). Stewart is a two-time NASCAR champion, winning the series championship in 2002 and 2005, and started his own NASCAR team, Stewart-Haas Racing, for the 2009 season. And Columbus residents still occasionally see him in town.

D. B. Reddick

ONE DEAD SCOOTER
by D.B. Reddick

D.B. Reddick is a Camby, Indiana, writer. His previous Charley O'Brien short stories have appeared in Racing Can Be Murder*(Blue River Press) and* Medium of Murder *(Red Coyote Press).*

I punched up line one on my radio console.

"Are you the Charley O'Brien who worked at KMOX?" the voice on the other end of the line asked.

"That's me," I said, scratching my balding head as I glanced at the clock above the control room window. 1:47 a.m. *Who's calling me at this hour to reminisce about St. Louis? Damn, that was more than 30 years ago. My first news side job in radio. I worked at KMOX for six months before moving down I-70 to Kansas City and KMBZ.*

"Charley, it's me, Scooter McClure."

"Scooter who?"

"Oh, sorry. That's who I am now. In St. Louis, I was Jim McClure."

"The sports guy?"

"The one and only."

"What are you doin' in Indianapolis?"

"Covering the Brickyard. Got a call yesterday from a guy at Speedway Motorsports. Said one of his turn announcers developed a case of laryngitis and he wants me to fill in for him. I've done this job for the Motor Racing Network in North Carolina for a dozen years now."

"Sounds like fun."

"It is, Charley. I travel the Nextel circuit with MRN four or five times a year. And it doesn't really interfere with my regular sports show on WFNZ in Charlotte."

"Still doin' the sports thing?"

"Yup, guess I'm a born jock," McClure said, laughing loudly. "Thought about doin' news once, but I didn't want to chase ambulances the rest of my career."

"Boy, you got that right," I said, remembering the numerous times I crawled out of bed in the middle of the night to rush to an accident scene.

"Listen, Charley, I'd better get going," McClure said. "I checked into the Westin a half hour ago. Flipped on the radio in my room, and there you were yakking away."

"That's me, an insomniac's best friend," I said. "Gotta go myself. Got airtime to sell before the 2 o'clock newsbreak. But before I do that, I'm sure my listeners would love to know who you think is going to win the race on Sunday."

"Tough question. Jimmie Johnson and his pit crew have been running real good of late, but so have Tony Stewart and Junior. And Jeff Gordon always runs well here. But if I had to pick, I'd say Tony Stewart."

"All right, we're going to hold you to that prediction," I said as I motioned for my producer, Zach Berman, to punch up a commercial.

"Still there, Scooter?" I said once we were off air.

"Yeah," he replied. "Listen, I've got a couple of driver interviews later this morning, but once I'm done with them, I'll have some free time this afternoon. Let's get together for lunch. I'd love to see you again. Why don't you meet me in the Westin lobby around 1:30?"

"Sounds like a plan," I said, never one to pass up a meal. "By the way, how's Ginger?"

"She and I split up six months ago. A real nasty divorce. But, hey, I'll tell you all about it at lunch. I need to get some sleep."

I woke up just after noon on Saturday. Short night. I didn't get home from work until six. But I took a quick shower, dressed and drove over to the Westin. After parking my trusty '94 Cadillac Deville in the hotel's underground lot, I used the elevator to reach the hotel lobby. I walked up to the registration counter and politely asked the female clerk standing there to call Scooter McClure's room.

She stared blankly at me. I repeated my request, this time enunciating each word very slowly. As I waited to see if she'd make the call, a guy leaning against the counter a few feet away spoke up.

"Did I hear you correctly? Are you looking for Scooter McClure?"

"Yeah," I said, glaring at Mr. Busybody. "Why are you asking?"

"I'm Detective William Floyd," he said, reaching into his plaid sports jacket and pulling out a police badge. "Can we talk over there?"

The detective and I walked over to a pair of plush leather chairs just off the lobby and sat down.

"Mind telling me who you are?" the detective asked as he shifted in his chair, trying to get comfortable.

"Sure, I'm Charley O'Brien. Scooter and I are old buddies. We used to work together in St. Louis. What's going on?"

"I'm afraid I've got some bad news," said Detective Floyd, looking me sternly in the eye. "A housekeeper found Mr. McClure lying dead in his bed a couple hours ago. He'd been stabbed in the chest."

"Damn," I said, rubbing my head in disbelief. "I talked to Scooter on the air earlier this morning."

"When was that?" the detective asked, pulling a notebook from his coat pocket.

"Just before two. We only talked for a few minutes. He called my talk show on WZMN. Said he was in town to help broadcast the Allstate 400 at the Brickyard."

"Know if he's got any next of kin?"

"He was married for a long time to a gal named Ginger. They met in St. Louis, but Scooter said they recently divorced."

The detective took down my personal information, including my cell phone number, and said he'd get back to me if he had further questions. Scooter's death ruined any thoughts of enjoying a nice lunch, so I wandered back to the parking garage and drove home.

As I stepped from my car in front of my house in the historic Lockerbie Square neighborhood, I spotted Matthew Malone sprinting toward me. And it looked like my neighbor was holding a plateful of homemade muffins in his hands.

"What's up, Charley?" Matthew said, stopping midstride. "You look kinda blue."

"Blue isn't the word," I said, letting out a long sigh. "I just learned an old radio buddy of mine was stabbed to death at the Westin."

"Omigod, what happened?"

"Don't really know," I said. "Apparently a housekeeper found him dead in bed."

"I'm so sorry for your loss," Matthew said, putting his arm around my shoulder. "Let me help you inside. You should lie down for a while."

I took Matthew's advice and fell fast asleep on my couch and didn't wake up until after five. As I sat up, I started thinking about Scooter and why somebody would want to kill him. I wandered into the kitchen, picked up the phone, and asked the operator to give me the number for WFNZ, where Scooter worked in Charlotte. Surely somebody there might be able to offer some clues.

"Lance Gruber show," the young guy who answered the phone said after seven or eight rings. "What do you want to tell Lance?"

"Is there anybody there who isn't in the middle of a radio show?" I asked. "I need to ask somebody about Scooter McClure."

"Afraid not. It's just me and Lance. What about Scooter?"

"He's dead."

"What? Is this some kinda sick prank? Hey, hold on a minute, I need to put through another call to Lance."

I held on the line. Hopefully the new caller would keep Lance Gruber busy talking about NASCAR or the approaching college football season long enough for me to pull some information out of his producer.

"OK, I'm back. Now, what's this about one dead Scooter?"

I told the producer who I was and how Scooter had been found dead in his hotel room earlier today.

"Damn, don't that beat all," he said when I finished.

"That's why I'm calling. Did Scooter have any enemies?"

"Mister, Scooter was a sports talk jock. Enemies? What do you think? He was always telling listeners where to get off. I'm sure he pissed off plenty of them. But I doubt any of them bothered to follow him to Indianapolis."

Good point. It probably wasn't a disgruntled listener who killed Scooter. More likely somebody he knew, but who?

"Let me ask another question before you get back to your show," I said. "What do you know about Scooter's ex-wife?"

"Ginger? Now, there's a wildcat if there ever was one."

"What do you mean?"

"Ginger became something of a local media darling a year ago after serving divorce papers on Scooter. She started talking to every reporter in town who'd listen. Told them some pretty embarrassing stuff, too. But then it came out that she'd been running around behind Scooter's back with NASCAR owner Barney Scott. I thought Scooter would get fired. Radio stations don't like being in the middle of scandals. But Scooter's ratings were tops in the afternoon drive time slot."

After hanging up, I reached into my freezer, pulled out a man-sized dinner, and popped it in the microwave. I was starving. As I waited on dinner, I began replaying the conversation I had with the WFNZ producer. He said Ginger's boyfriend was a NASCAR owner. When I finished dinner, I booted up my laptop and learned that Barney Scott owned the Number 83 car, and it was entered in tomorrow's race.

Maybe if I dropped by the racetrack, I could find Ginger and see what she knew about Scooter's murder. As I thought more about it, I remembered our station owner had sent out a memo earlier in the week telling everybody he had extra tickets to his suite at the track. I called Jerry Zimmerman at home and told him my story. I got lucky. He had one ticket left.

"Glad you can use it," the Z-man said, "But how are you going to find that woman in a crowd of 200,000 or more fans?"

I met the Z-man early Sunday morning in front of the Indianapolis Motor Speedway. He handed me his extra ticket and wished me luck. I definitely was going to need it. Once inside the track, I walked up to several security guards and asked them where I could find Barney Scott.

"Barney's probably hanging out in the garage area, but you can't get in there without a special pass," one guard informed me. Another said some NASCAR owners liked to watch the race from a suite, but he wasn't sure if Barney used one.

I was becoming more frustrated by the minute. Z-man was right. Finding Ginger and Barney Scott was like looking for the proverbial needle in a haystack. Maybe I should give up, drop by the Z-man's suite, and watch the race from there.

As I stood in front of the stands along the front straightaway, my cell phone started vibrating in my pants pocket.

"Is this Charley O'Brien?" the voice asked when I answered the phone.

"Who's this?"

"Detective Floyd. Where are you?"

"At the track."

"Good," he replied. "I'm here, too. Where are you? We need to talk."

"About what?" I said, wondering why Detective Floyd suddenly was interested in me.

"I talked to Scooter McClure's ex-wife earlier," he said. "You didn't tell me about once being romantically involved with her."

"What?" I said, nearly dropping my phone on the pavement.

"She said you and Mr. McClure used to compete for her affections in St. Louis, and you were angry when he ended up marrying her. I need to know more about that, so where are you?"

"Near the starting line," I said, still reeling from Ginger's comment.

"Don't move," Detective Floyd said. "I'll be right there."

The last thing I needed right now was Detective Floyd grilling me about Ginger. Sure, I thought she was beautiful. Ginger had long blonde hair and a curvy figure. But it didn't take me long to realize she was more interested in Scooter, and why not? He was tall and had the kind of long, wavy black hair that apparently drives women crazy. None of that mattered now. I needed to find Ginger and ask her why she lied to Detective Floyd. I also wanted to know what she knew about Scooter's murder.

I talked to several other security guards and finally learned the whereabouts of Barney Scott's suite. About 10 minutes later, I found myself at his doorway. The door was closed, so I knocked. A dark-haired woman in a bright red Number 83 sweat suit and a beer in her hand opened the door. She looked at me curiously for a second before letting me in.

"Wanna beer, sugar?" she asked in a thick Southern drawl.

"Sure," I said.

After she wandered off to fetch me a beer, I began scanning the room. That's when I spotted Ginger to my left. She didn't look much different from her days in St. Louis. Her hair was shorter and she'd put on some extra pounds, but she still looked good for her age. Ginger was standing next to a handsome-looking older man with silver hair. He was wearing a red exercise outfit. Must be her boyfriend, Barney Scott.

As I continued to stare, Ginger looked up. I could tell from the expression on her face that she didn't recognize me at first. Then it hit her. She formed a small smile on her face.

"Omigod," Ginger said as she approached me a moment later. "I can't believe it's you. Charley O'Brien. What are you doing here?"

"I think you know why I'm here."

"What's goin' on, honey?" the older man said as he walked up to Ginger and put his arm around her waist. "Who's this guy?"

"Barney, this is Charley O'Brien," Ginger explained. "We used to work together at KMOX in St. Louis a long time ago."

"Nice to meet you," Scott said, reaching out to shake my hand. "What can we do for you?"

"I want to ask you some questions about Scooter McClure. I talked to him Saturday morning and ..."

"Not here," Scott said, pointing toward the front door.

The three of us stepped into the hallway.

"Now, what's this about Scooter?" Scott asked.

"For starters, where were the two of you yesterday morning?"

"We don't have to answer that," Scott said sharply. "You're not a cop. Why don't you go and leave us alone."

"That's fine," I said. "If you won't talk to me, maybe you'll talk to a friend of mine."

I reached in my pants pocket for my cell phone.

"What are you doing, O'Brien?"

"Calling my friend, Detective Floyd."

"No, you're not," Scott said, reaching into his exercise jacket and pulling out a tiny black gun. "Put that phone away, or I'll blow you away."

"Barney, don't shoot him here," Ginger pleaded. "It will upset our guests."

"Yeah, Barney," I said. "Why ruin a perfectly good party by shooting me?"

Scott nodded and slowly put his gun away. He ordered me to begin walking down the hallway away from his suite.

"Where are we going, Barney?" I heard Ginger ask him.

"I don't know yet," he replied. "Maybe we'll take him over to the garage and get rid of him there."

I wasn't sure what Barney meant by that last comment, but it didn't sound too good. We'd just taken the elevator from the suites to the ground level when I looked up and noticed

Detective Floyd walking toward us.

"There you are," Detective Floyd said with a determined look on his face. "I thought I told you to stay put. Think this is some kind of a game?"

"No sir," I replied. "It's just that I ran into Barney and Ginger after we talked, and they invited me up to their suite."

"That's right, detective," Scott interjected. "Charley's a heck of a guy. No wonder Ginger thinks the world of him."

"Where are the three of you going now?" Detective Floyd asked suspiciously.

"I'm taking Charley over to my garage to show him around," Scott said. "Why don't you go up to my suite and enjoy yourself until we get back? We'll only be gone a few minutes."

Detective Floyd now had a puzzled look on his face, but he let Barney, Ginger and me continue on our journey.

"That was some mighty fine sweet talkin' you just did," I told Scott when we were out of earshot of Detective Floyd. "Ever thought of going into radio?"

"Shut up, O'Brien, or I'll blast you right here," he said, jamming the tip of his gun into the small of my back. I got the message.

Once we arrived at the garage, Ginger turned to Scott and asked, "What are we going to do now?"

"I'm not sure. I wasn't counting on running into that detective. That complicates everything. Now we've got to make Charley's death look like an accident instead of just shooting him."

"Well, we can't wait too long," Ginger said. "Detective Floyd will get suspicious and come looking for us."

"Shut up, Ginger," Scott said, still holding his gun firmly in his hand. "Don't you think I know that? Give me another minute. This accident needs to look convincing."

Barney needed to abandon this crazy talk about me being in a deadly accident and walk back to his suite for a drink. But somehow I figured he wouldn't listen. I started to get nervous when I saw him looking fondly at the hoist near the practice car. Being crushed beneath a NASCAR race car didn't sound very appealing. But I didn't have to worry about that. Just then, the garage door flung open and in charged Detective Floyd and three uniformed officers.

"Put down the gun, Scott," Detective Floyd ordered.

Scott looked up from the hoist and pointed his gun at the officers. Bad idea. One of them fired a shot, winging him in the right shoulder. He fell to the floor. Ginger rushed to his side as did the cops. As Detective Floyd rushed past me, he said, "Don't go anywhere, O'Brien. We need to talk."

A half hour passed before two ambulance attendants carted Barney off to the nearest hospital and the uniformed officers handcuffed Ginger and took her away. That was when Detective Floyd finally walked up to me.

"So, how did you figure out Barney and Ginger killed your friend, Scooter McClure?"

I shrugged. "It started with Scooter saying something on Saturday morning about going through an ugly divorce. And then a guy at WFNZ told me how Ginger made a big fuss about the breakup. She obviously had some unresolved issues. I figured it could have been enough for her and Barney to kill Scooter."

"Good reasoning on your part, O'Brien," Detective Floyd said. "But real dumb of you to get involved. You could have had your head blown off."

"Tell me about it," I said, scratching my head. "So if you also suspected Barney and Ginger, why didn't you arrest them when you ran into us earlier?"

"I figured they were up to no good, but I needed to catch them in the act."

"I'm glad you showed up when you did," I said, glancing over at the hoist. "So why did they kill Scooter?"

"We need to question them some more, but I figure it's probably got something to do with money," he replied. "We've heard rumors that Ginger thought your friend hid money from her before they were divorced. She wanted her share. And Mr. Scott agreed to help her. They must have learned Mr. McClure was in town for the race. We suspect they confronted him in his hotel room, and one of them stabbed him."

"But that still doesn't explain why Ginger tried to pin the murder on me."

"Simple," Detective Floyd said. "The clock radio in Mr. McClure's room was still playing when the housekeeper found his body. Ginger must have recognized your voice and decided to implicate you if she was asked about the murder."

"Wow," I replied. "Ginger is really a wildcat, just like that producer in Charlotte said."

"I don't know anything about that," Detective Floyd said. "All I know is she and Barney Scott will likely spend the rest of their lives thinking about what they did to Scooter McClure."

"If you're done with me, detective, I'd like to go watch the rest of the race."

"Afraid you're too late. One of the ambulance attendants told me it's over. Tony Stewart won."

I smiled. "Scooter would be happy."

A HOOSIER IN NASCAR – RYAN NEWMAN
by Diana Catt

Although many people are unaware of the fact, there is another prominent Hoosier in NASCAR's top series: Ryan Newman of South Bend.

Newman entered the NASCAR scene in 2000. In 260 Sprint Cup starts through the 2008 season, Newman has earned 43 pole positions and has led the series in pole wins four times – with six pole positions in 2002, 11 in 2003, nine in 2004, and eight in 2005. He has earned at least one pole position each year since the 2001 season, when he was running a partial schedule.

His impressive résumé has him tied with Buck Baker for 10th on NASCAR's all-time pole list, while ranking second in poles among the series' full-time active drivers, also based on statistics through the 2008 season.

In addition to his consistent qualifying ability, Newman has proven to be an equally adept racer, including winning the series' biggest race, the Daytona 500, in 2008.

Before the end of the 2008 season, fellow Hoosier Tony Stewart named Newman to drive the second car in the new Stewart-Haas Racing team, which entered NASCAR in 2009.

When not racing, Newman is an avid sportsman and enjoys fishing as well as restoring his classic cars. Newman and his wife, Krissie, play an active role in the Ryan Newman Foundation, which they founded in 2005. The mission of the Ryan Newman Foundation is three-fold: to educate and encourage people to spay/neuter their pets and to adopt dogs and cats from animal shelters; to educate children and adults about the importance of conservation so the beauty of the great outdoors can be appreciated by future generations; and to provide college scholarship funding through the Rich Vogler Scholarship program, of which Newman himself was a recipient, to students interested in auto-racing careers.

A LUCKY GUY
by D. L. Hartmann

Dee Hartmann teaches English in prisons for Ball State University. She started college at age 39 and graduated in 23 months. She has written Home Sweet Funeral Home—*a young adult mystery, seven produced plays, and also features and theater reviews for the* Muncie Star Press *for 15 years. She is a member of the National Association of Pen Women and the American Association of University Women.*

Sandy would tell you she didn't think about NASCAR, didn't know what the initials stood for, but she knew the drivers were sexy and the cars were cool, like they were spray painted with testosterone.

She spotted the fat bald guy glued to the computer in the library and saw the big letters NASCAR on the screen in front of him.

She took the seat at the next computer, logged on, and typed in the word NASCAR, all caps. Lots of hits. She scrolled down to find a list of drivers. Even the names sounded sexy: Tony Stewart, Kyle Busch, Clint Bowyer, Jeff Gordon and rookie Blaze Hollis. She printed the list, went back, clicked on another site and got a list of race locations: Daytona, Atlanta, Bristol, Phoenix, Talladega, Darlington, Indianapolis Brickyard. Print.

The fat guy noticed. "You a NASCAR fan?" he asked.

"Yeah," Sandy said, giving him a warm smile. "You?"

"Honey," he said, "I'm more than a fan. I'm an expert." He eyed her, paying close attention to the way her pink top hugged her ample breasts.

"Gee, I would love to know more about Tony Stewart and Jeff Gordon."

He took a deep breath, looked at his computer screen, then closed out. "How about I buy you a cup of coffee and tell you all about them?"

She smiled broadly, revealing sharp white teeth between her hot pink lips. "I'd love that."

"Harley Wilson," he said as he stood.

"Sandy Brown." She offered him her hand.

He shook, holding her hand a little too long.

In the coffee shop Sandy leaned forward in fascination as Harley held forth at great length about Tony Stewart, his favorite driver.

"He's an Indiana boy, born in Columbus, they call him the Rushville Rocket. I tell you, dirt, concrete, asphalt, he can drive anything with a set of wheels. He started out as a kid racing go-karts, and everyone knew at an early age he was something special. Hey, he's done it all. Won Indy cars in '98, IRL champ, and then transferred to NASCAR."

"Wow. You know a lot about him. Do you go to a lot of races?" she asked.

"Nah, I watch on TV. Don't like crowds and all the noise."

"Then how do you know so much about it?" she looked confused.

"Hey, honey, I know plenty. Trust me. I get all I need watching on TV."

She smiled. "You're an interesting man, Harley Wilson."

He grinned like a kid, sucking in his breath to swell his chest and make his belt loosen a little.

After an hour Sandy looked at her watch. "Gee, I'm sorry, but I have to go. This was great. Thank you."

He stood as she did and stared at her. "You're welcome. It isn't too often I find a woman who really cares about NASCAR the way I do." He paused, then went on quickly. "Maybe we could get together again some time, you know, to talk and all that."

Again she gave him that stunning smile between hot pink lips. "Gee. I would really like that."

"Maybe tomorrow?" he asked, wiping his handkerchief over his sweating head.

"Sure," she said. "I'll meet you in the library. How about 7:00?"

He nodded. "Anytime you say."

She wrote down a number. "Here's my cell phone. Call me."

He met her in the library almost every day after that. She wouldn't tell him where she lived so he could pick her up and take her out to dinner like a real date, but Harley Wilson didn't insist. He liked a little mystery in his life.

He finally convinced her to meet him at Serena's Supper Club and felt like he had won the race for the chase.

"Sandy," he said after dinner at Serena's, "why don't you let me take you home tonight? I hate putting you in a cab."

She patted his hand. "Harley, you are just a darling, but those are my rules. If you keep asking, I'll just have to stop meeting you."

He swallowed hard and wiped his head. "No. No, you don't need to do that. I'll get you a taxi anytime you go out with me. OK?"

"OK." She waited while he fidgeted. "Now tell me again about how you bet on the Brickyard."

He really liked that about Sandy. She was a great listener, always seemed fascinated when he talked. He grinned and told her about the race. He had it all figured out. He was going to win a fortune.

"How do you know?"

He hesitated, looked around the restaurant, then whispered, "I've got some inside information. I bet for some big people."

"Wow," she whispered. "That's fantastic. If you bet for people, does that mean you're a bookie?"

"No, no," he protested with a whisper. "Not me. I know a guy; he's the money man. I just have to be careful right now."

"Why?"

He shook his head and sighed. "The guy who handles the money …"

"The bookie?" she asked, eyes wide.

He looked around again. "Not so loud," he whispered. "The guy who handles the money used to do all his business by computer, you know, he deposited winnings in off-shore accounts, but right now he can't do it like that. His computer may be watched."

"Is that why you use the computer at the library? Is someone watching yours?"

He wiped the sweat off his head. "Yeah, maybe. I can email the bets, but when we win I have to collect in person. He can't put it off-shore right now."

Her eyes widened. "Will the guy have to pay you in cash?" She looked horrified. "That's really dangerous."

"I know," he said, "I know. But I don't have a choice. There's too much riding on the race." He shrugged and took a deep breath. "That's a joke."

She smiled.

"I just have to pick up the money and deliver it to my clients."

She patted his hand. Her long red nails gleamed in the candlelight. "What if someone is watching you? Didn't you say you thought there was a man watching us when you got me the cab last night?"

He wiped his sweating head. "I don't know. Maybe. That's why I have to get my friend Cliff to pick up the money."

"Can you trust him?" she asked, looking deeply into his watery hazel eyes.

He shook his head again. "I don't know. I hope so. It's a bundle. I have a couple of days before the race to decide."

"Well," she said, "I just hope he's OK. I hope he's a really good friend. It would be awful if he tried to rob you after you win all that money."

That evening for the first time Sandy went back to Harley's apartment with him. In the morning she left early. "I have to catch the bus, Harley. But I had a wonderful time last night." She patted his round cheek. "You are a terrific lover."

He reached for her and hugged her as if he had found a treasure beyond price. "I hate to let you go."

"I have to get to the shop. I've got clients coming in early today for perms," she protested, kissing his bald head. "But I'll meet you tonight."

"I want to pick you up," he said. "Maybe we can watch the race tomorrow afternoon."

She pulled away and studied him seriously. "OK."

He grinned like a child. "Really?"

"Really," she said and gave him her address on East Third Street. He felt as if he had already won the race.

When he drove up in his old Plymouth she was waiting for him. She came out of the vestibule and got into his car. She leaned over to give him a kiss. "You got to upgrade this car," she said with a laugh.

"I intend to as soon as I get some money. Then I'll treat you in style."

She grinned. "That sounds good."

"Will you stay tonight?" he asked in a husky voice.

"Of course, darling," she whispered.

The next afternoon before the race began, Harley and Sandy curled up together on his worn couch. "Tell me about the race," she said stroking his hand.

He cleared his throat and explained, "No matter how good or how fast your car is, you have to draft to win and you have to depend on other cars. So guys team up for the draft. I'll show you when it starts."

"How do you win?"

"You can bet on a single NASCAR race, or you pick your top 10 drivers and whoever has the most points is the winner until the race for the chase—every driver, there are odds on his winning."

"So what do you do, bet on the points or on the driver?"

He nodded. "Both actually, but for this race it's on the driver."

"With those cars following each other that way, how can you tell anything?" Sandy asked.

"That's what I was talking about. Cars line up in a row. There's wind resistance, so if there are two cars with one right behind the other the resistance is cut and two cars linked up together can get more speed and momentum. Drafting partners are in sync until the end when it's every man for himself. The lead car is pulling everyone behind him. They all stay high or low and they take turns leading the draft. A guy in the back pulls out of the draft and shotguns to the front to take the lead."

She smiled adoringly at him. "That's fascinating."

During a commercial Harley acted more nervous than usual. Finally Sandy asked, "What's the matter, darling?"

"I been doing a lot of thinking, and I need to ask you a favor," he said.

"What do you want me to do?"

He cleared his throat again. "I need you to pick up the money."

"You said that would be dangerous," Sandy said hesitantly. "What about your friend?"

He swallowed hard. "I kept thinking about what you said. I don't know if I can trust him." He looked miserable. "It would be dangerous. The man with the money is in the basement of a bar on the near east side. It's a rough place—actually it's a hooker bar."

She blinked. "That's scary."

"I know. If the feds are watching me I don't dare go for the pickup. Even if they saw you with me, I don't think they'll be following you."

"You want me to go alone?" Her voice cracked.

"Hey, baby," he said, "you're the only one I can trust. If our guy wins, there's going to be a bundle. After I pay off my people, we'll still have plenty for ourselves. I could even get a better car."

She thought it over, frowning. The race resumed and Sandy watched the TV for a full minute. Finally she nodded. "I'll do it."

He glowed. "You're the greatest."

Two cars went in the wall at the Brickyard. Sandy sat on the edge of her seat on the lumpy couch next to Harley, who was so caught up with the race he forgot to paw her. The mesmerizing circle of speed kept them both holding their breath. They may have missed the press of the crowd, the unique smell of food, sweat, beer and gasoline that made addicts out of race fans, but even on television the power of the race stirred them. The right result would make Harley a fortune. It was better not to think about the wrong result.

Sandy heard Harley whisper, "Come on, Blaze."

Then it happened, so fast Sandy almost missed it. Blaze Hollis pulled out of the draft and started around the lead car just as behind him a tire blew and spinning cars went in all directions as everyone tried to avoid the carnage. Yellow flag meant caution. Meanwhile, just before the crash Hollis had moved into first and stayed there. Pandemonium ruled.

The caution stayed out until the wreckage was cleaned up, leaving only two laps remaining. Hollis stayed in front.

"That's it! It's over and we won," Harley chortled.

Sandy hugged Harley. "He was your man?"

Harley shook and nodded in shock as Hollis took the checkered flag.

"How did you do it? Did you know about the wreck?"

He wiped his head with his handkerchief. "You can't fix the race."

"OK, but something just happened. Hollis pulled out and took first just before the tire blew, like he knew it was coming."

"Well, maybe the tire that blew might have been compromised."

"You're kidding."

He smiled. "Baby, I just made 300 G's and 50 of it's ours. Now we need to pick up our money."

She rubbed his cheek. "This is so exciting." She kissed him. "I'm scared, but I'll do it—for us."

He glowed. "Listen, honey, the bar is in a bad part of town. You won't be able to get a cab to take you down there. Can you borrow a car? You can't use mine if the feds are watching for me to make the pickup."

She nodded, looking scared. "My friend Tiffany will let me borrow hers. I'll call her and have her pick me up down the street. I'll take her home and use her car. OK?"

"Yeah, but be careful. Don't try to talk to anyone. Have the man call me and I'll give him the OK to turn the money over to you. Ask the bartender for Sam and he'll send you downstairs. When I verify, he'll give you the cash." He got his lucky satchel out of the closet. "Take this and put the money in it. Try to get out as fast as you can and I'll come to your place." He studied her face. "You OK?"

She gave him a wan smile. "I'm OK."

She left five minutes later, looking scared but determined. He gave her a hug. "Call me as soon as you make the pickup, and hey, thanks, baby, you're the greatest. I'm a lucky guy."

After she left he waited, pacing the floor, sweating. When the phone rang he almost dropped it. "Yeah," he answered.

A voice growled a question. "Yeah, she's OK," he said.

He waited, but Sandy didn't call. He prowled his shabby apartment sweating, wanting to vomit, needing to pee. He checked his watch and imagined Sandy dead in a ditch, stopped by the feds, having trouble with Tiffany's car. He called. Her cell phone went straight to voice mail.

Harley waited a half hour before he went to East Third Street to her apartment. He remembered when she waited in the vestibule for him, but no Sandy waited today. He crawled out of his car and went in. None of the mailboxes in the vestibule had her name on it.

He pushed the speaker buttons on the mailboxes and in a cracking voice asked everyone who answered for her apartment number. None of the neighbors knew her. Big surprise. He staggered back to his rusting Plymouth head down, feet dragging. Sandy knew the men who gave him money to bet for them would be in touch soon. They would not be amused.

He couldn't pretend any more. He was a fool. He knew days ago, but he was an idiot. How could he ever hope a woman like Sandy would fall for a guy like him? Stupid. He didn't know anything about her, where she came from, what shop she worked in. She never talked about herself, and he never noticed because he loved talking about himself.

According to her plan he would never see Sandy or his lucky satchel again. He pulled his cell phone out of his pocket and dialed.

"Cliff? Where is she?" He paused. "OK. I'll be right there. Don't let her get away with the money. It's worth 25 g's to you." He sighed. "Yeah, right, and your life. See you in a few."

Harley Wilson got into his old Plymouth and drove downtown. You win a few, you lose a few. At least he would live. He knew he was a lucky guy.

JOE GIBBS RACING: AIMING TO WIN AT THE BRICKYARD

by Jaci Muzamel

The Three Stooges, the Three Musketeers, Three's Company, Three Days Grace, Third Time's a Charm, Threepeat … The "Rule of Three" is a principle that suggests things coming in threes are inherently more satisfying.

Joe Gibbs certainly has known the power of three. As head coach of the NFL's Washington Redskins from 1981 to 1992, Gibbs led the team to three Super Bowl wins and had only three losing seasons. But at the end of the 1992 season, Gibbs looked for a new direction to channel his leadership abilities.

He turned his attention to his newly formed NASCAR race team. Joe Gibbs Racing (JGR) had its first start in 1992 in NASCAR's biggest race – the Daytona 500. Dale Jarrett was behind the wheel of the Number 18 Chevrolet, but an accident on Lap 91 ended his day early. He finished 36th. But the "Coach," as many still refer to him, had begun to assemble a racing team that would become a powerhouse.

Gibbs Racing has three Brickyard 400 wins through 2008. Team driver Bobby Labonte drove the Number 18 Pontiac to a win in 2000. Indiana native Tony Stewart crossed the "Yard of Bricks" in the Number 20 Chevrolet for wins in 2005 and 2007.

The team also has three NASCAR championships. In 2000 Labonte won the championship when it was known as the Winston Cup series, and Stewart won it in 2002. Stewart won again in 2005, after the name had been changed to the Nextel Cup series.

Gibbs has two sons and all three are involved with Gibbs Racing in different capacities.

THE COLLECTORS
by Tamara Phillips

Tamara Phillips moved to the Midwest in 1985 after growing up and living in Alaska for 30 years. She has a published short story in Racing Can Be Murder. *Tamara has worked for the federal government, owned an antique shop, and been a fundraiser for public radio and television. Currently employed as an insurance adjustor, she has a degree in journalism, three daughters and three grandsons.*

Carl Miller's freckled hand stroked the cellophane packaging of his prized Dale Earnhardt Sr. mint-in-box, die-cast, Limited Edition, Winston Cup 25th anniversary silver stock car. He adjusted its position on the shelf just enough so that it caught the tiny spotlight from his recessed lighting.

"There ... just right," he said quietly and rolled his chair back to admire the effect.

"Carl, where are you," Fonda yelled, as she tossed her keys on the counter. "I came home for lunch today, thought I'd surprise you. Carl, did you hear me?"

Fonda stuck her head into the half-open door of Carl's Dale Senior shrine, "I said, where were you today? Oh, for God's sake, Carl, you didn't take Princess out! Again!"

Princess danced around Fonda's legs as she made her way back to the kitchen.

Carl heard the distant jangle of the dog chain as it was yanked from its hook by the kitchen door, and then he heard the door smack closed. His lips turned up slightly as his eyes moved over the wood-and-glass shelving displaying his collection of NASCAR, and in particular, his Dale Earnhardt Sr. metal die cast cars.

He had a nice little collection. Not the same caliber as his friend Ray's. But Ray had the money to buy whatever he wanted, whenever he wanted it. He hadn't lost his job like Carl had. Building and maintaining a collection had been more difficult for Carl, but now, thanks to Ray, he'd just about completed it.

Fonda was so exasperated she was talking to herself as she absentmindedly pulled the little dog up the street. Carl hadn't worked for almost a year—since he was laid off from Thompson Electronics. He had no interests except NASCAR and his precious Dale Earnhardt Sr. car collection. He did nothing around the house—forgot to walk Princess—what was going on with him!! She wondered if he was depressed. He'd weathered layoffs before, but this was different, being so close to retirement for him. She'd had to take a part-time nursing job just to get by, and now with the economy on the downturn, maybe she'd have to think about full time.

Fonda started briskly toward home, the little Shih Tzu doing her best to keep up. About a half-block from home, she saw Dede, their neighbor Ray Gilliam's new (well a year anyway) wife, pull up and get out of her car. Fonda felt a little guilty as she slowed her steps so she wouldn't get so close that she'd have to stop and have a conversation. Dede was OK, just so much younger that they didn't really have much in common except that their husbands were best friends. She knew Dede casually and didn't feel up to hearing about how great Dede and Ray were doing.

She and Carl had been close friends with Ray and ex-wife Mary Beth for over 20 years. Carl and Ray had maintained their friendship after the divorce, mostly through their shared enthusiasm for NASCAR. Dede was the typical trophy wife, and Fonda had never really gotten to know her. Now with the part time job and all, she really did not have time for socializing. Fonda watched Dede swing her long legs, one by one, out of the car, pull a couple bags from the passenger seat, and head up the walk toward her front door. She lifted her hand with the keys, gave a little wave to Fonda, and turned to go inside.

Relieved, Fonda waved and smiled, automatically picking up her pace again and headed for home, Princess trotting behind.

She was almost past Ray and Dede's walk and getting ready to cross the street to home, when a scream brought her to an abrupt stop.

"Help, help me! Something's happened to Ray," Dede shrieked, as she stumbled out the front door.

"Dede, what's the matter?" Fonda said as she turned and ran toward where Dede stood in the open door.

"I think Ray's fallen ... he's just lying there not moving."

Fonda pushed Dede aside and stepped in. Ray lay in the middle of the living room, part of a shelving unit lying across the lower half of his body, and metal die-cast cars and mangled boxes fanned out around him. A small pool of blood framed his head like a halo. Another shelving unit was tipped over, and the miniature metal cars and boxes were strewn under and around it as well.

Fonda moved her feet sideways to push the colorful rubble out of the way, and leaned down to see if she could find a pulse. Nothing.

"Dede, where's your phone?" Fonda looked up to see Dede holding a car out to her.

Shaking, Dede pressed it into her hand, and Fonda heard a voice say "Hello? Hello? What is your emergency?"

She raised the car to her ear and spoke into it.

"There has been an accident at my neighbor's house; I think he's dead. Please send someone right away." Fonda gave the address, which was just one number off from her own.

Fonda put an arm around Dede's shoulders and pulled her in. "Just hang in there, Dede, they are sending paramedics and police to help. Do you know what happened?"

"He was like that when I came in from shopping. You saw me come in. I think he must have been putting a car away or getting one out, and the shelf fell on him."

She gently turned Dede toward the couch, which was as far away from the body as possible. She had thought about having Dede lie down, but that would mean crawling over all the cars and smashed boxes.

"Just sit right here; they'll be here any moment," Fonda said, gently pressing down on Dede's shoulders.

As she was speaking, Fonda looked over Dede's shoulder in horror, not just at Ray's body, but at the house in general. She had not actually been here since Ray and Mary Beth split up, and what she saw took her breath away. Everywhere she looked was NASCAR. The house looked like it had been entirely redone by a NASCAR-crazed decorator.

Floor-to-ceiling glass shelves lined three walls of the living room (two of them now on the floor) and were filled with all kinds of NASCAR memorabilia. Even the picture window was covered up, curtains and all. The showcases were lighted, which gave an other-worldly glow to the whole room. The coffee table was a display case, too, glass covered of course. The wall behind the couch was filled with Dale Earnhardt Sr. autographed flags, plaques and photos. The open door to the bedroom revealed a race-car shaped bed with a car hood headboard and a life-sized cutout of Dale Earnhardt Sr. holding up a Coke bottle and smiling crookedly stood just outside the door as if beckoning you in.

They sank onto the couch together, and Fonda looked toward the front door, seeing Princess, who had been abandoned in the excitement. Princess let out a yip and chose that moment to squat on the black-and-white checkered tile floor.

Fonda automatically leaned forward toward the dog, but Dede grabbed her arm.

"Don't leave me, don't leave ..."

"Of course not," Fonda said. She turned over the car she still held in her hand, punched in her home number, and held it to her ear.

"Carl, you need to come over to Ray's right now. Something awful has happened to him. I'm pretty sure he's dead. I don't know... I've called the police. Yes, Dede's here."

After Fonda hung up, she asked, "Is there anyone you need to call? Someone to come and stay with you maybe?"

"No one. He's dead, isn't he? I'll call my sister, but she lives out of town and probably won't be here for a day or so. Ray doesn't have any family except for his ex-wife, and I don't really know her."

"I'll call her later for you," said Fonda, thinking she hadn't spoken to Mary Beth since right after she and Ray were divorced.

Fonda watched Carl cross the street and arrive at the same time as the police car, followed by an ambulance and paramedics.

Carl and two policemen came in the open front door. The taller policeman took charge and motioned the paramedics through the smashed boxes and brightly colored cars. The one who reached Ray first looked up and shook his head. "He's been dead for a while—don't know how long, but there's nothing we can do."

"OK, our forensics van will be here in a few minutes. Will you wait and talk to them?" the tall officer asked the paramedic.

"You three," the officer nodded his head at Dede, Fonda, and Carl, "go into the kitchen, and my partner and I will be in to speak with you shortly. Was there anyone else here?"

"Just Dede, Ray's wife. I came in right behind her. And Carl just got here. Can we take our dog home? We live right across the street," said Fonda.

The officer said it was OK, so Carl took Princess home and came back within a few minutes to wait.

Carl held Fonda's hand as the three of them sat on swivel stools at the kitchen counter waiting to be interviewed by the officers. The seats looked like tires, and the NASCAR theme was repeated in here as well. Dede sat on one side of Fonda and Carl on the other. Dede's stool was pushed close to Fonda's, and she occasionally laid her head on Fonda's shoulder and sniffled. There was a lot of activity going on in the living room where the body was, but Ray's widow and best friends hardly moved on their stools—all lost in their own thoughts.

"OK folks, I'm Sergeant Paul Webster, lead investigator." He stuck his hand out to Dede, who looked up and took it. "Sorry for your loss, ma'am. I'm going to talk with you first. I know it's going to be hard for you to answer questions right now, but we need to find out all we can as soon as possible."

"Ray just fell, didn't he?" asked Dede, her eyes filling up.

"Well, we don't know for sure yet. We've just started our investigation. By the way, did you happen to notice if anything is missing?"

"No, it's all such a mess; I have no idea if anything is missing."

"Again, we are still investigating. I understand some of those cars in there are pretty pricey."

Dede nodded and then looked up sharply, as if suddenly understanding what the officer was saying. "You think someone was trying to steal Ray's collection? Like maybe he was killed during a robbery? Oh my God," she said and looked back and forth from Fonda to Carl.

"Carl would know about the values, and maybe even what Ray had, right?" she looked at Carl.

"I might be able to help with that. "

"Mr. Martin, are you familiar enough with the deceased's collection to tell if anything is missing?" Webster asked.

"The Dale Earnhardt Sr. stuff I could. At least the rare pieces. Ray and I both collected the cars, but Ray collected all kinds of Earnhardt Sr. stuff, plus NASCAR-related items in general. I couldn't begin to tell you what was missing there."

"What about an inventory?" Fonda asked "You keep an inventory of everything you have, Carl. Do you know if Ray kept an inventory?"

Carl didn't respond. Sergeant Webster looked at Dede, and she shook her head no.

"All right," said Webster, "Carl, I'd appreciate your help going through Gilliam's stuff once our lab is through with everything. Right now, I'm not sure what happened here, but it's possible all these NASCAR things are part of it in some way. Now I'd like to speak with Mrs. Gilliam alone in the dining room, and as soon as we're done, I will need to speak with the two of you. While you're waiting, you might make a list of anything you can think of that might help and an itemized list of your activities since, say, yesterday evening for starters. Include names, addresses and phone numbers of anyone who can verify your whereabouts. It'll just make things go quicker."

"OK, Mrs. Gilliam, we'll go into the other room here to have some privacy." He stepped back and stood at the side of the door and had Dede go in ahead of him toward the dining table.

Carl reached into the breast pocket of his shirt, pulled out a small notebook, and took two automatic pencils from the half-dozen that were clipped there.

"Here you go," he said, handing Fonda a pencil and ripping out a couple pages.

"What in the world did you mean you *might* be able to help? You must know Ray's collection backward and forward."

"Shush, Fonda."

"Why the two of you ..."

"Fonda, just wait, I'll tell you when we get home." He shot his eyes sideways at the door the officer and Dede had just gone through.

"You better tell me now," Fonda said, leaning toward him and lowering her voice to a whisper, "if it's something that requires privacy, because Dede's staying with us."

"What? You've hardly exchanged a full sentence with her since Ray married her and now you're inviting her home?"

"Her husband, your best friend, has just died," Fonda hissed, "and she can't stay here with this mess. Plus she told me she has no relatives or anything. I feel sorry for her."

"Don't be feeling too sorry for her. According to Ray, things were not going well between them. He told me today she was downright mean about his collecting and had threatened to burn the whole house down with him in it. Ray was starting to be real nervous about her. That's why ..."

"Well, I'm ready to speak to you folks. You first, Mrs. Miller." Dede followed him out and leaned down to speak to Fonda.

"He," she said glancing at Sergeant Webster, "wants me to stay at a hotel tonight, with a guard, just in case. I'll need to come back tomorrow for some things, but thank you for offering to let me stay with you."

Fonda patted Dede's hand and got up to follow the sergeant into the dining area. She glanced back and saw Carl writing in his tablet. He didn't even look up as she left.

The sergeant didn't have many questions for her and all she could tell him was that she had seen Dede enter her house and a few seconds later come out screaming. They had called the police. She had pushed some of the cars and boxes out of the way to check to see if Ray was breathing, but nothing else had been moved. Fonda had been at work all day, yesterday, too, and hadn't seen a thing last night. Yes, it was a part-time job, but she worked two twelve-hour day shifts—Friday and Saturday, the hospital's busiest days.

Fonda was glad when it was over. "I'll see you at home," she said as she passed Carl on her way out. She had come out in time to see Ray's white sheet-covered body being rolled to the ambulance. She waited as the ambulance drove silently away.

It was dark and had started to drizzle as Fonda started back across the street to her house. The house was lit up; Carl hadn't even turned the lights off. Fonda was surprised at the number of neighbors out in their yards and others walking at this time of evening. They must have been out watching the ambulance, too. Several of them came over to talk to her before she got to her front door.

She had begun to tell them what she knew when a stranger walked up and started asking questions. A reporter. She turned to the friend standing closest and said, "I'll talk to you tomorrow; I need to let Princess out."

Fonda snapped on Princess' leash and went out the back way. It was a fairly light drizzle, and she figured she would get back about the same time Carl was done and then they could talk.

She walked around the back yard a couple times and then set out on her usual route. Surprisingly, no one was lying in wait for her and the walk was uneventful.

If Carl was talking to Ray today, it was very possible that he was the last person to see him alive. And why was he being so cagey about his knowledge of Ray's collection? They both had enjoyed the collectible market. Actually Ray would even defer to Carl's judgment and relied on Carl's expertise. Carl knew Ray's collection as well as his own. Carl dabbled a bit in investment cars, but that was mostly buying the current race winners track sanctioned cars and reselling them on EBay. He hadn't even done that since he was laid off. Ray, on the other hand, was into it big time, and swore he could live fine on his earnings from buying and selling NASCAR collectibles. Ray used to like to show off his collection and Fonda remembered Carl saying several times that he would like to get his hands on some of those early Earnhardt items to round out his own collection. Ray had hinted some of them were worth a small fortune and Carl had agreed.

What was going on? Could they have gotten in an argument over those stupid cars? Carl had been acting funny lately. It didn't seem possible. Not Carl.

Fonda got back before Carl, took a shower, and curled up in her chair with her new Bubbles Yablonski hairdresser detective book to wait up for him.

She was so worried she couldn't keep her mind on the story, so she got up and pulled the blinds back just a little. Two police cars and a van were still across the street. No sign of Carl yet. She set the book down and went back to Carl's collection room. She flipped the light switch and looked around at the neatly arranged cars. Fonda had jokingly called this room the Dale Earnhardt Sr. shrine. After seeing Ray and Dede's décor, she was mentally downgrading this entire room to a Dale Earnhardt display. One car stood out more brightly than the others, and it didn't look familiar. One of the recessed lights made whatever car was in that spot look like it was in a spotlight. Carl would purposely set his newest car in that spot so he could enjoy it. But Carl hadn't been able to afford any new cars for some time.

Fonda looked at the car carefully. The box was in immaculate condition. She didn't want to touch or move it. She knew there wouldn't be a name on it anywhere or any distinguishing mark to show ownership, as this would lower the value. Neither Carl nor Ray would consider marking their most valuable cars even to protect them from thieves. Especially their most valuable cars.

She hesitated for a moment and then sat down at the small desk. The desk was purposely painted in Intimidator black with touches of red and white so it would not stand out and take away from the cars. She reached down and opened the file drawer. Carl, the meticulous keeper of records, had a manila folder labeled "inventory." Fonda scanned the list. There was complete information on all his cars, and they were listed in chronological order by date of purchase, with additional columns for "purchased from", "amount paid", "description" and "condition". The last three columns were blank for the majority of the entries. They were "date sold", "sold to", and "amount".

It crossed her mind that these inanimate objects were as well documented as any purebred in the American Kennel Club.

She flipped to the last page. The final entry was dated today. Purchased from Ray Gilliam, 1:24 scale, silver stock car Winston Cup Limited Edition, $200.

Fonda closed the file, put it away, and left the room. "No, it can't be," she said aloud. Not Carl.

There has to be an explanation. He would never have hurt Ray .... but how did he get the car? Or maybe he went back over for some reason, found Ray dead, and took the car. That would explain everything, except who killed Ray. Fonda couldn't believe what she was thinking. She could see him as a thief, but not a murderer, and hopefully she was right. If she had found his inventory book, the police would, too. She needed to confront Carl with what she had found.

But first she needed to talk to Dede.

Fonda woke up the next morning at 6 o'clock. Carl was sleeping soundly on his side of the bed. She had pretended to be asleep last night when Carl had finally come home.

She dressed quietly and headed downtown to the police station for her 8:00 meeting with Sergeant Webster that she had arranged the night before. She left a note for Carl telling him where she was going and that she had thought of something else she needed to tell the police. She was confident Carl would never think it could be about him.

The meeting took longer than she expected, but she pulled her car into her driveway at 11:00 and walked across the street to what was now Dede's home. Dede's police escort had dropped her off a few minutes earlier to pack a bag. Fonda thought she might ask when Dede's sister would be arriving and offer to pick her up at the airport.

The front door opened as she reached the bottom step.

"Come in, Fonda. I don't have a lot of time. Sergeant Webster said you were going to pick up some paperwork from Ray's files for Carl."

"Yes, should just take me a moment. Carl didn't get much sleep last night, and I guess the police are anxious to find out what, if anything, is missing."

"I don't know anything about all these toys, but of course if there's anything valuable there, it will help me get this all settled and start over," Dede said, her eyes sweeping the room. "It's too bad about Carl, though. I never thought he would have hurt, Ray."

"What are you talking about? Carl and Ray were best friends!"

"Well, I guess it won't be a secret for too much longer," Dede said. "Sergeant Webster mentioned to me this morning that they are looking closely at Carl. He was the only one who knew the value of this stuff, plus he was over here yesterday, which makes him the last one to see Ray alive."

"Well, what about you?" Fonda countered. "You hated Ray's collecting, and I understand the two of you hadn't been getting along too well. Ray thought you might do something to hurt him or destroy the collection he loved."

"And he was crazy, wasn't he? Look at all this junk. Who lives like this? Why wouldn't I hate it? And besides, you were a witness. You, yourself, saw me come home and find him."

"Well, yes, I did," Fonda said carefully. "But you could have been home earlier, maybe after Carl was here. Maybe you didn't mean to kill him, but I bet you meant to destroy his NASCAR collection; did he try to stop you? Did you give him an ultimatum and he chose his collection?"

"So what if he did. It just proves he was crazy," Dede said, moving closer to Fonda. "And it was an accident. I just couldn't stand living like this anymore. I started throwing those cars at him and couldn't stop. Ray was bending over to pick them up when I pushed the case over. It all happened so fast. Once I realized he was dead, I started on the second case to make it look like a robbery. Ray couldn't help bragging about how valuable his collection was. He and Carl talked to all kinds of people at swap meets. Who knows who might have decided to come over and help themselves."

"Why didn't you just leave, if you were that unhappy?" asked Fonda.

"I would have, but it was only fair that I have a little money to start over with. I've asked and begged him to get rid of some of this stuff, but he wouldn't even consider it. When I first met Ray, I thought he was so interesting, and he had this nice little house and a good steady income. He had just gotten divorced, and I knew I didn't have to worry about his running around; he had only one real interest in his life—NASCAR."

Fonda nodded. She understood.

"But my life turned into a NASCAR hell. Everything was related to Dale Earnhardt Sr. and NASCAR. There's even a poster of him over our bed. My sheets are checkered; heck, my socks and underwear are checkered. Even my birthday present, a black leather jacket, had the Dale Earnhardt team logo and number 3 on it. When he started collecting Dale Earnhardt Jr. I knew it was over for good, and I had to get out of here." Dede paused and took a breath. "But you're the only one who knows, and no one will believe you anyway. They'll just think you're trying to protect, Carl. Thank God NASCAR is out of my life forever!"

"That's not entirely true, Dede. You see that life-size cut-out of Dale in the corner? That Coke bottle he's holding? There's a microphone hooked up behind it, and I expect the police will be here any minute."

On cue, Sergeant Webster and two other officers came through the front door, handcuffed a crying and sputtering Dede, and took her out to a waiting squad car.

"Well, Mrs. Miller, you've been a big help. I don't know if we would have figured this out so quickly without you. I do believe we would have solved this, though. Our rationale would have been a little different, but thanks. Oh, and tell Carl I'll call him when he can start organizing all this. I spoke with Ray's ex-wife, who, by the way, is still the executrix for his will, and she said she'd be grateful if Carl would handle all this for her. She said to have him call her and they would work something out."

Fonda walked into her house and went straight to Carl's collection room. He was leaning over his desk with a car in one hand and a magnifying glass in the other. He set both down as she came in and turned to face her.

"Carl, it is all over, Dede killed Ray, and you are no longer a suspect," Fonda announced.

"I was a suspect?"

"Yes, but I went to the station first thing this morning and convinced Sergeant Webster that an advanced, discriminating collector like yourself would never have taken a car out of its original box or damaged the original packaging. All that destruction that occurred at Ray's could not have been done by a fellow collector." She paused and then added, "I never said a thing about you taking that car—the one I saw entered on your inventory yesterday. You can probably figure out a way to put it back when you are helping catalogue Ray's collection."

"Fonda, I'm glad you didn't believe I would have murdered Ray, but I didn't steal anything from him, either. I was trying to tell you last night. I bought the Silver Winston Cup stock car from Ray. He was actually downsizing his collection, like Dede wanted him to do. He was getting a kick out of practically giving them away. He knew she would have a fit if she knew he was selling some to me for a fraction of their value. He was just selling his duplicates and I was helping him determine values. He sold me that Winston Cup die cast for what he had originally paid for it. I know it was still more than we could afford, but I sold a couple duplicates of my own. I didn't want you to know I was spending money we didn't have, especially when I'm not working. And if you'd taken a closer look at my inventory, you'd see that I've added more than the one car from Ray's collection to mine. It wasn't the money with me and Ray. We enjoyed finding the rare cars and talking about them and sharing what we knew with other collectors. I'm sure going to miss him."

Fonda patted Carl on the shoulder, thinking that as far as vices go, collecting was the most agreeable one she could think of.

She thought back to her last glimpse of Ray and Dede's front room as she left this morning. She had turned back for a second and locked eyes with the life-size Dale Earnhardt Sr. cutout. She could have sworn that little half-smile was a satisfied smirk and that he was holding that Coke bottle up to her in a toast. She couldn't help but smile back. That cute little grin of Dale's was growing on her. If she could figure out a way to buy that cutout, she had just the spot for it.

Maybe she would begin her own Dale Earnhardt Sr. collection.

DALE EARNHARDT, SR.
by Brenda Robertson Stewart

Dale Earnhardt Sr. won the 1995 rain-soaked Brickyard 400. As often happens in Indiana, rain from the remnants of an Atlantic hurricane came down in torrents on race day, delaying the race for four hours. ABC's broadcast ended nearly an hour before the race began. While a couple hundred thousand race fans saw Earnhardt take the checkered flag at the Brickyard, thousands more didn't get to see the finish on TV. The fans let loose their wrath on the network's affiliate stations. Those fans who endured the rain and hung around the track saw a fast race with only one caution. Earnhardt led the last 28 laps and won by 0.37 seconds. Known as "The Intimidator," Dale Earnhardt Sr. was a fan favorite wherever he raced.

TARNISHED LEGACY
by Andrea Smith

"Tarnished Legacy" is Andrea Smith's fourth published short story. Smith writes mystery and romantic suspense with strong, resourceful women protagonists. She's currently looking for a publishing home for, Kill the Messenger, *a romantic suspense novel featuring Chicago press secretary, Jade Gillette. Smith holds a master of arts in novel writing and publishing, and has had an extensive career in corporate communications. Originally from Chicago, she's called Indianapolis home for thirteen years.*

Nate was so focused on the TV monitor he didn't notice me come up beside him in the pit stall. I looked at the monitor; Rose's yellow Chevy was gunning out the second turn.

After two years of watching her race, I still marveled at how she handled a stock car. She was a brave soul. Just the thought of traveling 200 miles an hour gave me the shakes, which was why I managed our NASCAR team and Rose was behind the wheel.

"Wow! She's burning up the track." It made me giddy because I'd just met with our marketing gurus who'd guaranteed they could make Rose a household name if she just finished the Brickyard 400 in the top 10. If she drove like this on Sunday, she could have a shot at winning the darn thing.

Nate threw me a glance. "Drives just like her daddy."

Whoa. Did he just compliment Rose? I narrowed my eyes at him. "Are you feeling all right?"

Nate looked at me fully. He adjusted his headset, cupped a hand over the mouthpiece. "We got a problem."

I frowned. "Do I really need to know about it?"

Nate rubbed a gnarled finger across his wrinkled forehead as if trying to erase a headache. "It's the tires, Kayla. Threads being eaten up after just two laps when they ought to last five."

"I'm confused. Why is this an issue? The crew can pick up the time on our pit stops."

Nate inhaled deeply. "Not worried about the time. We got our pit stop clicking on 12 seconds. I'm scared one of them suckers is gonna peel and make her spin into the wall. I'm not sure those tires can make it through even two laps when Rose hits her top speed during the race. We should switch to H&M."

"Switch? As in pull out of our deal with Davis Automotive?"

Nate raked a hand through his snow white hair. "Rose didn't like the idea, either."

"I guess not. Sheldon Davis is our biggest local sponsor."

"Yeah, well his tires are garbage. You gotta convince Rose we need to make the change."

Now it was my turn to sigh. "Why do I have to be the bad guy all the time?" My whining was in jest–sort of. "Maybe I need to wear a bullet-proof vest when I tell Sheldon Davis to forget about the media exposure we guaranteed."

"Already told Davis' mechanic. He was here while you were at your meeting, and I'm sure he gave his boss the message. Got tires coming from H&M this afternoon."

I was still going to have to grovel to assure Davis we'd give back his investment. Rose really had to finish strong if we were going to have the money to do that. "Least you could do," I told Nate.

A hint of a smile touched his lips before he focused on the monitor again. He cocked his head, listening to what Rose was telling him in his headset, then yelled to the crew waiting patiently to service the car when she finished her practice laps. "She's coming in early. Get that baby in quick as you can. We got work to do."

Then he said to me, "Don't worry. She's got winning in her DNA." He gave me a wink and sprinted out the pit stall and started walking toward our garage.

I stepped out, too, and surveyed the fans who'd come out for a sneak peek at the race. Women poured into hip-hugging Daisy Duke shorts waved hand-painted signs – love notes to their favorite drivers. Shirtless guys had used their bare chests for a canvas, painting them with the number of their favorite car. The pageantry of NASCAR was almost in full swing.

Rose came roaring onto pit road. Full throttle.

Crazy girl. Why is she going so fast?

She came up on our pit stall and VROOOM! shot past it. Right at Nate.

Poor Nate didn't even have a second to sense the danger. The Chevy plowed into him, sending his 70-year-old body arching into the air and slamming into the dirt, twisted like a pretzel.

The Chevy careened down pit road, making the crews scatter before crashing into the pit stall on the end. Black clouds of smoke billowed from the car like clouds.

Rose! Nate! My heart cried.

I wanted to move but my feet felt glued to the ground.

Everything, everyone seemed to stand still.

The guys who expected to be handling routine maintenance on their teams' cars sprang into a different kind of action. Some sprinted toward Nate, some to the Chevy. Media stalkers hoisted their cameras and galloped to get shots to lead their evening newscasts.

Finally able to pick up my leaden feet, I bolted toward the Chevy. Alfred, our crew coach, got to Rose first. He yanked the car door open and pulled Rose out and away from the smoking car. Marcus and John ran up with fire extinguishers, and although there were no flames, started dousing the Chevy.

"Rose!" I cried when I reached them. Amazingly, there was no blood on her silver uniform. She snatched off her helmet. Her green eyes were round with horror.

"Are you OK?" I searched her face. No cuts or bruises, but that didn't mean she hadn't suffered some kind of internal injury. "Rose, are you hurt?"

She shook her head. She tried to speak but her words were garbled.

"Stay with her, Alfred. I'm going to see about Nate."

"I got her," he said.

I elbowed my way through the crowd that Speedway police officers were holding back so the medical teams always on duty at the track could help Nate.

"Kayla Lucas. He's my crew chief!" I told the cop who was using his thick arm as a barrier.

"Oh, sorry, Ms. Lucas." He let me through.

My breath left me when I saw Nate on the ground. His eyes were open. Blood trickled from the corners of his mouth. I watched through blurred vision as the medics tried to get Nate to respond. Finally, one of the medics looked up at the police officer. "Sorry. He's gone." Then he barked into his radio for the wagon to come around.

A scream brought me out of my teary trance. I thought it was me. But it was Rose, who was gripping my arm as if to stay on her feet.

This wasn't real. Minutes ago Nate was winking at me. Now he was dead.

"Hot damn, Miss America. When you make a promise, you sure keep it. You murdered the old man."

My head snapped around. The ugly words had come from Eli Riley Jr. He was always accusing Rose of trading on being a woman and on her father's reputation even though she'd logged more respectable finishes than he had. In truth Riley was a lousy driver. He was on a NASCAR team only because his daddy owned it.

"What's that you say, Riley?" asked a Speedway cop whose name tag read "Sergeant Martin." I'd never seen him before at the track; this must be new detail for him. But I wasn't surprised Riley and the cop were first-name friendly. Riley had the whole city charmed by his fake hometown-boy-makes-good image.

"Miss Universe here and the old man were just about brawling on the track this morning. She told him she was gonna flatten him like road kill."

Rose had no trouble finding her voice now. "You're a lying germ. It was the car, Kayla. The accelerator stuck and the brake wouldn't catch. I couldn't even steer the damn thing."

"How bad was this, eh, fight?" Sergeant Martin asked Riley.

My blood pressure started to rise. "Oh come on, you couldn't possibly be taking his ridiculous claims seriously."

Riley folded his arms so they rested on a belly that seemed to swell more each race. He was a Snickers bar away from being fat. "Hey, I'm not the only one who saw 'em arguing. There were a lot of other crew folks around at the time."

Rose got in Riley's face. "Why are you lying? Payback because I wouldn't go out with your lard a—"

"Rose!" I said to shut her up. The media sharks were taping every word. It would crucify her with these images.

Sergeant Martin cleared his throat. "We're going to need to talk to you about this accident, Ms. Canzone. Away from here."

"What? You're arresting her?" I was incredulous.

"We call it an interview, Ms. Lucas. My officers are gonna have your crew move the car to your garage. We're gonna secure it as a crime scene. Nobody touches the vehicle until our technicians have had a chance to go over it and see if there was a mechanical problem."

He gestured to Rose. "The squad car is this way."

Rose's body stiffened with defiance. "No way. This is fucking crazy!"

Oh yeah. Rose was definitely past shock.

"Now, now, Ms. Canzone. It's just an interview."

Rose still didn't move. Just glared at him. She was taller than him, which obviously made him feel a tad inadequate. He stuck out his chest, agitated.

"I don't want to put handcuffs on you, Ms. Canzone."

Rose balled her fists. "No, you don't want to *try*."

Sergeant Martin puffed his chest out again and moved toward Rose. I jumped between them, facing her.

"There's nothing to worry about. You go with the officers. We'll figure this out."

I had no idea how we'd do that but hoped my saying it would coax her into going quietly before the antsy sergeant felt forced to prove he was in charge.

Rose gave her long red ponytail a righteous shake. "All right. But if I'm not back in an hour, I expect you to show up with a knife in a cake."

Sergeant Martin reached to touch Rose's arm, but she snatched away from him. I watched as Martin and another officer flanked her and marched her down pit road, media trailing like a pack of dogs chasing a porterhouse steak.

"Looks like Daddy's princess won't be joining him in the record books this go round. Such a shame."

I glared at Riley. "I get it you're scared witless she's going to smack you down on the track. But accusing her of hitting Nate on purpose is low even for you."

Riley smirked. "Well, if there was ever a chance of her doing that, it's gone now that she mowed down your crew chief."

He jiggled off before I could hurl an appropriate insult, his cackle ringing in my ears.

Out of the corner of my eye, I saw a reporter and a cameraman stalking my way. I pivoted on my Nikes and took off for our garage, jogging past the crews working to untangle the Chevy from the pit.

I was alone in the garage. The scent of gasoline and tire rubber that had become comforting smells now almost made me gag, and a mixture of sorrow and fear flooded me.

Owning a NASCAR team was the last thing I thought I'd end up doing with my life. And when Rose, who'd worked in my office for a quick six months, first asked me to be her partner, I told her she'd lost her mind. She was a dare devil, had grown up in the sport. I was more comfortable behind my IRS desk. Or so I had thought.

"Come on, Kayla. You hate chasing tax cheats. We'll be trailblazers, the first woman-owned NASCAR team. I know I can win. It'll be like having a party every day."

Still reeling from my husband's death from a suicide bomber in Iraq, I needed something to block the pain, so I kissed my government holidays and pension goodbye. And Rose, with her fiery red curls and freckled face, and I with my milk-chocolate skin and natural twisted tresses, became the salt-and-pepper team of the NASCAR circuit. It had been tough getting people to take us seriously, but it had been a blast.

Until today.

I snatched my BlackBerry from the holster clipped to my jeans and called our lawyer, Sam Pierce. Sam had practiced criminal law until the harsh realities of it gave him insomnia and ulcers. I sighed with relief when he answered his cell. I told him about Rose, and Sam said he'd cancel his appointments and head for Speedway police headquarters right away.

Relieved that Rose wouldn't be alone too long, I stood in the garage dreading the next call I had to make. I took a deep breath to calm my nerves, but my hand was shaking when I punched in the number for Rose's mom. When she answered, the bad news tumbled out my mouth. Then I listened as Celia Canzone did what I wanted to do.

She cried.

"I want to see her," she finally said.

"I'm sure Rose will be calling soon to let us know she's been released. I'll let you know the minute she does." I was doing my best to sound reassuring.

I was disconnecting from Celia when the garage door began to clank up. The mangled front of the Chevy stared at me from the bed of the tow truck. I winced thinking about Nate's crumpled body. Alfred hopped from the truck's passenger side.

"That was fast," I said when he came into the garage.

"Yeah, cops made it clear we had to get a move on."

The truck made a grinding squeal as Marcus lowered the bed so the Chevy could be pushed into the garage.

"I don't get it. How did we let the car out with so many problems?" I asked Alfred.

Alfred looked at the floor, embarrassed. "I swear I don't know. Nobody ever touched this baby without Nate's say so. No way this car hit the track with accelerator and brake issues. No way."

"Well Rose said there was. Were you here this morning with Nate and Rose?"

Alfred looked at the other crew members who had the Chevy in place now. "They did have some heated words this morning about the tires. Rose told Nate she didn't want to use H&M because their tires were fossils. Like him."

Ouch. Rose and her razor tongue. "How'd he take that?"

"I never saw Nate get excited about much. But this time he was rattled. He said he was going to take it up with you. That really made Rose blow. She told him not to forget he worked for her, too, and she could give him his walking papers. It really got heated. Then they took it outside."

It was just like Nate not to make a big deal about just how angry Rose was about the change. Still, their disagreement was hardly enough for Rose, even with her hot temper, to want to run him over.

Alfred's expression turned wistful. "He was a good man. Me and my family appreciated what he did for us."

I walked around to the front of the Chevy. "How fast do you think you can get us back up and running?"

Alfred's eyebrows went up in surprise.

"You know Rose," I said. "Stubborn and tough. She'll want to race if she can."

"Can't say until I've had a chance to see what needs to be done."

I nodded. "When the cops get here, watch everything they do and call me the minute they finish examining the car.

"Absolutely," Alfred said.

I stepped out into the blazing summer sun. I needed to find a quiet place to check in with Sam to see if he had made it to the Speedway police station. Deciding my Ford Fusion—my rolling office—was the best bet, I grabbed one of our team caps to hide my face from the media vultures I knew were still circling and headed for the employee section of the parking lot.

I went from a walk to a trot when I got near Riley's team pit stall. I was not a violent person, but I might be tempted to wipe that smirk off his face with my Dooney & Bourke tote bag if I had to listen to his wild accusations again.

Riley wasn't in sight, but someone else I didn't want to see was. Sheldon Davis, our tire sponsor, was heading in my direction.

Rats. I was not ready to grovel. His investment was gone, and I had to figure out how we were going to pay him back. If Rose didn't race, and win, I didn't know how we were going to do that. I ducked my head, stopped behind two Speedway cops flirting with ladies in Daisy Dukes.

To my relief–and surprise–Sheldon turned and headed for Riley's pit stall. He sure wasn't wasting any time trying to line up a new deal. But then who could blame him.

I hurried to my Ford. In the quiet of my car, I watched fans streaming in. The practice laps had kept going. Had to, since as they say, the show must go on. The race was happening on Sunday—day after tomorrow—no matter what.

My thoughts ping-ponged. My mind replayed every disagreement I'd witnessed between Rose and Nate. Rose's reaction to my announcement that her dad's former crew chief had agreed to work with us had totally thrown me. Nate Alexander was a NASCAR legend; he'd helped her dad cross the bricks three times. I thought she'd jump for joy. Boy, had I been wrong. Although she finally agreed to hire Nate, she never had a kind word for him. Seemed to resent him telling her what to do. I chalked it up to Rose just being so headstrong. But when I thought about it, what did I really know about Nate other than what people said about his skills as a crew chief? I hadn't looked into his personal life or anything. Maybe he was a kook. There was a reason Rose hadn't liked him.

I unholstered my BlackBerry and hit redial. Maybe her mom could give me a clue.

"It's Kayla again," I said when she answered.

Celia gasped. "Have they let Rose go?"

"No. I haven't heard anything more yet. But I wanted to ask you about Nate Alexander."

"What … what about him?"

Why did she sound apprehensive?

"Well, you knew him a long time. I was hoping you could help me understand why Rose disliked him so much."

"Rose wouldn't hurt anybody. I'm surprised you would think such a thing, Kayla. You know Rose better than that."

That bruised my feelings. "Celia, you know Rose is my best friend. You know how much I owe her for keeping me sane when Robert was killed. I wouldn't have made it through those dark days without her help. I'm just trying to be as good a friend to her as she was to me. I know her hitting Nate was an accident. It's just that Rose seemed to hate Nate. And if the police don't find anything wrong with the car, they might decide she disliked him enough to run him over. Don't you want to prevent that?"

Celia was quiet. I'd never known her to act so strangely. What was she hiding?

I heard Celia sniff. Finally she said, "She blamed Nate for her father's death."

Whoa. "What? How could she hold Nate responsible for her dad's accident?"

"It's my fault," she said, sorrow in her voice, "for not telling Rose the truth in the first place. Danny had started to drink. He wasn't winning as much and he was worried he'd lose his standing. Nothing Nate or I said could make him stop. He was drunk the day he died. He crashed because he lost control of the car."

Her voice caught and she paused to regain control. "Nate, bless him, didn't want Danny's memory tarnished. It would have been horrible for NASCAR and for Danny's estate if the real reason for the crash had come out. So Nate took the blame. Told NASCAR he'd made a mistake and missed a problem with the engine. NASCAR made sure it was ruled an accident."

Oh wow. "I still don't get why she blamed Nate."

"She told Nate she overheard us talking. She thought we were hiding Nate's mistake."

"But you were covering for her father."

"Rose loved Danny so much you would have thought he invented ice cream. She was his shadow. He'd drive around the track with her on his lap sometimes, even though he knew I was scared to death of him doing that. I wanted Rose to remember the good things about him. Not as a drunk who got himself killed and paralyzed a man.

"I didn't know she'd overheard us and misunderstood. I never knew her hatred ran so deep until you hired him. He told me she'd confronted him. Told him he was the reason her dad died. I called Nate yesterday because I wanted us to tell Rose the truth together. It was time for her to understand her dad was no saint and that Nate wasn't the devil."

Celia began sobbing again. "Nate wouldn't do it. He was still protecting Danny."

Wow, wow, wow. If the Speedway police found this out…

I disconnected. Now I was really scared for Rose. The police would definitely consider her hatred of Nate a powerful motive. And they'd love to be able to claim they solved a murder. Her only hope was if the examination of the Chevy proved someone had tampered with it.

And if it had been, how would we find out who'd done it? Who desperately wanted Rose to fail?

I pushed out my car and ran to Riley's garage. His team was bustling around the Ford Riley would be driving, adjusting issues that came up in the practice laps. It was all shiny with no dents. The green monster of jealously gave me a pinch. That's what our team should be doing right now. Instead they were watching the cops perform an autopsy on the Chevy.

I felt eyes on me as I made my way over to Riley. Folks still weren't used to women teams, and working for a Neanderthal like Riley didn't make them see us as anything more than a novelty. The oaf was hunched over the work table in animated conversation with one of his crew.

"Cops charge Ms. World yet?" Riley smirked when I approached.

I bit back a snippy answer. "Can I have a word with you? Outside?"

Riley's eyebrows went up. He looked around at his crew, grinned as if I'd asked him for a date. Then he said, "Yeah, sure."

Outside the garage, I said, "You had a visit from Sheldon Davis earlier. Are you working with him?"

Riley's eyes widened in surprise. "You know how it is; everybody wants to ride on the bumper of the car that's gonna win. Wants to be a sponsor." He waved his chubby hand in a dismissive gesture. "I'm not about to hook up with a loser who's going under."

My heart stuttered. "How do you know that?"

"Davis offered us a deal a few months ago. My dad had him checked out. His company's been struggling for a while."

I absorbed this revelation for a minute. Davis Automotive was in the red. Then how could Sheldon Davis sink so much money into sponsoring us? He'd taken an even bigger gamble than I realized. And our pulling out probably hurt more than I knew.

Nate had told Sheldon Davis' mechanic about the change. Maybe Sheldon's plan was to destroy Rose's chances at winning and grab a deal with Riley. Maybe he had his mechanic get to our Chevy.

That was a crazy thought. Alfred said Nate wouldn't let anyone else near our car.

"So you never used his tires? Never heard about any problem with them?"

Riley shook his head."Never even thought about it. Hey, since you won't need that crew of yours for the race how 'bout you send 'em my way? I could use guys like Alfred and Marcus. They can make an engine sing."

My blood pressure went up. He wasn't stealing my crew. I smiled. "Actually they'll be too busy getting Number 33 ready to leave you in our rubber debris."

I was walking back to our garage when my BlackBerry buzzed. I paused near a vendor who was hawking NASCAR hats and other trinkets. Sam's words spilled into my ear in one big rush. "Speedway police say their techs didn't find anything wrong with the car. They're grilling Rose like she was a serial killer and talking about charging her."

"What? Bunch of Barney Fifes. She didn't hit Nate on purpose. What are we going to do?"

"I'm waiting to talk with the lead investigator. You learn anything more?"

"Nothing good. Our crew coach saw Nate and Rose arguing this morning, too." I told Sam what Celia had told me.

"Sheesh. That's damaging. Call me if you find out anything else."

I almost wanted to stop looking; everything I turned up hurt Rose's cause instead of helping. I looked at my watch. No time to get weary; the cops wanted to charge Rose.

Sheldon Davis' image flashed in my mind. Odd he hadn't tried to contact me after he'd learned we weren't going to use his tires. Anyone who'd sunk as much money into a team as he had into ours would have been on the phone ranting at the person–me–who'd talked them into the deal. Yet he'd not dialed my number.

So I dialed his.

I was surprised when Sheldon answered. I wondered if he was still at the track trying to scare up deals.

"Sorry for not reaching out sooner. It's been—"

"A little busy, I imagine. What a bad break for you ladies."

Bad break? Getting caught in a caution zone during a race was a bad break. Being suspected of mowing down your crew chief on purpose was something else entirely.

I took a deep breath and groveled. "I want to make sure you understand our team's going to pay back every cent you put up to sponsor us."

Sheldon laughed. "We can deal with that later. You've got enough problems."

Huh? He was going under, and he wasn't worried about getting his money back?

"Besides, I just landed a whopper of a contract with Powell Motorsports."

"Wow. One of the top teams on the circuit."

Do they know about your little tire problem? "Congratulations. Do you want us to return the tires we didn't use because of the tread issue Nate found?"

I emphasized *tread issue*. Couldn't wait to hear the answer to that question.

"Thanks. The deal doesn't kick in until next year but we're happy about it. I'll have my guys pick up the tires. We had independent safety tests run on every batch we've made and got a total pass. That problem Nate had was a fluke. Good luck to you gals."

Yeah, good luck to us gals, I thought as I punched off the call.

Even with his deal with Powell, Davis was out of the running for this year's race. He didn't stand to gain anything from destroying Rose's chances except revenge because we pulled out. What would be the point of that?

My head felt like it was near exploding as I tried to come up with someone else desperate enough to tamper with the car. There just didn't seem to be anyone who could have gotten into our garage. Rose was the only one in control of the car. Rose …

I shook my head to dislodge that ugly thought.

Rose was not a killer. Someone had gotten to our Chevy.

Alfred's words replayed in my mind. *No one touches this baby unless Nate tells 'em to.*

That only left our own crew. Nate had handpicked every one of our guys. They all worshipped him. Still, what did I know about Bates, Carson and Jesse except that between them they'd been with racing teams for more than 30 years. Alfred had grown up on the circuit, like Rose. Marcus and John weren't rookies either.

I sprinted back to my Fusion, which doubled as a mobile office. I kept sponsorship contracts, insurance policies, marketing plans and personnel files in a plastic crate in my trunk so I'd always have information I needed handy.

I pulled the files on our crew and slid into the front seat to go over them. I got teary reading about Nate and how he'd guided Rose's dad to victories. If Rose had known the truth about her father's death, there's no way she would have hated Nate.

My BlackBerry buzzed. It was Sam.

"They're definitely charging Rose."

His words left me speechless.

"Kayla?"

I sighed. "I'm here. What do we do now?"

"Pray I can get bail."

My heart was hammering after Sam clicked off. I sat in my car, file folders about to fall from my lap. I couldn't crumble now.

I opened my file on Alfred. I was reminded he'd been a mechanic on his father's team when he was just a teenager. He'd left the circuit when he was 20, after his father stopped racing, and didn't come back to the circuit until Nate made him his second in command six months ago.

Alfred was in his early 30s now. He'd stayed out of racing for over 10 years. Odd for someone with so much talent and who loved the sport so much.

"Nate did so much for me and my family."

What had Alfred meant when he'd said that?

I called Celia a third time.

I got right to my question so she wouldn't have a chance to ask me for an update on Rose. No way was I going to tell her Rose was about to be charged. "Who was the driver Danny hit in the crash that killed him?"

"Larry Ingalls. Such a sweetheart. Oh God, it was awful. His wife, Marcy, couldn't deal with what happened and left him. His sons took care of him as best they could. It was heartbreaking. Nate kept in touch with Larry's boys. I think he felt responsible for letting Danny race while he was drunk."

My thoughts splintered in a million directions as I took in Celia's words. "Is Larry still alive?"

"No. Nate said he died a few months ago. Why are you asking about the accident, Kayla? You don't think …"

I didn't want to tell her what I thought. I didn't like what I was thinking.

After our conversation, I considered calling Sergeant Martin to tell him what I suspected. Nixed that idea; I had no proof, so he'd probably want to pat me on the head and send me on my way.

I called Sam but got his voice mail. Looked like I was on my own.

Heart pounding, I stalked toward our garage. Practice laps had ended, and the crowds in the stands and those roaming the track had thinned.

Marcus and John were stacking tires. Alfred was bent over the engine of the Chevy.

"Good news. I think we can have this baby ready for Sunday," Alfred said, straightening up and grabbing a towel to wipe his hands. I stared at our R&K logo on his yellow team shirt. Nate had placed a lot of trust in him.

I tried to keep a normal tone in my voice. "It's great news. I still don't understand why the cops didn't find anything wrong. Rose may not be a mechanical genius like you, but if she said the brakes and the steering failed, somebody got to our car and made it happen."

Alfred shook his dark hair out of his eyes. "No way. Like I told you, nobody worked on our car unless Nate told 'em to."

"I know. You also told me no one was in the garage that shouldn't have been there."

He tossed the towel behind him at the work table. "That's right. It was just me and the guys."

"Where was Nate?"

Alfred squinted at me. "He was here until they started arguing."

"And that made Rose snap. I mean, we all knew she hated him. He was responsible for her father's death."

Alfred's expression was unreadable, but I saw his jaw give a slight twitch. "Nate was a good man."

"This must have made how your plan ended even more difficult after all Nate did for your family."

Alfred flicked a gaze at Marcus and John who couldn't hear what we were saying and were giving us curious glances.

"Don't know what you mean," Alfred said, shrugging his skinny shoulders.

"Larry Ingalls was your dad, right? I heard he was a good driver."

He narrowed his eyes at me. "He was a great driver. So?"

"So Rose's father was responsible for him being paralyzed."

Alfred kept the blank face. "It was a tragic accident. Dad didn't blame anybody."

"But you did. And when Nate asked you to work on our team, you saw it as your chance to get even by hurting Rose, even though she was a kid and not responsible for what happened."

Alfred blinked. "I don't know what you're talking about. You're starting to sound a little like your unhinged partner."

"Am I? How does this sound: Nate was eaten up with guilt for hiding Danny's responsibility for the crash so he sought you out for the team. He was still trying to make up for your loss.

"Rose was supposed to crash like her dad. You drained the fluids so she'd run into trouble on that last practice lap. We might have chalked it up to the bad tires, but she came in early and lost control on pit road instead. Poor Nate was an unfortunate casualty. It must have really galled you to have to pull Rose alive from the car you'd rigged to cause her death."

A darkness came over Alfred's face. He stepped toward me.

My mind said move, but my feet rejected its message. My eyes darted around for Marcus and John. He wouldn't dare try to do anything to me with them here.

Alfred's voice was low and threatening. "I'm gonna be out of here. If I was you, I'd go back to my cushy desk job. You don't belong in NASCAR. And neither does your daddy's girl driver."

Alfred stepped toward me. I stretched my 5 feet 2 inches as if that would block him. He shoved me and I went down. My handbag flew out of my hand. My BlackBerry popped from its resting place on my hip and clattered into pieces. I slid across the greasy floor, landed with a hard thump on the leg of the work table.

"Hey! What's wrong with you, Al?" From my spot on the floor I saw Marcus drop a tire and run over to me while Alfred bolted out the door.

I scrambled up. "I'm OK."

I took off after Alfred. When I made it outside, I saw him hustling down pit road.

The two cops were still flirting with the Daisy Duke lovelies. "Quick! I was just assaulted by a murderer. There he goes in our yellow R&K shirt." I pointed at Alfred, who was zigzagging through the fans.

One went after Alfred; the other pulled his radio and barked out an alert.

"I need to get to a phone," I said, and the blond Daisy Duke wearer handed me one. I used it to call Sam.

The cops caught Alfred trying to make it to his truck in the parking lot. Speedway's finest shocked me by getting a confession, even getting him to admit he replaced the fluids before the police team had a chance to examine the car.

Our crew worked round the clock to get the Chevy repaired in time for the race. Alfred's plot of revenge turned out to be marketing gold for Rose; everybody—including big national companies—wanted a piece of the story of a daddy's girl about to make it big on the racing circuit. Even if she didn't win, we'd be able to pay Sheldon Davis and bankroll our next race with ease.

Marcus, now our crew chief, did a final check, and Rose slipped behind the wheel of the Chevy. A long heart-to-heart with her mom had helped her accept the truth about her dad. But the pain she'd carried all those years had been replaced with regret for all the blame she'd heaped on poor Nate. Regret that he'd lost his life because of her.

I hoped in time she'd accept that Alfred owned Nate's death, not her.

"You're sure you're ready?" I asked.

Rose's expression was rueful. "Sitting this one out won't change what happened. Besides, I've got quite an ugly legacy to live up to."

I smiled. "Something tells me you're about to create your own."

LIPSTICK AND TIRES
by S. Ashley Couts

When Frank Christian's pretty wife, Sara, drove his number 71 Ford in a three-quarter-mile "strictly stock" race at Charlotte Speedway, she altered history. If anyone thought she'd break a nail and give up, they were wrong. In 1949 she was the United States Drivers Association Woman Driver of the Year and in 2004, she was inducted into the Georgia Automobile Racing Hall of Fame.

However, it wasn't skill that brought women into NASCAR. It was a promotional gimmick dreamed up by master promoter Bill France Sr. In July 1949 he recruited Ethel Mobley, a sibling to the famous Flock brothers, and Louise Smith. They raced against Sara Christian at the Langhorne Speedway in Pennsylvania sponsored by the National Championship Stock Car Circuit, the forerunner of NASCAR . The Flocks also recruited the women to race in Atlanta.

Ethel Mobley was named after the gasoline her father used in his taxicab. In 1948 her brother, Bob Flock, built the Atlanta Motor Speedway near Jonesboro. Ethel, a dimpled brunette, raced a car modified by another brother, Fonty. She competed in 100 races at that track.

Louise Smith, a spirited and aggressive driver, joked that France recruited her because of her reputation for outrunning the Greenville, South Carolina, police. She had never seen a stock car race and didn't know what the checkered flag meant. "They had to wave a red flag to stop me," she once told a reporter. In the next decade, she won 38 modified races in the Grand Nationals series.

In 1947, on a whim while traveling, she entered the family car, a new Ford Coupe, in a beach race and wrecked it. Before quitting as a driver in 1956, she broke almost every bone in her body, racked up 48 stitches, and needed four pins in her left knee. She was involved in racing as a sponsor until 1971.

THE MISSING CD
by M. B. Dabney

Award-winning journalist M. B. Dabney is an avid race fan whose writing has appeared in the Indianapolis Star, NUVO, The Indianapolis Business Journal, EBONY *magazine, and BlackEnterprise.com. He is an officer in the Speed City Indiana chapter of Sisters in Crime and recently completed,* A Murderous Dispatch, *a mystery novel set in a black newspaper. He lives in Indiana with his wife, two daughters, and their dog, Pluto.*

Barbara Jean was the best waitress at Rosie's Roadside Diner on Highway 77 north of Talladega, Alabama, near the interstate. She knew all the regulars and was cheerful and welcoming to a fault. And she was particularly happy about having her one-time high school sweetheart, Bobby Lee Stevenson, having breakfast at the diner.

Barbara Jean offered Bobby Lee a big smile as she approached a booth near the back. She carried a plate full of flapjacks in her right hand, and on her forearm balanced a plate of fried eggs sunny-side up, four strips of bacon, and an order of grits. She set the glass of orange juice in her left hand on the table before placing the plates of food in front of Bobby Lee.

"Here you go, darlin'." Barbara Jean called everyone 'darlin' these days. "You need anything else?"

"No, Barbara Jean. Thanks."

One of the old men up front in the restaurant yelled to Bobby Lee.

"Why you down here, boy?"

Bobby Lee, who looked a lot like Cary Grant early in his film career, hadn't lived in Alabama since his father moved their struggling NASCAR team, Johnny Eldon Stevenson Racing, to North Carolina 10 years earlier.

"Just visiting some family. One of my cousins is sick," he said, charging headlong into the food. "You know him. My cousin, Eldon, named after Grandpa. And we got a weekend off this week before heading up to Indianapolis for the Brickyard."

Another old guy said, "You guys looked pretty good last weekend. If it weren't for that damned fool Tony Stewart crashin' Kevin out you might have won that Chicago race."

"We'll get 'em next weekend," Bobby Lee said. "Our guy's a pretty good driver. We'll get there."

The good folks of Talladega considered the Stevenson's a hometown team and no one wanted to mention the team's fall from grace. For lack of sponsorship, the team was forced to hire a third-rate driver named Kevin Holmes, who came with his own sponsorship money from a Southern grocery store chain. That deal, which Bobby Lee arranged, financially saved the team.

Rosie's was surprisingly busy for midday on a Tuesday. A regular crowd of senior citizens was up front having donuts and coffee and talking NASCAR with two truckers, who were having full meals. But there was a lone man, a stranger, sitting at the counter toward the back eating the steak-and-eggs special, enjoying black coffee and reading the local sports page. He was tall and thin and wore blue jeans. His cowboy hat was on the counter next to him.

"You finished, darlin'?" Barbara Jean asked Bobby Lee when she saw that he was done. Then she added with a slight flirt, "You need anythin' else?"

"No, I'm fine, Barbara Jean," he said, ignoring the come-on. "Just leave the check on the table for me while I go hit the john real quick."

She nodded, wrote the check, and left it on the table as he headed to the restroom.

Bobby Lee spent a few moments in the restroom. No one was looking his way as he came out. And no one noticed he was carrying a white business-sized envelope in his right hand. As he passed the stranger at the counter, he dropped the envelope on the red vinyl stool next to him. The man didn't look down and Bobby Lee kept walking. Once at his table, Bobby Lee grabbed his check and headed to the front to pay.

The cash register was on the end of a counter near the entrance, and Bobby Lee had the crowd's attention as he walked up. He gave Barbara Jean a knowing smile as he paid the bill and tipped her more than 25 percent.

As everyone else in the joint was fawning over Bobby Lee, the stranger reached for the envelope, opened the flap and looked inside. He saw the left half of 10 nonsequential 500 dollar bills and a picture of a newspaper sports columnist from Indianapolis named Henry Rennert.

The man with the cowboy hat tucked the envelope in his inside jacket pocket and motioned to Barbara Jean to refill his coffee. It was bitter-tasting because it had been sitting on the warmer too long, but he drank it anyway. He was facing a 10-hour drive and needed to stay awake and alert. And once he arrived at his destination, there was work to do before he completed his job.

Three days later, on Friday morning, Henry Rennert was found dead in his Speedway home. Police said Rennert apparently was shot after walking in on someone burglarizing his home.

"Hank. Hank. Hannah!"

Hannah Watkins was sitting in the front row in a chapel at Stewart's Mortuary on Illinois Street and hadn't heard her best friend, Kia, call her name. Hannah's eyes were fixed on the spot where Henry Rennert's casket had been. The funeral was over and most people had left to accompany Henry to his final resting place in Crown Hill Cemetery. Hannah decided she couldn't handle the burial and stayed behind. She planned to visit the grave privately to say her goodbyes.

Kia sat in the chair next to her. "You OK, Hank?" Kia asked, calling Hannah by the name she used everywhere except on-air.

"Yeah, I'm fine," Hank said, dabbing tears from her eyes. "I just can't believe he's gone."

"Come on. Let's head out," Kia said, bringing Hank to her feet.

They went out a side door and crossed the parking lot to Kia's Ford Focus. Kia drove downtown to a fashionable condo on Meridian Street, across from a downtown park. It was an expensive residence, but then, as the lead anchor on a local station's 5 p.m. and 11 p.m. telecasts, Hank could afford it.

"You want me to come up?" Kia inquired as she drove up to the building's entrance.

Hank looked at her friend, offered a weak smile and said, "No. I'll be all right. I'm a professional and I'll be in to work. I can't let you screw up my broadcast."

"I'm a good director, and you know it," Kia said in mock protest.

"See you at five."

Back in her condo, Hank ventured into her bedroom and sat on the bed. On the nightstand was a framed picture Henry gave her from their vacation together in the Colorado Rockies the previous winter. She liked the picture because they were in it together, and the shot perfectly framed her face.

She stood and looked out the large window. Through the trees, she could see across University Park to the *Indianapolis Star* where Henry had worked.

Despite Kia's recommendation that she take the day off, by 4:30 p.m. Hank was sitting in a makeup chair in a room down the hallway from the main studio at Channel 13. The makeup artist noted the puffiness around Hank's eyes but said nothing. She applied some eye gel and some concealer under her eyes before adding makeup.

"There," the artist said as she finished, moving to the side so Hank could see herself in the mirror.

It was perfect and not a smudge was on her cream-colored blouse. "You are a genius," Hank said. "I look better than the day I was born."

In the mirror, Hank noticed two men approaching. They showed no expression. They were serious men in dark suits. The suits virtually shouted, "We are from the government."

"Hannah Watkins," said the shorter of the two. His voice was amazingly high pitched for his body, which resembled a fire hydrant with a head on top. "May we have a word? In private."

Hank looked first at her makeup artist, who offered no help, and then at a clock. It was 4:33 p.m. She had perhaps 12 minutes before she was due in the studio. She made the decision quickly.

Rising out of the chair, she first addressed the makeup artist. "Tell Kia I will be in the anchor chair on time." She pointed toward the door when she spoke to the suits. "There's a small conference room around the corner. We can talk there without being interrupted."

The conference room walls were lined with pictures of the station's on-air celebrities and with promotional pictures of all the network's shows. Hank sat on one side of an oblong conference table, and the suits pulled up chairs across from her.

The tall one, who was white, was obviously the silent type because his short black partner did the talking.

"My name is Special Agent Adair of the FBI," he said. Despite his many efforts, Adair couldn't get a mellow Southern drawl out of his voice. "And this is Special Agent Larsen."

"Am I in some sort of trouble?" Hank asked.

"No, ma'am, you are not," said Adair.

"But we would like for you to answer a few questions," Larsen spoke for the first time. His accent was East Coast–Philadelphia, perhaps New York.

"Have you ever heard of a man named Chuck Creighton?" asked Adair.

"No, I haven't. Should I have?"

"Should you have," Larsen echoed in an unbelieving tone that made Hank visibly uncomfortable.

Adair glanced over at Larsen but said nothing to him. He turned his attention back to Hank. "Perhaps not. But look at this picture."

Reaching into his inside breast pocket, Adair pulled out a black-and-white head shot of an unsmiling, gray-looking man with thinning hair. Hank examined the photograph and handed it back, shaking her head.

"He was from North Carolina," Adair said, accepting the picture.

Hank noticed Adair spoke of Chuck Creighton in the past tense. "What's he got to do with me? I don't think I have ever met someone by that name."

"He died several weeks ago in an auto accident," Adair said.

"His death was suspicious, which is why we are involved," Larsen put in.

"When? Where? And what's this got to do with me?" Hank looked quickly back and forth between them, trying to determine what was really behind the questions.

Adair pushed back his chair and rose. He looked about the room at the pictures on the wall, taking several moments to admire the portrait of Hank sitting at the anchor desk with her co-anchor. He turned back to address her.

"This is an ongoing federal investigation and I am going to have to rely on your discretion. You cannot discuss this outside this room," Adair said.

"OK. It's a big secret," Hank said.

"The accident was on a road outside Mooresville. He was alone at the time," Larsen piped in.

"He had no identification on him, and it took local law enforcement a while to positively ID him. At first, they just thought this guy was speeding and lost control on a dark road. Later they noticed his brakes hadn't just failed. They were sabotaged," Adair said.

"Once they ID'ed him we got involved. We had been watching him for some time. We are probing possible problems at his employer," Adair said.

"Who did he work for?" Hank asked.

"Since you apparently didn't know him and this is a sensitive investigation, I'm not going to name his employer at this time," Adair said. Hank accepted the mild rebuff. "But while they found no identification on him in the accident, they found something interesting in his pocket."

As if on cue, Larsen reached into his pocket and pulled out a business card and handed it to Hank. Surprise swept across her face.

"You say you never met the man. Why, then, would Chuck Creighton have your business card in his pocket," Larsen asked pointedly.

Hank was at a loss for words.

"I don't know how he got it," she said, not taking her eyes off the card.

"Turn it over," Adair said.

Hank did and got another shock.

"Is that your cell phone number written there," Adair asked.

"No," she said, choking back tears. Her emotions were welling up but she didn't want to lose it and spoil her makeup only minutes before going on air.

"And whose was it?"

Past tense again, but Hank didn't appear to notice. She looked at Adair, who was clearly the more sympathetic of the two.

"Henry Rennert," she said softly.

Even as the day of the race approached, there wasn't a lot of traffic on Crawfordsville Road past midnight. In fact, once west of Interstate 465, Crawfordsville Road was a pleasant experience which Bobby Lee completely enjoyed. And few people noticed the sleek, black-skinned 620-horsepower Saleen Dark Horse Mustang with North Carolina plates as it prowled through downtown Brownsburg heading west.

Five miles up Crawfordsville Road it entered Pittsboro, which claims NASCAR star Jeff Gordon as a hometown hero. Reaching Pittsboro from Brownsburg should have taken nearly six minutes but speeding down the highway past cornfield after cornfield, Bobby Lee made the trip in just over three.

Just a block and a half before Pittsboro's only stop light, Bobby Lee turned left into the parking lot of a small tavern. He parked in back, where the Dark Horse couldn't be seen from the street. Once inside, Bobby Lee's eyesight adjusted quickly to the low lighting and he spotted his man sitting in a booth near the back, his cowboy hat resting on the table next to his Budweiser.

There were few people in the small town tavern so late on a weeknight. Bobby Lee slid into the seat opposite the man. Unlike his hired killer, Bobby Lee liked having his back to the door. Though the NASCAR circus was already in town only a few miles back down Crawfordsville Road at the Speedway, it was unlikely anyone would recognize him in this place. But he didn't want to take more chances than were necessary.

"Well," he asked without preamble.

"We don't have it yet," the man answered. "And I'm not sure where it is, although I have a good guess."

"I'm not paying you to guess," Bobby Lee said.

There was irritation in his voice intended to intimidate. But the man with the cowboy hat wasn't one to be intimidated. When he spoke there was a sharp tone in his voice not unlike the sound of a knife being pulled from a sheath.

"You haven't fully paid me at all," the man reminded Bobby Lee, who backed down.

"So then, how do we proceed? There isn't much time. The race is coming up this weekend. The crews are already here. I need this totally taken care of," Bobby Lee said.

"I've been here a while. I think I know how to find the material," the man said. Then he added, "But I'm gonna need you to help."

The idea of direct involvement terrified Bobby Lee, but time was short and the alternative was equally scary.

"What do you need?"

The man outlined the plan.

Miles away, Hank and Kia were sitting in Hank's living room going over the day's 5 and 11 o'clock newscasts, reliving Hank's afternoon conversation with the FBI and trying to enjoy a bottle of red wine.

"They asked me how I knew Henry and if we were involved," Hank said.

"And what did you tell them?"

"I told them the truth, that we had been involved for about a year, although given our high-profile jobs, hardly anyone in town knew about it. We kept it very quiet."

"What else did they want to know?" Kia asked.

"They asked whether I knew what Henry was working on, particularly anything pertaining to NASCAR," Hank said. "But I said while we were both journalists and not in direct competition, we generally did not discuss work when we were together. In fact, that was the point of being together–not to have to talk about work."

Hank lifted her glass and swirled the liquid around inside. She took a sip and enjoyed the warm taste and slightly smoky flavor.

"Did you ever find out who this Creighton guy was," Kia asked.

"No, it was a busy evening, and I didn't have time to surf the Internet. Let's go now to see if there's anything."

They got up and went to Hank's spare bedroom, which served as her office at home. It was pristine, as if it were about to be shot for a layout in some fancy magazine that showcased the home interiors of the wealthy. Everything had its place on her desk, in the bookshelves and on the walls. The CDs and DVDs were neatly arranged alphabetically near the entertainment center.

The laptop was on the desk. Hank sat in front of it while Kia pulled up a chair next to her. Once Hank was online, she typed "Charles Creighton and North Carolina" into the search engine.

"They called him Chuck, but I hope his real name was Charles," Hank said.

They didn't have to wait long. There were 57,400 variations of the name and state, but it was the first one that caught their eyes. It was a story from the Mooresville (NC) Tribune. The headline read, "Accountant's Body Identified."

Hank clicked the link and they read the story.

MOORESVILLE – Police Tuesday identified the body of Charles Creighton, who was killed last week in a single-car accident on Rt. 152 near Brumley Road.

Creighton had no identification on him when his body was discovered inside his wrecked car on the morning of July 2. Authorities made a positive identification through dental records.

Creighton, 46, had been an accountant for Johnny Eldon Stevenson Racing since the beginning of the season. A statement by the team said, "Everyone at Stevenson Racing is saddened by the loss of one of our own. Chuck's wife, Sarah, and their two children, Scott and Abigail, are in our prayers."

While police say the road was dark and wet around the time of the accident, the cause of the crash has not been determined, and an investigation is still underway.

"I guess that's why they asked me about the NASCAR connection," Hank said. "But Henry never talked about what he was working on."

"Well, it's late and I have to get going," Kia said. "I've got a dentist appointment in the morning. See you at work. You should get some sleep."

"Sleep is all I do these days. I haven't even been in this room or on the computer in more than a week," Hank replied.

Hank escorted her friend to the front door and after a quick hug, they said goodbye. Hank then went back to her computer and read as much as she could about Chuck Creighton. She didn't know what the connection was between Henry and Creighton, but she was sure there was one.

It was just before three in the morning when she noticed there was a white envelope in her letter holder with Henry's handwriting on it. She didn't remember putting it there. Reaching for it, Hank opened the flap and pulled out a handwritten note from Henry. It was dated the day before he was killed. It was the last night he had spent with her.

It read:

Hey, babe. If you are reading this, then something has probably happened, probably something bad. Otherwise, I would have retrieved this note before you saw it.

I have been getting some threats lately-I get them all the time, actually. I'm a columnist. What can I say? Generally they're harmless, but I thought it prudent to take a few precautions. I'm spending tomorrow night at home and then Friday night with you because of our plans for shopping in Brown County on Saturday morning.

If something happens to me, there is a CD with some very important information that I hid and you will need to find. I will leave it up to you what you do with it. You can find it where I took you to impress you on our first real date. I can't say more right now.

I'm sure everything is fine and I'm just being silly. But in case I'm not, always remember, Hannah, I love you with all my heart and soul, and will forever.

Love, Henry

She cried after she finished reading and cursed Henry, herself and the world, though not necessarily in that order. She walked to her bedroom without turning off the laptop, fell on the bed, and cried until she went to sleep, fully dressed.

The sound pierced the silence of her bedroom and she first thought it was her alarm clock, which read 9:37 A. M. But it was her telephone. The caller-ID said it was Kia.

"Hello?" Hank said, her voice hoarse, her mouth tasting like a dirty gym sock. "Kia?"

"Hannah, it's me. Kia Marie." It sounded like she was crying. And she rarely ever called Hank by her given name. "I am so sorry."

Kia paused as if to collect herself before continuing, "My car broke down on the way to the dentist and I need you."

Hank sat up, her mind beginning to function again. "Did you call your motor club?"

"I called and they're coming, but they can't take me to where I need to go. I am really sorry, and I understand if you can't come. Really," Kia pleaded.

"Of course I can come. Where are you?"

"In the parking lot of my apartment complex."

"Don't worry. I'll be there in about 20 minutes."

Hank got up and surveyed herself in the mirror. She didn't have time for makeup and she pulled her shoulder-length hair back into a ponytail. After splashing some water on her face and brushing her teeth, she changed her top and put on another pair of jeans. As was her habit, she checked her teeth again in the mirror near the front door and gave herself one last look. She slipped her BlackBerry into her back pocket and grabbed her car keys.

Her building parking lot looked cold and impersonal as it always did, and her heels clicked on the pavement as she walked to her car. But just before she reached it, she heard then saw a stranger in a cowboy hat approach. It was quick and threatening. They were alone in the garage.

When he showed her his gun, her eyes nearly popped out of her head.

"There's a white van sitting over there. I want you to calmly walk over to it, open the door and get in back. If you don't, I will shoot you on the spot."

Hank could see he was serious and she walked over to the van with the man walking casually behind her. She grabbed the handle and yanked. The door slid open. Inside she saw Kia sitting on a bench along the wall. Her hands were tied, a strip of gray duct tape was across her mouth, and tears were rolling down her cheeks. Next to her was a man who looked like a young Cary Grant.

Hank got in and was followed by the man with the cowboy hat, who pulled the door behind him.

"Who are you and what do you want with us?" Hank said.

"Who I am is not important at the moment," Bobby Lee said. "What is important is what you can do for me. If you do it, you may live. If not, well, things don't look good for you."

She noted his Southern accent.

"You can have anything you want. I don't have much money on me but you can have it. Please, just let us go," Hank said.

Bobby Lee moved closer to Hank, who backed away from him until she bumped up against the man in the cowboy hat. She was trapped, which was exactly what Bobby Lee wanted.

"You really are much prettier in person than you are on television," he said, reaching out to touch her face. She turned her head away from him as he touched her left cheek. "It would truly be a shame if something happened to that pretty face."

She looked at him in horror as the gravity of his threat settled on her.

"I see I have your attention. So hear me. If I don't get what I want, my friend here will cut your face. If you survive, you will never work in television again. Understand me?"

She was trembling but nodded yes.

"Well then, let's talk business," Bobby Lee said, easing back away from her. "Your friend Henry Rennert had something of mine. It was a CD. I want it back. Where is it?"

"I don't know what you're talking about," she said. He reached over and slapped her hard in the face, leaving a red mark.

"He must have told you something," Bobby Lee barked. Hank recoiled.

Bobby Lee turned to face Kia, who was shaking with fear. "Your boyfriend died for the secrets he held. Do you want me to have her shot, and her dead body dumped onto the interstate before I get what I want? I will do it, you know."

At that, the man with the cowboy hat pulled out his gun and pointed it directly into Kia's face. Her eyes grew wide as she stared at the gun and cried.

Then Hank remembered.

"I think I know what you want," she said rapidly. "I think I know."

"Good," Bobby Lee said, calming down. The other man lowered his gun.

"But I'm not sure where it is," Hank said.

"Don't mess with me," Bobby Lee said, eyeing her with suspicion. "I will kill you."

"I believe you. I'm not sure where it is, but I think I may know," she said, looking toward Kia, then back to Bobby Lee. "I promise to cooperate, but you need to at least take the tape off her mouth."

Bobby Lee considered it for a moment and then took joy in ripping the tape off. Kia let out a scream of agony.

Bobby Lee looked her directly in the eyes.

"Another sound out of you and you're dead. You got me?" he said. Kia nodded but kept her mouth shut.

"He left me a note which mentioned some sort of tape or CD. He said he hid it somewhere. Somewhere he took me to impress me on our first date."

Kia couldn't keep quiet. "He took you to Harry and Izzy's for your first date, didn't he? That's a nice restaurant."

"Yes, but I wasn't that impressed. I had eaten there before," Hank said. "Besides, that was our second outing. Where did we go the first time?"

Hank paused, head down, as she thought. She looked up suddenly.

"I remember now. We picked up a couple of deli sandwiches at Shapiro's downtown and headed out to the Speedway," she said to Kia. "He took me to" ... she and Kia said it together as the realization struck ... "The Speedway Museum."

Bobby Lee couldn't help but to smile at the irony.

"I've been there before. Wonderful place. And I have to get out to the track this morning anyway for the beginning of practice for the race," he said. "Do you know where the CD is? What I'm looking for?"

"I'm not sure, but I know where he took me."

"OK then. Let's go see. But any funny business, any at all, and you are both dead. Got it?"

They nodded that they understood as Bobby Lee spoke to his assassin.

"We'll tie them both up in the back here. You drive the van out to the Speedway. You know the way, don't you? Good. I'll follow you in the Mustang. Park in the museum parking lot and I'll meet you there," Bobby Lee said. He added, "And if they give you the slightest trouble, well, uh, you know what to do."

The man with the cowboy hat smiled at the prospect.

"How do I know you'll let us go once you find what you're looking for?" Hank asked. Kia merely added, "Yeah," for moral support.

"I've given you no guarantees. You'll just have to trust me," he said, smiling even bigger than before.

After securing both women's feet and hands with duct tape, Bobby Lee got out and walked to the street where his Dark Horse was parked. Once he saw the van pull out of the parking garage and head for Meridian Street, where it turned left, Bobby Lee started the Mustang and put it in gear.

Inside the van, the women tried to stay calm.

"I'm so sorry I got you into this, Hannah," Kia said in a voice barely above a whisper. They were in the very back of the van, and the man in the cowboy hat couldn't hear them.

"They broke into my apartment this morning. My building isn't as secure as yours. I wouldn't have called you, but they forced me. They would have killed me. I tried to plead with you not to come. What are we going to do now?" Kia asked.

"I'm thinking about it," Hank said.

Kia then said what they both knew but didn't want to say aloud. "We've seen their faces. Once they have what they want, they'll have no reason to keep us both alive. What do they want?"

"I did some research online after you left last night, plus I discovered a note Henry left me," she said. "Creighton was an accountant for some racing team, and I think he discovered or took part in some illegal activities that would show up on their books. That's probably what's on the CD they want. They must have killed him to get the information back."

The women were knocked to the floor of the van when it turned left off Meridian onto 16th Street. The man looked in the mirror and smiled as they righted themselves.

"Henry really did impress you with where he took you. How are you going to get around that?" Kia asked.

"I haven't figured that out yet either," Hank said.

The van was still east of the Speedway when they crossed over the White River and the Mustang sped pass them.

As the van neared the Speedway town limits, it went under a railroad viaduct, and then the massive Turn Two grandstands came into view. The race was still several days away, but cars were on the two-and-a-half-mile oval nearing the end of the weekend's first practice session. The van turned right at the main gate and down a tunnel which took them under the track between Turns One and Two. They heard the muffled roar of several 650-horsepower engines pass over head as the van emerged from the tunnel. The museum was directly ahead.

The Dark Horse was near the front, and the van parked over to the far right. Bobby Lee walked over and got in once the van had stopped.

"This is how this is going to play out," he said to Hank. "You and I are going to go in there and find my CD. Then we're going to come back out."

"It's going to take all of us," Hank said.

"What?" Bobby Lee said.

"Trust me on this. It's going to take all of us."

Bobby Lee at first was gripped with indecision, but he had come too far to be stopped now.

"OK, we all go in. But one wrong move and your friend here dies on the spot. Got me?"

"Yes," Hank said.

"Then let's go."

The cowboy assassin cut the tape off of the women and they all got out and walked toward the entrance, the men flanking the women. No one spoke. Once inside the museum, Bobby Lee forked over three dollars for each of them to get in.

The first car they reached inside was the yellow Marmon Wasp, the car that won the first Indy 500 in 1911. The museum was full of racing cars and antique cars, from A.J. Foyt's record-setting Coyote in which he won his fourth Indy 500 in 1977, to the 1965 Le Mans-winning Ferrari 250 LM.

"Now where?" Bobby Lee asked.

"This is where we have a problem and why we need all of us," she said. Anger flashed in Bobby Lee's eyes as she continued. "There are probably six dozen cars on display here, but the exhibit is rotated often. The rest of the cars–dozens of them– are in storage downstairs. And that's where he took me to impress me. He has a good friend who works here and he took me downstairs. It's incredible down there. And it isn't open to the public. I was impressed."

"So, what do we do?"

She looked over to a doorway along the back wall that led to a corridor. Bobby Lee followed her gaze. There was a rope across the corridor entrance, and an elderly woman in a dark red jacket was sitting there on a stool.

"We can get to the basement on an elevator down that hallway. But first we need a distraction," Hank said.

The man with the cowboy hat took the cue, grabbing Kia's forearm and dragging her away. "I can handle that. Give me five minutes."

Five minutes later there was a racket over near a rare 1935 Duesenberg convertible passenger car, and several museum staffers went to investigate. Hank and Bobby Lee slipped into the corridor unseen. They walked down the hall and, glancing back and seeing no one, took another short hallway to the left that led to an elevator. They pushed the button, entered when the doors opened, and rode it down.

When the doors opened, they were in a large space with countless racing cars, all looking as shiny as on the last morning they were raced.

"It's over here," Hank said, indicating to their left. Down a row along the wall was a car Bobby Lee instantly recognized. It was the bright-colored DuPont sponsored machine Jeff Gordon drove to win the first Brickyard 400 in 1994. "I think whatever we are looking for is in there."

Bobby Lee went over and looked around. He didn't see anything until he looked carefully inside, and there, taped on the floor on the passenger side, was a small case that held a CD. "Crawl in the window and get it out," he told Hank.

Once she got the CD and climbed out of the car, he looked at her and said, "Good. You may live yet."

They left the same way they came in and no one saw them.

Back in the museum, all four of them gathered again and Bobby Lee showed the assassin he had what they were looking for. "Now everyone, back outside and into the van," Bobby Lee ordered.

They were walking down the steps outside when they saw several police cars with lights flashing coming up from the Speedway entrance. And to their left, Special Agent Adair had his gun drawn when he barked, "FBI. Hold it right there."

The man in the cowboy hat already had his gun out but hidden. He raised it, firing off three shots. Special Agent Larsen was hit in the leg and fell to the ground. Adair returned fire, hitting the assassin in the chest, killing him instantly.

It happened so quickly the women were frozen in place. But Bobby Lee ran to his right and reached his Mustang before Adair could stop him. The powerful 302-cubic-inch Ford V8 roared to life, and Bobby Lee burned rubber as the Dark Horse leapt forward. Seeing that other officers were on the way and Larsen was only hit in the leg, Adair ran back to his Crown Victoria to give chase, followed by two police cruisers with sirens wailing.

People scurried out of the way of the speeding Mustang. It ran past a line of team tractor-trailers with Adair following. Bobby Lee turned right and headed north, breaking through a fence and heading through a part of Gasoline Alley. People on foot and in golf carts scattered to get out of the way.

At the end, he turned left and headed directly toward the track. Adair continued to follow. When the Mustang reached the pit lane, Bobby Lee turned left again and mashed his foot to the floor, burning more rubber as he accelerated down the pit lane. He entered the track just before Turn One.

Bobby Lee raced up through the gears as he went down the one-eighth-mile short chute between Turns One and Two. He briefly noticed the corporate suites on the outside of the track as he went into Turn Two. He hit the apex of the turn perfectly and drifted back out to the wall at the exit just like he'd seen race car drivers do countless times.

Like the Speedway's front stretch, the back stretch is five-eighths of a mile long. Reaching 150 miles per hour, the wind roared past as he drove and the engine screamed near its red line. But there was a quiet calm in the car. For the first time in more than a week, Bobby Lee had time to sit and think. And in the more than 17 seconds it took him to drive down the back stretch, Bobby Lee's predicament became clearer. The Feds and the police were no match for the Mustang and were falling back. But the Speedway is an enclosed track. He had no hope of escape.

"This car's handling is smooth," Bobby Lee said to himself as he approached Turn Three. He braked at the entrance to the turn but again hit his mark at the apex. He was going about 110 and the lateral G-forces made it feel like he was going to be pushed out of the car.

In the short chute between Turns Three and Four, Bobby Lee checked his mirror again. The Feds were so far behind he couldn't see them. He turned into Four and headed for the main straightaway.

In the distance, the tall grandstands on both sides made the 50-foot-wide race track seem narrower than it was. The wind sock on top of the scoring tower showed he was heading into a slight headwind. A line of vehicles with flashing lights was placed at the yard of bricks at the start/finish line. But Bobby Lee barely noticed. He had already turned left to head for pit lane.

He slowed to the pit road speed limit of 60 miles per hour by the time he reached pit-in. The eyes of every member of every team were on him as he drove through the pits. Everyone was stunned.

The Stevenson Racing pit was located four stalls before the timing and scoring pagoda, and he pulled in directly behind his driver's race car. Bobby Lee turned off the engine and looked up at his driver. He had a look on his face that said, "What am I going to do now?"

Hannah and Kia were still shaking an hour later when someone brought in two bottles of water and sat them on the conference room table in front of them. They were on the second floor of the Speedway's administration building. Adair and another agent sat across from them.

"Are you all right now?" he asked them. Kia nodded. Hank spoke up.

"How did you find us?"

"You hit the emergency button on your BlackBerry and the call went out. Smart move. The police tracked your phone's GPS signal. Since you were on our watch list, they alerted us.

"This is what he was after," Adair said, placing the CD on the table.

"Is it an accounting ledger?" Hank asked.

"Yes, he was cheating his company, embezzling hundreds of thousands of dollars. He was using two sets of books to hide his theft. He apparently needed the money to pay off some gambling debts. But I think the accountant found out, which is why he was killed. But he must have talked to Mr. Rennert first and gave him the missing CD. Mr. Rennert was going to break the story before the race this week."

"And that's why he was killed," Hank said. "Who did it? I have to know."

"Probably the guy I shot. Roland Sands. He was an enforcer for a gambling outfit up in Raleigh, North Carolina," Adair said.

"I'm going to need some more information from both of you," he said, taking out his notebook.

"That's fine, but I have to make it out of here by three at the latest," Hank said.

"You still plan to do the news today?" he asked.

"It's my job."

That evening at Rosie's Roadside Diner, Barbara Jean watched the story unfold on ESPN.

"I always knew that boy was up to no good," she said, standing behind the counter with a pot of coffee in her hand.

"More coffee, darlin'?" she asked an old customer. She poured the coffee, then let the man eat his pie in peace.

CHEVY VS. FORD
by Jaci Muzamel

There's no denying that Americans are loyal. Brand loyal.

Ask anyone and they will have a favorite–soda, beer, clothing, hardware store, and baseball and football teams.

But nowhere, perhaps, is brand loyalty stronger and marketing competition more fierce than with the automobile. Who can't still hear the voice of a father or grandfather saying, "I'm a Ford man," or "I'd never own anything but a Chevy!"

Many car brands have been raced in NASCAR, from Oldsmobile, Chrysler, Dodge, Pontiac and Buick to legendary names like Hudson, which won three stock car championships. But the greatest competition is between Ford and Chevrolet.

Or is it?

Since the inception of NASCAR racing on a dirt track in 1949 through the 2008 "three-peat" championship by the Number 48 car of Jimmie Johnson, Chevrolet has won 25 NASCAR championships, compared with only eight for Ford.

There are similar statistics for the first 15 years of the Brickyard 400 at the Indianapolis Motor Speedway. Chevrolet has 10 in the win column to only three for Ford. Pontiac and Dodge each notched a win.

Chevrolet has obviously dominated at the Brickyard 400 and in the NASCAR Sprint Cup series championships. And an interesting statistic is also obvious in the numbers. While Ford and Pontiac each won the NASCAR championship once after a win at the Brickyard 400, eight of the 10 times Chevrolet has won at the Brickyard, it has also won the series championship.

Superior automobiles? Better teams and driving? Or does winning at the Brickyard give an edge?

PICTURE PERFECT
by Victoria A. Stewart

Victoria A. Stewart was born in Long Beach, California. She grew up in southern Indiana and now lives and works in Indianapolis. Currently she works for the United States Department of Agriculture as an administrative assistant. Her interests beyond writing include reading, word puzzles and history. She is working on a novel that takes place in central Indiana with two timelines, one present day, and the other in the late 1800s.

I had yearned to be his girlfriend in high school, I endured being his wife, but I will love being his widow. My lust and desire for Tucker Owens had run its painful, humiliating course, finally.

"Are you sure you're OK, Shelly?" Dawn asked. My sister was searching my eyes for any clue to my state of mind.

"I'm sure … I'll just be glad when the wake is over and I can have a few moments to myself." Keeping direct eye contact with Dawn, I could see her begin to ease the furrow of her brow.

The breaking point came with the last dalliance. I'd been patient and forgiving over and over again. But the last one was young enough, if we had had children, to be his daughter. The older he got, the younger they got; at this rate, his next conquest would step down into the pedophile range.

"Is there anything you need me to do in the kitchen?" Dawn asked.

"No, I hired extra help, so Sarah and William will see that everything is taken care of, but thanks."

After three hours the crowd was dwindling, and those left were making their way to the main foyer. With the last goodbyes said, I was able to take off my Manolos and rest my aching feet. Dawn was coming out of the study with a note in hand.

"I didn't want to bother you while you were saying good-bye, so I took a message for you from a Detective Kelley McAllen. She wants to come by tomorrow afternoon at two. I told her if that wasn't OK you would call her for another time."

"Did she say what she wanted?" I asked, fiddling with the flower arrangement *Sports Illustrated* had sent. It was massive, but I hadn't expected anything less from one of Tucker's biggest clients.

"No, but that there were a few things she needed to go over with you. She said it was just routine."

"OK, I'll be home all day so it should be fine."

"Do you want me to spend the night and stay until the detective leaves?" Dawn asked. I could see the searching again.

"No, I'll be OK."

"Shelly… did you do anything to Tucker?"

"No, why would you ask such a thing?"

"I don't know… I guess I didn't expect you to be this strong."

"Tucker drained everything he could from me, and when that wasn't enough for him, he came back and took more. What you see isn't strength, it's emptiness. With Tucker gone, I'll have to try to locate what is left of me, if anything."

"Was he at it again?"

"Tucker's indiscretions were getting closer and closer together. I thought he would at least give it his customary year, but yes, he was 'at it again.' His latest was an 'apprentice' who is in a work-study program at Herron High School. They have a fine arts program. See the little waif over by the fireplace?"

Dawn made a quick glance in Erica's direction. "The one with the red blotchy face?"

"Yes, but that's because she's in mourning."

"Why did she come?"

"I'm sure she doesn't have the slightest inkling that I know. Tucker didn't. She probably thought it would look odd if she didn't come."

"She looks like she's 12!"

"I know, but she turned 18 this April. To celebrate, Tucker took her with him to Phoenix for NASCAR … Erica Lesure, she followed him around like she was a starving puppy and he was wearing pork chop underpants."

"I'm sorry you had to go through this again."

"Yeah, me too, but at least I won't have to ever go through it again." Knowing that was true made me smile, a real smile for the first time in months, perhaps even years.

"OK … but you will call me as soon as the detective leaves?" Dawn asked.

"Sure, I'm certain it's routine like she said."

As soon as Dawn left and Sarah and William had gone to their apartment above the garage, I ran up to the master suite charging into Tucker's closet. On my hands and knees I reached to the back of the bottom drawer and felt for the sealed plastic bag… it was still there. I pulled it out, and the soggy, yellow-ish, heat wrap was still encased. With wobbly knees and trembling hands, I put on a pair of latex gloves and stripped before I opened the package of death. I took a pair of scissors and cut the heat wrap and plastic bag into tiny pieces, flushing the toilet every few minutes until it was completely gone. Then I clipped until the gloves followed the fragments.

I then stepped into a hot shower. Standing there with so many feelings raging through me … fear of getting caught, worry about the consequences if caught, and the prospect of relief if not. The steam swirled about my body; it was such a compassionate friend, holding me and giving comfort during all the years I needed kindness. Now, allowing the tension to drain from my weary frame, letting my mind retrace all my actions, giving me absolution for the terrible act I had committed …

I'd been cautious … careful with every detail. I had planned it for so long, I had done all the research at the public library, using the free pass codes to log onto the internet, wore gloves when I read the books on nicotine poisoning. Who knew nicotine is three times more toxic than arsenic? I had bought the carton of cigarettes while in Chicago, six months ago, the same brand Tucker had smoked years ago. Hiding the remainder of the carton in Tucker's closet where it would be found … if looked for. I had managed to get one of Sarah's discarded hypodermic needles she used for her daily insulin. It had been a perfect way to inject the distilled nicotine into the heat wrap. Nicotine is most effective when absorbed by direct contact with skin.

It had seemed like such a clever way to end the humiliation that had become my life. The years had passed too quickly; in high school I was envied by even the most popular girls. Even though he was pushing his mid-forties, he was still such a pretty man. I had worked hard to keep my body in good shape … I could still fit into the clothes I wore when we first were married, but it wasn't enough for him. Tucker worked out and was in good shape physically, but like his morals, his back was weak. It was only a matter of when, not if, both would fail. After twenty-three years of disgrace, I'd had enough.

It took a while to perfect the technique of injecting the nicotine into the heat wrap. I had to inject the poison without opening the heat wrap, or the heating process would begin too soon. It couldn't be soggy either, since Tucker would notice that too. A quick trip to the other side of town to dispose of the needle along with my "practice" heat wraps went smoothly. Trash collection ensured that these materials were now resting in the city dump.

I was a little sad, but only a little, remembering how Tucker had staggered out of his dark room on that last night. He was livid, screaming for some Valium and the heat wraps for his back. His eyes were wild and he was sweating so much I thought maybe he would have a heart attack and collapse right there and die. He had refused any treatment for four days after his back started giving him pain. I continued to wait.

Then on Friday evening, my opportunity had come. I had been downstairs in the game room pretending to be watching TV when Tucker started yelling and cursing for help. *What an odd way to ask for anything.* I called out for William; we struggled up the two flights of stairs finally getting him to our room. While William helped get him into bed, I got the "special" heat wraps. During my planning phase, I'd dumped all the Valium, so that I would have to send William to the drug store to get the refill, giving me time to change the "special" heat wrap for a non-nicotine-laced one and to store the other in a zip-lock bag in Tucker's closet.

I knew Sara wouldn't come near Tucker when he was like this; she was a timid, quiet person like I had been for most of my life. So I would be able to oversee his exit in private. He kept screaming as long as he could get enough breath to do so. He was in pain, he could taste metal, he vomited, then he started foaming at the mouth. It was an ugly death, but after years of enduring his lies and infidelities, his 30 minutes of agony seemed justified. That would be the last thing Tucker would take from me, my compassion.

I could see that his heart was giving out as he slipped into a final convulsion. As soon as his body quieted, I called 911. The EMTs did try to revive him, but it was too late. I then became the grieving widow. Not hysterical, but a respectful dignified mourning.

He had wrenched his back on the day of the race, yet he spent every moment he could in his studio. He wouldn't even let Erica in. Tucker had been so tense, teetering on the threshold of out-and-out paranoia. Now he was at peace … and so was I.

His last week was anything but peaceful. I hadn't seen him like this since we had moved back to Indianapolis six years ago from California. Every few months, while we lived in California and before that New York, Tucker would get crazy. I credited this weirdness to his work as a free-lance photographer. He had managed a few extremely profitable years getting pictures of megastars and selling them to the highest bidders. After a while, though, he had said he wanted a different challenge, so he made the switch to sports photography. He had always loved racing; he wanted to go home to Indianapolis.

During the month of May, he was in paradise. But when he started to follow NASCAR, he was sure he had found what he was looking for. For the last six years he had been gone an average of 20 weeks out of the year. Since this was business, he insisted that I stay home, According to him, I would be too much of a distraction. He didn't go to every event, but each year he would pick some of the major races and some of the smaller events. Tucker would be gone for three or four days and be home the Monday after the race. He didn't follow any particular team, just NASCAR in general.

He would be sure that he was being followed, and he would change his entire routine for a month or two. As quickly as the madness had descended upon him, he would return to his normal self in which the universe orbited around him and him alone.

Three minutes before two, Detective McAllen was at the door. William showed her into the study. This was my room; I had filled it with great books and comfortable chairs. I always felt at ease surrounded by these books that had the power and authority to take me somewhere else, to somewhere safe where there was at least a possibility for contentment.

After the introductions had been made, beverages offered and declined, we sat across from each other. Detective Kelley McAllen had an easy manner. I'm sure it was a skill that had been highly honed to allow criminals to feel they could open up to her, confide, confess, and unburden themselves.

"Mrs. Owens, I'm sorry for your loss."

"Thank you, Detective. But please call me Shelly."

"OK, Shelly, the reason I'm here is that IMPD received a package from your husband yesterday morning, and after looking at the information enclosed, I need to ask a few questions."

"I don't understand," I said, working on controlling my breathing and never breaking eye contact with her.

"Well, it appears that your husband was afraid that someone was going to kill him." Detective McAllen pulled out a manila envelope from a small satchel.

"Can you tell me about your husband's photography business?"

"I really didn't have anything to do with his business. I didn't even know how much he made until the end of the year when he wanted me to sign the tax returns. We were married for 23 years, and for at least the last 20, money wasn't often discussed. He was very generous with me. Anything I wanted, he would either give me the money or make arrangements for whatever was needed to be delivered. Is there a problem with Tucker's business?"

She ignored my question and continued on with hers.

"Did Mr. Owens have any visitors since the race?"

"Well, let me think … Um, yes, the day after the 400, the winner came by. I thought he wanted to see if Tucker had gotten any good shots of him during the race. Tucker had introduced him, Nathan Welsh. They went to the studio and were in there for about a half-hour, not more than 45 minutes."

"Did Mr. Owens seem nervous before or after Mr. Welsh left?"

"Now that you mention it, Tucker was tense ever since the race. He used to get that way when we lived in California and New York." I explained how Tucker would get so irrational, certain he was being followed.

"It appears that Mr. Owens had a side business along with the photography. He was attempting to blackmail Nathan Welsh. May we search your husband's studio, or do I need to get a search warrant?"

"You don't need a warrant; you can search anywhere you need to, Detective."

"Thanks, Shelly, I'll call the forensics team and we'll start the search."

The detective excused herself and walked over to one of the large cherry bookcases. She made a quick, hushed phone call to get the forensics team started with the search. After a few minutes, she returned to where I was sitting.

"Detective, what exactly are you looking for?" I asked.

"We'll be looking for any pictures and negatives from the race this last Sunday and especially of Nathan Welsh and his racing team." Flipping through a small notebook, Detective McAllen said, "The Red Brick Racing Team. We also need to look at his business records for at least the last month or so. We might need to go back further in his records."

"Sure. I'll show you to the studio and where the records are kept."

"It'll take 30 minutes to an hour for them to get here. Has Nathan Welsh come by since the day after the race?" Detective McAllen asked, with her pen at the ready.

"He was here yesterday for the wake. He was one of the first ones to arrive and the very last caller to leave."

"Shelly, do you remember what rooms he was in yesterday?"

"There were a few hundred people who came through the house yesterday, but most milled about in either the dining room, sitting room or the game room downstairs; and of course there are bathrooms … on the main floor as well as downstairs. I don't remember anyone going into other parts of the house. I think he was in the game room most of the time he was here."

"Where is Mr. Owens' studio?"

"Downstairs. His studio takes up about three-fourths of the area, and the game room is in the southwest corner of the basement. I can show you where everything is."

"Yes, I'd appreciate that."

"I'll get the keys for the studio. They should be in Tucker's closet."

"Do you mind if I come and have a look around upstairs?" the detective asked.

"No, feel free to come with me." I detected the slightest tremor in my voice. Detective McAllen didn't give any indication she noticed. Another skill I'm sure she has honed over the years.

While in the master suite, the detective made a cursory pass through Tucker's closet. She remarked how orderly his closet was. His shirts, jackets, slacks, all lined up like little soldiers awaiting orders from the commander. Even his jeans were perfectly creased and hung in their assigned location. That was his side, mine looked quite different. I didn't freakout if a blouse was hung up with the skirts or a pair of jeans was not hung with precision. For all of Tucker's faults, he was obsessively neat.

The bottom of the spiral staircase opened up directly into the game room, and to the right behind the mahogany double doors was Tucker's studio. I put the key in the lock and swung open both doors.

"Does anyone else have keys to the studio?" Detective McAllen asked.

"No, there is only one key, and Tucker would have it with him, except at night when he put it in the bowl on his chest-of-drawers. And he wouldn't do that until he was sure that our bedroom door was locked."

"When was the last time you were in the studio?"

"Friday night. Tucker came staggering out of the studio screaming with pain from his back and needing help to get upstairs. After William and I got him upstairs, he insisted that I come back and be sure that the studio was locked."

"And that is when you did it?"

"Excuse me, did what?" I asked.

"Came and locked the door?"

"Yes. It was locked, though, just like always."

Detective McAllen carefully scanned the first room then asked, "Does anything look out of place?"

Nothing looked different; it was an area that Tucker would allow clients into. It contained several comfortable chairs and a table with magazines. The studio could be entered from the lower level of the house or by French doors that opened out to the pool area. Both the game room and this part of the studio opened out to the pool. The rest of the studio was cloistered underground with no windows or doors.

"No, everything looks as it should," I said.

"Where does this go?" Detective McAllen asked, pointing to another set of double doors.

"There is a small room to take photos and a room for records, where business records and all his negatives are kept. There in the very back is a dark room and a room to view his proofs."

"Did Mr. Owens have many clients come to the house?"

"Sometimes, not often, though. Usually when someone was coming for photographs, he would come through the patio, so I can't be certain how often someone would come. Very little of Tucker's work was portraits; he sometimes did that for friends."

I unlocked the second set of doors. The detective asked me to check these rooms to see if I could see anything abnormal. Everything was in its place until we reached the room with the light table.

"The light table and stool have been moved," I said.

"How do you know?"

"Detective, you saw Tucker's closet: He was just as particular with his studio, anything that was his. As soon as an item was brought into Tucker's world, it would be assigned a place, and that is where it would reside, always. I thought he needed medication, but he was able to function, so I didn't push him."

The table isn't at a perfect 90-degree angle from the wall, exactly five inches from the wall, with the stool pushed up to the table … exactly in the center. See the table is farther away on this side?"

"It is barely different from one end to the other."

"Yes, but it is different, and Tucker wouldn't have left the room like this."

"When you came down here last Friday night, did you notice this?"

"No, the outer door was locked so I didn't come in," I said.

When I started to move the light table back into the proper position, Detective McAllen firmly told me not to move the table.

"Do you see anything else that seems wrong in the room?" she asked.

I pointed out that the access panel on the light table wasn't closed; Tucker wouldn't have left the room like this.

"I think someone has been in this room besides Tucker."

"Let's check the rest of the room again."

We went through the office and the darkroom. I was certain that most of his latest race photos were gone as well as the negatives.

The forensics team combed every inch of the studio, taking several brown paper bags with them. After five hours they left, but I was given strict orders not to go into the studio. The double mahogany doors as well as the French doors were now decorated with yellow police tape.

Detective McAllen said that she would be in contact in the next few days. As she was leaving, she gave me her card. I noticed she was assigned to the Homicide Division. My short experience with the police had taught me that they were excellent at asking you questions, but extremely reserved when answering them. When I asked about what exactly was in the packet that Tucker had sent, I was ignored. There was no debate about my request; it was just quietly, politely ignored.

Two days later the detective called and said that she would need to take Tucker's light table to the lab for further testing. The forensics team came back and removed a few more sacks and the table. This time they only took about three hours. They spent about half of the time upstairs in the master suite. They found and took the case of cigarettes.

I wasn't eating or sleeping. My appearance was that of a terrified person who was going to be spending the rest of her life in the Indiana State Women's Prison. This look was being mistaken by all as a grieving widow. I had instructed my attorney to start drawing up paperwork that would allow my sister Dawn to become my power of attorney. He was also to open a trust for Sarah and William; they had worked for us for 20 years, even moving across country with us. They deserved a good retirement.

Next I received a request from the detective for yet another visit. She asked if I would be sure that William and Sarah would be present. The appointment was again set for 2 o'clock. When I told William that the Detective wanted to speak to both him and Sarah, he was concerned that they would be busy with the weekly household shopping. I assured him that the groceries could wait until after the detective had left. After several minutes of hemming and hawing, William consented to be present the next day for the meeting.

Exactly three minutes before two, William showed the detective into the study.

"Mrs. Owens, I would like to speak with Sarah first and then William, before speaking with you, if that is OK?"

Sure, I thought, *like I had any choice in the matter.* "Whatever you need, detective, I'll be in the kitchen."

"Thank you, Mrs. Owens." *Uh-oh, I'm now Mrs. Owens, not Shelly.*

Oh well, maybe I can claim diminished capacity at my trial. Instead of going to the kitchen, I went to the game room, went behind the bar, and made myself a large screwdriver. It was as much vodka as orange juice. Knowing that the drink wouldn't solve or even help my problems didn't deter me. I was anticipating at least a little bit of softening of the knotted muscles; if they got any tighter I wouldn't be able to stand up straight when the detective handcuffed me. While finishing off my drink, I wondered exactly what a person wears when being arrested.

After waiting for what I was sure was hours, but a quick glance at the clock revealed was only 20 minutes, the detective came into the kitchen for me.

"Thank you, Mr. and Mrs. Knowles. If you could get the packages together, I'll stop by your apartment after I'm finished with Mrs. Owens," Detective McAllen said.

"Like I said, there are several, but I'll get a box for you to carry them," William said.

Neither Sarah nor William made direct eye contact with me. They seemed anxious to get to their assigned task.

I desperately wanted to stall, to completely avoid this conversation, so I asked, "Detective, you said that Tucker had had a packet mailed to your office. Who mailed it?"

"William. It seems this isn't the first time Mr. Owens had committed blackmail. Once he had taken a photo that could be used in his side business, he would compile a packet with pictures and negatives of the mark and give instructions to William. If anything happened to Mr. Owens, William was to send the packet to the police. Once the monies had been paid and he felt safe, he would tell William to destroy them. But William kept them, said he felt uneasy destroying them since Mr. Owens was so troubled when he would give him these packets. He said that he has packets going back fifteen years. That's what I'm taking with me."

I guess Tucker had more secrets than I thought.

"I want to thank you for your patience, Mrs. Owens. We have a clearer picture of exactly what happened to your husband. It has been determined that Mr. Owens didn't die of natural causes; he was poisoned."

At this point the room was spinning and I was beginning, against all my resolution, to hyperventilate.

"Please sit down, Mrs. Owens."

"Please call me Shelly." If she was going to take my freedom, I thought she should at least use my first name.

"OK, Shelly, can I get you something, or maybe call someone to come be with you? I know this is a shock; it is always difficult to learn that a loved one has been murdered. But we will be charging the perpetrators within the next day or two." I could see genuine concern in her eyes. *Oh, she was good.*

I had done this to myself, so I wouldn't drag anyone else into this final act. I told her that I just needed to sit down... not even wanting to guess what would come next.

"The medical examiner was concerned and took some blood samples from your husband. The results came back this morning."

At this point, what difference did it make? I was going to jail. But I wanted to know.

"The nicotine level... what was it?" I managed to croak.

I saw a questioning look pass over Detective McAllen's face. But she obliged and flipped through her notes. She said there were trace amounts of nicotine in his blood.

"Excuse me, what did you say?"

"There were trace amounts of nicotine in his blood. It seems he had taken up smoking again, but there wasn't much in his blood. And the ME reported that his lungs weren't damaged from smoking. But he was concerned because your husband's lungs were full of pneumonia. It had come on so suddenly he sent samples for additional lab testing, or this wouldn't have been noticed."

"Poison?"

"Yes, Mr. Owens died of mercury poisoning. We found remnants of mercury in the light table your husband used in his studio."

At this point all I could do was sit in a semi-comatose state. I did manage to close my gaping mouth.

"Nathan Welsh was being blackmailed by your husband. On race day, Mr. Owens took several pictures of Nathan in the pit area before the race. He caught him slipping a small cartridge into the gas tank when his crew was able to distract the pit official for a split second. According to Mr. Welsh, it was a fuel enhancement that was in time-released packaging. It released during the race, but was completely burned off before the end. We are still trying to determine what was added to the fuel tank. The enhancement wasn't detectable during the post-race inspection, but it did give him enough advantage to win."

By now I was beginning to tremble. Could this really be true?

"When we brought Mr. Welsh in for questioning, he rolled on his owner. When your husband contacted the driver with a demand, he contacted the owner," she said, flipping through her notes.

"… a Mr. Darcy. Mr. Darcy made some phone calls, and within a short period of time, Mr. Welsh was given a bump key, the mercury and specific instructions. He was to put it on a small tray and put that in the light table. He did that when he came the day after the race and then removed it at the wake. As the lights in the table heated the mercury, it became a deadly vapor. The effects of the vapor could manifest as psychosis. The concentration of mercury vapor would account for all your husband's symptoms. All the things you told the EMT's when they arrived…the metallic taste, foaming at the mouth, his inability to catch his breath, grabbing at his chest. The ME ruled that the cause of death was ventricular fibrillation due to acute mercury poisoning."

"I'm stunned." That was all I could say.

"Are you sure that there isn't someone I could call to come be with you, Shelly?" she asked.

"If you could call my sister, Dawn, she'll come over."

The detective used her cell and called Dawn.

"Is there anything else I can do?"

I was beginning to regain my balance. "No, detective, you've done so much. I'll now be able to have some peace knowing what really happened. Thank you for everything."

SPEEDWAY MOTEL CLOSES
by M.B. Dabney

It was an institution to race fans for decades: the Brickyard Crossing Inn, more commonly known as the Speedway Motel.

Indianapolis Motor Speedway officials ended years of speculation and rumor in December 2008 when they announced that the motel would be demolished.

"We do this with a heavy heart," Speedway spokesman Fred Nations told local television station WRTV Channel 6 at the time. But, he added, the cost to upgrade and maintain the motel's 96 rooms was too much.

The Speedway Motel was built in 1963, just outside Turn 2 at the track, on the southeast corner of the property. And over the years it became a mainstay for many visiting the track.

Actor James Garner, an avid race fan who starred in the film *Grand Prix*, reportedly always reserved the same room at the motel whenever he visited the track for a race. Part of the 1969 Paul Newman film, *Winning*, was shot at the motel.

NASCAR star Jeff Gordon was part of Speedway Motel lore. Gordon ordered a pizza and enjoyed it in his motel room in 1994 hours after winning the first Brickyard 400.

Signs of the motel's physical decay were visible for years before the decision was made to tear it down. But the supply and demand for hotel rooms in the area played a significant part in the decision.

"When it was originally built, there were really no motel facilities here on the west side serving the Speedway," Nations told Channel 6. "Marion County now has 30,000 hotel rooms."

Fifteen people lost their jobs when the motel was torn down. But the adjacent pub, conference center and pro golf shop stayed. And at the time of the announcement, Speedway officials had not decided what to do with the space, leaving the door open for another, more modern facility to take the motel's place.

ROADKILL
by Suzanne Leiphart

Dr. Suzanne Leiphart is an Indianapolis, Indiana, psychologist and mystery and nonfiction writer who was born and raised in Michigan. She is the author of the psychological thriller, Love the Evil *(2000, by Xlibris Corporation), to be re-released as* Deadly Handsome, *as part of her new Deadly series of romantic thrillers.*

As Richard Jones sipped his beer and eyed the shy, tight-jeaned beauty sitting at the bar with her two friends, he knew he'd found the right NASCAR fan. He was certain she was his type, a lady. She didn't laugh loudly like her friends, her top wasn't quite as low cut, not as much midriff showed, and her soft-blond hair wasn't as big as theirs. No noticeable tattoos, either. He liked her fancy Western boots with the jeans tucked in.

Shapely figures like hers were easy to find around a NASCAR track; in fact her companions had similar good looks. What appealed most was the uneasiness about her as she fidgeted with her hair, half smiled at her girlfriends' jokes, kept her head down, slouched a little.

He liked them submissive, reeking of low self-esteem.

Absentmindedly, he clicked the gold pen in his shirt pocket that started and stopped the hidden recorder, fiddled a moment with the buttons on his expensive jacket, and headed for the bar.

A tall chair next to the woman he desired was open now, but he politely asked her if the spot was taken. Her slumped shoulders straightened a little, and her eyes lit up when she saw his face. They always liked the way he looked. But then she turned away, passively, back toward her friends.

"Would you mind passing me the nuts?" he said to the country-western beauty. When she looked at him, he gave her his warmest smile. She smiled back as she slid the bowl of peanuts toward him but had difficulty holding eye contact.

"Thank you." He nodded at the baby blue NASCAR cap lying next to her beer and cell phone. "You must be here for the Brickyard race."

She agreed as her two friends curiously turned their heads his way.

"Hi, I'm Louise," called the oldest and grittiest looking of the three over the droning background voices in the busy honky tonk and a motor-sports channel on the TV behind the bar. She was sitting the farthest from him. "We're going to the 400 tomorrow at the track."

Forcing a gleaming grin, he replied, "I'm Richard." He wasn't the least bit interested in the young woman's friends.

Louise extended her hand. "This is Fran." Louise nudged her friend with her elbow. Fran looked him up and down with approval. "And this is Tammi," she said as she leaned toward her tongue-tied friend.

"Tammi. What a pretty name. Bartender, another round for the girls."

The four chatted for a few minutes. The women were Indianapolis natives. All of them were looking forward to an exciting 400-mile race at the Brickyard.

"Have you been to Daytona?" Tammi asked Richard. "We went down there to the 500 this year for the first time. It was great!"

"Terrific race this year in Daytona. I've been a few times."

"Afterward, we drove on Daytona Beach," Tammi continued, animated. "Never knew sand could be hard enough to drive a car on."

Richard took a sip of his draft beer and drank in Tammi's flawless skin. "I'm planning on going to the race in Pocono after the Brickyard, and then Watkins Glen."

"We were talking about doing that, too. We want to be NASCAR groupies," Tammi giggled.

Richard grinned and decided right then that he wanted her all to himself. She was perfect.

"I'll be right back," Tammi said as she stepped down off her seat and headed into the shadows of the lively restaurant area.

He watched as Louise barely sipped her beer. The way she seemed to look at him suspiciously sometimes bothered him. But she seemed to be the protector watching over her close friends Tammi and Fran. He nodded at her and she waved back. *I'm just paranoid,* he thought. *No need to worry.*

"Hey, look. There's Jeff Gordon." Richard, excited, pointed to a slim, dark-haired man coming in the front door. When Fran and Louise turned to look, Richard grabbed Tammi's cell phone off the bar and put it in his pocket.

"That's not Jeff Gordon," Fran teased. "Don't look anything like him. You need glasses," she laughed.

"It's not?" He chuckled along with her, then eased off of his bar stool. "Any idea where the men's room is?" Fran pointed the way.

Once inside a stall in the plain but surprisingly spotless bathroom, Richard pushed a few buttons to program Tammi's phone, then left, hoping to beat her back. He did and quickly placed the cell phone on the bar.

"Hello, Tammi," Richard said, his eyes lighting up when Tammi returned smelling sweeter than ever, freshly made up. He couldn't wait to taste her shimmering pale-pink lip gloss.

"God Bless the USA" started to play on Tammi's cell. She answered as Richard's phone vibrated silently in his pants pocket. He smiled to himself. He loved the spy phone he'd purchased from his favorite online spy shop. The connection was working. "I've got a call, too," he mouthed to her as he stood and walked several feet away to listen in to her call. His lips moved like he was speaking to a caller on his phone.

"Honey, can't I see you tonight?" Richard listened as the deep, slurred voice continued to beg for Tammi's company.

"No! We broke up. You need to let go. I'm moving on."

"You'd better not be."

"Don't threaten me! I'm getting on with my life. You need to do the same. It's been over for two months."

"I'm warning you, Tammi. You're not moving on without me. Where are you, anyway? Oh, never mind. I can tell by the noise in the background. I'm coming over now, and you'd better be there!"

She hung up on him. Slammed the phone shut.

Richard kept acting like he was busy listening to his caller while he plotted his next move. He liked having an edge, always being prepared.

"What's going on, hon?" asked Louise. Fran had taken notice, too.

"Ryan just won't let go. I need to get out of here. Said he's coming over to find me. I'm done with him."

"Go on home. I'll talk to him when he gets here," Fran said.

"We'll take care of him for you, especially if he gets mean," Louise said, giving a bold wink.

"*If* he gets here," Tammi said. "Sounded like he'd had a few."

Richard walked back over to them. "Everything all right?" He gave Tammi a concerned look, gently touched her waist.

"It's my ex. Won't leave me alone," she said nervously. "He's on his way here, and I don't want to see him."

Richard shifted his weight closer to her. "Any way I can help? Would you like to go somewhere else?" He looked at Fran and Louise. "Let's all go."

"No, we're going to wait here for him, me and Louise. Someone needs to set Ryan straight."

Tammi grabbed her phone and NASCAR cap off the bar, started to leave. Richard immediately ordered a diet cola to go.

"Call me when you get home," Fran said. "We'll make him leave you alone."

"Let me walk you to your car." Richard rested his hand on her lower back. He grabbed the soft drink with his other hand.

"See you guys tomorrow, but let me know if there's any drama. It's almost closing time, so he might not make it."

Richard followed as Tammi hurried out of the tavern. Once out the door she stopped to put on her hat and fish for keys in her bulging bag.

"My truck's right over there." Richard pointed to a big, shiny vehicle parked a few yards away.

The lot was almost full. "Would you like to go get something to eat?"

Tammi caught her breath when she saw the stunning new truck. "Well," she hesitated. "It's late."

Richard stepped toward her, looked at her closely. "Tell me what happened. Is this guy dangerous?"

"Not really. Mostly a jerk." She continued on with the details of their break-up as Richard edged her toward his rental vehicle.

"You deserve better than that. You've got such a wonderful quality about you, and you're gorgeous. You could have any man you want."

"Really?" She blushed. "I never thought so. But I'm not settling for anyone like him anymore. Drinks too much. No ambition." She shivered in her flimsy top, holding her arms tightly around herself. It was an unusually chilly summer night for Indianapolis.

"You're cold. Let's sit inside and talk for a few minutes." He opened the passenger door for her, and she eagerly stepped up and slid onto the smooth leather seat. He reached over her to show her how to use the seat heater, then walked contentedly around the back to the driver's side, fumbling in his pocket for the tablets he always kept stashed, and rapidly put a couple into the diet beverage before he got in.

"Let me start the car and get the heat going for you."

It didn't take Tammi long to unwrap her arms and lean back on the head rest while Richard placed the doctored drink in the cup holder.

"Are you warm enough?" He touched her thigh briefly.

"Yeah, thanks. I never sat in a heated seat before." She beamed as she took in the perfectly detailed interior. "What do you do for a living?"

"Business. Different things." He let his hand rest on her leg this time.

"Oh." She didn't move away.

Richard reached over to push a few strands of hair out of her eye. She bent her head so it rested in his hand. He leaned over and kissed her tenderly, feeling her mouth submit to his, knowing he had her.

Immediately he thought about driving away with her into the country, northeast to Pennsylvania toward his next NASCAR stop at Pocono. She'd enjoy the trip. The last one hadn't. What to do if this one got spooked like some of the others had? Maybe this relationship would last, and she would truly be his dream girl. She was so pliable and never suspected he'd heard every word of her phone call from her ex, Ryan.

He reached for the diet cola and held it out to her. "Would you like a sip?" It was time they got out of town, he'd decided.

"Sure. Sounds good." She put her lips to the cup, then again a few more times.

Richard surveyed the parking lot. Another couple was making out in a small pickup. No sign of anyone who might be hotheaded Ryan. He didn't notice the two men slouched down in the seats of the dirty white van several spaces away.

Richard watched with pleasure as Tammi put her head back and closed her eyes. Those pills really packed a fast punch. If she behaved, she would be a great traveling companion for him. They could follow the entire NASCAR circuit.

Tammi's head fell to his shoulder and rested. Richard couldn't believe his luck. He stopped in the night spot's driveway to wait for traffic before he headed east. It was too bad they'd have to miss his favorite race tomorrow at the Brickyard. Pocono would be almost as good. He tossed her phone out the window before he pulled out. Didn't want anyone tracing their movements through the cell towers or GPS.

They reached the Ohio state line by taking I-70, while Tammi slept next to him. Richard took the first Ohio exit and turned off on a familiar gravel road. *Looks pretty isolated,* he thought. I can play with her here. She belonged to him now, and absolutely no one else would ever know what was about to go on between the two race fans. He opened the glove box that lit up his favorite game pieces, brass knuckles and a .45, and reached for the roll of duct tape, not really wanting to cover her tantalizing pink lips that shimmered in the dim light from the compartment, but there was no other way. He kissed her one last time, then tore off just the right amount of tape with his teeth.

"Not so fast, sucker!"

Richard froze in shock as Tammi grabbed his wrist, digging in hard with tough, cemented-on acrylic nails as she grabbed the gun in her boot with her other hand. Pointing the weapon with both hands toward her captive's chest, she carefully maneuvered herself away from him over to her door. Her silent intensity helped keep him in his place as the minutes passed.

Suddenly the driver's-side window cracked. A heavy automatic weapon broke through and completely shattered the glass. Richard felt his heart in his throat as he started for the .45 in the storage box. Too late. Tammi moved faster. Her gun smashed into his skull, knocking him down to the seat.

As he lay there blanking in and out, the barrel stayed pressed against his temple. He could see a huge, blurry man now, holding the firearm outside the car window with a dirty white van right behind him.

The passenger door swung open, and a second man handed Tammi a pair of handcuffs.

"You do the honors, Special Agent Fuller."

"FBI at your service," she told Richard as she snapped on the cuffs. "We despise serial killers."

"You OK, Tammi?" Richard recognized Louise's voice from the tavern.

"Agent Lusco. Glad you could make it." Tammi got out of the truck and hugged Louise.

"We finally got him."

"Look what we got here." Another agent held up a dirty shovel he'd found behind the seat of the truck. There were also several heavy plastic bags, a rifle, hunting knife, leather gloves, and more duct tape. He stared hard at Richard who was trying to sit up. "Probably got some DNA here from some of the other victims, too."

"Let the men take this sicko lover boy away, hopefully forever." Louise gently smoothed Tammi's tangled hair as other federal agents removed Richard from the truck. Lots of back-up support had arrived. "Feel free to throw the bum out on the highway and turn him into roadkill, guys," she shouted as they led him away. "That's what the mother deserves."

During his interrogation Richard was disgusted with all the evidence the feds thought they had related to multiple murders he'd allegedly committed. They'd learned about most of the aliases he'd used, that he was from old money in Rhode Island, Ivy League educated. He didn't like how they'd invaded his privacy, followed him, taken pictures, bugged his phones, accessed his email, monitored his web movements, pried into all of his financial accounts and records. His rights had been violated, he was sure of it. They knew very personal specifics about the type of women he liked, his favorite race tracks and watering holes. He admitted to himself that he'd become careless over the years with his exploits, but the FBI had set him up with those three bitches in Indy.

As he sat and listened to the investigators' garbage, he knew he was smarter than all of his accusers put together, and his lawyer, Martin York, was one of the best criminal defense attorneys in the nation. He'd gotten off that stupid attempted murder charge years ago. Had a clean record except for those two batteries when he was 20 because he hadn't wanted his abusive father's help. He turned his head away and sneered. What could they really do to him?

Weeks later, after the preliminary hearing, Mr. York spoke candidly with his smug client. "We're going to have to try to plea bargain. You don't want to go to trial." The star litigator pressed on with Richard, who was clearly still in denial regarding the irrefutable evidence against him. "You could easily end up serving tandem life sentences. Or worse. With all the DNA evidence they have, there's absolutely no way out."

JEFF GORDON:
RACER, CHAMPION, PHILANTHROPIST, WINE LOVER
by M.B. Dabney

Jeff Gordon started on his road to NASCAR greatness at a tender age, guided first by his stepdad, John Bickford. Born Jeffery Michael Gordon on Aug. 4, 1971, in Vallejo, California, Gordon stepped into a quarter midget at age 5, and Bickford had the youngster running laps on a makeshift track near their Vallejo home. Gordon's skills as a racer showed almost immediately. By age 6, he had won 35 main events.

Gordon and his family moved to Pittsboro, Indiana, in his early teens and started racing 650-horsepower sprint cars. By his midteens, Gordon had been racing midgets and sprints for years, but he and his family eventually decided there weren't enough opportunities for him in open-wheel racing. So he turned to the Buck Baker Driving School at Rockingham Speedway in North Carolina, where he got his first taste of the much heavier stock cars.

At age 19, Gordon raced in a couple of NASCAR Busch Grand National races in 1990 but made a big splash the following year when he was named the Busch series Rookie of the Year. By then Gordon had gained the attention of legendary car owner Rick Hendrick.

Gordon's first full season with Hendrick Motorsports in NASCAR's top division was in 1993, when he won Rookie of the Year honors again. Over nearly 20 years, the relationship has proven to be one of the most successful in NASCAR. Gordon has four NASCAR championships and, with Hendrick, is the co-owner of the Jimmie Johnson's championship-winning Number 48 car.

Driving a Number 24 Chevrolet with DuPont sponsorship, Gordon won his first points-paying race in 1994, the Coca-Cola 600. He also won the Brickyard 400 that year, the first of four wins at the Indianapolis Motor Speedway.

Through mid-2008, Gordon had won 82 races, making him sixth on NASCAR's all-time win list, and 67 pole positions, ranking him fourth. He was the winner of the All Star Race three times and the Daytona 500 three times.

But Gordon has also thrived for a balanced life. He and wife Ingrid Vandebosch were married in 2006 and welcomed daughter Ella Sofia into the world in June 2007. They live in Charlotte, North Carolina.

In 1999 he started the Jeff Gordon Foundation to support children battling cancer. The foundation works extensively with the Jeff Gordon Children's Hospital in Concord, North Carolina. And in 2005 Gordon started working with Briggs & Sons Winemaking Company in Calistoga, California, to offer the Jeff Gordon collection of fine wines.

LADY LUCK
by S. Ashley Couts

Shirley Ashley Couts from Greenwood, Indiana, holds a BFA degree from the Indiana University Herron School of Art and Design. She edited Literally *(Indiana Writers' Center); is an Indiana Writing Project fellow; has earned several visual arts grants; and is a Ruth Lilly Teacher Creativity scholar. Her written work has appeared in local, regional and national publications. She has performed poetry in several spoken word venues and is a retired Shelbyville Middle School visual arts teacher.*

Johnny Avatar, grateful for the smooth start, steered his yellow Daylight Steel Chevrolet into the first turn. His owner, Bryant Bright, had invested big bucks on this rookie's ability. But so far, Johnny hadn't performed up to expectation. Bad luck, bad tires, bad attitude and low qualification scores have plagued him all season. If Johnny's luck didn't change soon, he would lose his Number 66 ride. Everything depended on this race.

In the first turn Ace Harper's radio voice crackled inside the cockpit. "How's the car handing?" The microphone popped, then went silent. "So far so good, Chief." Johnny's gloved hands gripped the wheel as he drove through the short chute. The banked stands along the south end were packed to capacity. In all, over 250,000 fans filled bleachers, grandstands and the grounds. Johnny felt the crowd's vibrant energy. They stood as his car zipped into the second turn, battling for position on the straightaway. Absorbed, he didn't pick up the sound as they booed him.

The track disappeared under his wheels, and his attention flicked between the windshield view and the panel of gauges. His foot and mind worked in tandem with the accelerated power as he steered low into the fourth turn. His front end was inches off Tony Stewart's bumper. It wasn't exactly a gentleman's move, but he was blocked with no place to go.

On lap 66 the team's spotter, up high in the stands, reported an accident and warned of an impending slow down. Ace confirmed. They were going yellow. The caution light flashed on. The first turn spotter reported the crash location up on the 9-degree slant in the banked turn. Four cars involved— a messy scene. Debris was scattered around crumpled race cars.

Realizing he had just missed the wreck, Johnny shrugged in relief. Slowing to pace speed, he wedged the Number 66 Chevy into the string of multicolored cars weaving together and apart like restless but obedient school children. Huffing a bored and irritated sigh, he relaxed his stomach muscles and wriggled his compact body against the snug restraints that held him in place. Long ago, he learned to ignore the dull pain in his left knee—an old injury from open-wheel days.

With racing on hold, Johnny surveyed the streak-marked wall up ahead. At full speed, he would have reached it in mere seconds. The wall was pocked and gouged by unlucky drivers who missed the turn. Unfortunately, he was one of them. The remembered sound and the jolt of impact flickered back to him. He survived; the car didn't. The costly rebuild set the team back, and he was still working the bugs out.

He flexed his fingers inside flame-retardant gloves as the slow procession moved along the backstretch fence. Dwarfed by the towering enclosure, Johnny imagined the track as a giant oval-shaped playpen where big boys and girls acted out their danger games. The place had its ghosts. He sensed the tangible memories of those who, testing limits, taunted fate and lost. He figured if a ghost could return and haunt a place, surely Billy Vukovich Senior's spirit would hang out back here. A dribble of sweat trickled along Johnny's spine. *Bad luck, fate or someone's dangerous mistake?*

He'd watched the horrific videos on YouTube and the Internet. *The determined Fresno driver, his white helmet jostling as he came out of the southeast turn seconds before his death— violently, quickly it all changed for him.* Back in 1955, that fence wasn't there. Bleachers lined up close to the track, lots of trees and a metal footbridge structure extended across the track—all gone now. As Johnny's mind replayed the frightening video, he shivered inside the fire-retardant suit.

Wrecks that horrifically bad inspired new safety features. That white stretch of wall-high Safer Barrier skirting the taller wire-mesh screen was meant to reduce damage and prevent injury. It bore an archaeological record of mishaps. No telling how many lives the padded barrier had spared. *Too bad it wasn't there when Vuky zipped out of the short chute on the 30th day of May.*

Defying premonitions of doom, fueled by desire for a third win, the silent Serb—leading by 17 seconds—came up fast on slower-moving traffic. That's when things went bad. After that, rumors spread about a Speedway jinx. Even those who weren't especially superstitious had their precaution rituals.

A strong huff of southeastern wind suddenly buffeted the Daylight Steel car. A tremor passed through Johnny. *That came from nowhere. A clear blue sky. No wind at all. Is it a bad omen—a warning?* The 1955 catastrophe began with a similar gust of wind. It caught Roger Ward's car. He spun out of control and began to slide. That wind began a dreadful sequence of events.

The radio chirped suddenly, jarring Johnny back to the present. Ace's voice alerted that officials had stopped the race. Two wreckers, arriving to clear the track, had tangled. The fracas spewed more wreckage. Johnny halted the car at an eastern-facing angle. Wriggling his fingers, he flipped up the protective eye shield attached to his helmet and gazed straight ahead. *That's precisely where it happened.*

He followed along the fence line with his eyes. Beyond its wire grid, a strip of grass bordered a gravel access road and some utility buildings. Beyond that the lush greens of the Brickyard golf course sloped over a rise before dipping toward the railroad track. Johnny had played that course and knew that 11th hole. He peered through a stand of leaf-laden trees to where the sun danced through summer shadow. It was always, for reasons he couldn't explain, his most difficult hole.

Bored by the monotony, he strained for something more interesting to look at. Behind him was the infield packed with people, semi haulers and concession stands. But the HANS device, a thick, stiff guard meant to save his back and neck from injury, restricted movement in that direction. He was forced to look back to the spot where the roadster, its dead driver buckled inside, came to a rest.

Scenes from the video replayed across the screen of Johnny's memory. The snub-nosed roadster went airborne. Defying its weight, it rolled like a feather caught in a tumbling breeze. End over end it went for what seemed like an eternity.

Johnny Avatar imagined with searing clarity the blue and orange Number 4 Hopkins Special roadster as it plowed nose down. He could almost smell the acrid, black billow of smoke as the car burned.

What is that? For a second he wondered if the quick flash on the golf course was conjured by his imagination. It sparked like sun reflecting off something bright. It moved then along the hilltop. At first a small bright spot, it expanded to a quarter-sized glow. *What is that thing? A sunspot?* He scrunched his nose in a squint. The glow floated along the horizon, hung there a few seconds, and then, like a giant halogen spotlight, it beamed directly toward him. The glare spread across the smooth surface of the windshield. Johnny snapped the visor over his eyes to block the penetrating ray.

"Ace," he shouted after pushing the flat button in the center of his steering wheel, "did you see something back here?"

"Like what?" Ace asked.

"I don't know for sure. A flash of light or something?"

"It was probably the sun."

"This was too bright for that. Besides, it came from the East and it's way after noon. I wonder if it was some kid with a laser. Don't you think that could be dangerous? A light that bright could hit someone in the eye. Remember a few months back—someone aimed a laser light at a plane? The beam hit the pilot's eye and he nearly crashed."

"Nope. Didn't hear that. I think you saw the sun bouncing off parked cars or something." Ace queried the spotters placed in various positions around the track. One at a time they reported in. No one saw anything.

Johnny shut his eyes. Behind his eyelids, an image of dancing sparks splintered in a thousand tiny lights. When the show subsided, Johnny flipped the shield back up and strained to determine the light's origin.

Two figures in silhouette, diminished in size by distance, were now on the green. They scuffled over something. Johnny strained for a better look. He got a glimpse of flurried movement before the light flared again obscuring his vision.

"Aren't they about done with this cleanup?" Irritation tinged his tone. "I'm ready to go."

"A few more minutes. What's the problem?"

"There's this crazy reflection bouncing off something back here, and it keeps hitting me in the eyeballs. If it happens again, I won't be able to see to drive."

A few seconds later, Ace's triumphant voice boomed in. "Let's go race. There's the green."

The racec ars one by one moved out to resume the chase. Right away, Johnny's car got blocked in. Jimmie Johnson lapped him a second time. Jeff Gordon closed in on Johnny's bumper, then swung out, around, and took off.

Two cars ahead of him went sideways suddenly but straightened out in time. Seconds later, the red-and-white, decal covered, National Distribution-sponsored Ford, piloted by a hotshot rookie out of California, went squirrelly. Johnny, in the Daylight Steel Chevy, quickly steered right. Sneaked by just in time. Inches behind him, the sound of metal against metal exploded. Johnny plowed on. His rearview mirror caught, through a veil of white smoke, a fast view of the crumpled pile of numbered scrap.

"They're out," Johnny chuckled.

The crew chief's dry wit was evident in his return. "Yeah. It's like a demolition derby out there today. Tough luck for those guys."

"I'm crying." He didn't hide the spiteful tone. "I hope they clean up quickly. This yellow-light fest is bugging the heck out of me. I've got 850 horses and 3500 pounds of steel bucking to run."

"Hang tight," Ace instructed. "It's part of the game."

The green flag waved, starting lap 80. Johnny, entering the first turn, impatiently accelerated. A paper scrap swirled down from the stands. It caught a back draft of air, hovered briefly over the track, and then dived toward his face. Catching air, it skidded over his roof.

Relentless August heat scorched down from an unforgiving sun. Spectators fended it off with sun block, icy soda and cold beer. Those who had tuned in heard Johnny Avatar mutter a complaint about the litter on the track.

In the fourth turn, Johnny's tire picked up something sharp. In the pits, the seven-member wall crew rushed in. With speedy precision, the jack man lifted the car. The rear tire changer did his job. The gasman splashed a little fuel into the tank. In seconds Johnny was back on the track and moving into the first, then the second turn.

Entering the backstretch, his mind flashed a dark foreboding. He overreacted with a push of his foot on the accelerator. The gush of power sent the car into a sideways slide. Spectators in the short chute jumped up, hoisting binoculars and cameras his way. They didn't want to miss the action if he hit something.

"What's going on?" his excited spotter shouted.

"It's acting a little loosey-goosey in the turns," he reported back, covering the mistake.

On lap 100, Johnny made a sudden and recklessly dangerous move. Cars dodged and slid trying to get out of his way. He got slammed broadside.

His body reacted to the jolt by straining against the centrifugal force of an out-of-control spin. The second impact tensed his safety belt. The third shoveled him off the track where, bent and broken, the Daylight Steel Chevrolet came to rest in the grass.

Johnny Avatar poked up out of the window and hopped out. Plucking off his helmet, he muttered words best not repeated. He shucked off his gloves and smeared an arm sleeve across his sweaty brow.

Later, in the garage, Johnny caught sight of his disheartened crew. Bright caught him by the arm and shouted near his ear. "I don't know what's wrong with you, bud. But you better shake this bad luck streak before you jinx the whole team."

"I'll find a way to fix this," he told Bright.

"I don't care if you have to make a deal with the devil," Bright shouted.

Watching Bryant Bright stalk off, Johnny angrily picked up some tools. *I might just do that.*

Above the city, the Daylight Steel-owned Cessna gained altitude. As the pilot banked the plane toward the setting sun, Johnny leaned back for the ride. In seconds, he was sound asleep and dreaming...

A few hours after Johnny Avatar pulled out of the Speedway grounds, a dismembered hand was discovered near the golf course. Cut off at the wrist, five manicured fingers—nails alternately painted black and white—grasped a crumpled Brickyard ticket. Homicide detectives combed through natty weeds looking for clues. Street cops draped the area with streamers of yellow crime tape.

At that very moment, ABC News was breaking the morbid story of a "grisly Brickyard find." With impeccable timing, the NBC affiliate followed suit. They trumped ABC by going live, on site, with the Metro Police spokesman, who, with sad eyes and a solemn voice, reported they had very few clues to go on.

Fear ran rampant through the city. Parents stocked up on locks, security cams, Mace and weapons. Children were warned to stay in after dark, walk with friends, and keep cell phones handy.

A few days later, Johnny, enjoying the luxury of his trackside RV, tuned in to NASCAR highlights. His recent run-in with Tony Stewart, in wide-screen color, was easy to analyze. From alternating camera views, Johnny saw the crash he'd caused. Just in case viewers missed it, a big yellow circle and an arrow appeared on the screen. Johnny winced.

"That's what you call a creative move," announced the narrator."

"That guy's a demon on the track," the second announcer laughed.

His partner agreed, "Yeah, unless he learns how to drive, that rookie better pack up and go home."

"I'm not sure anything will help."

"Maybe he should make a deal with old Lucifer," the announcer chuckled.

Johnny clicked the remote and the screen went blank. Frustrated and exhausted, he closed his eyes and began to dream.

Meantime, back in Indiana, a jogger stumbled over the stump of an arm. It protruded, in ghastly horror, from mossy water near the track. A delicate charm bracelet encircled the slim wrist. Twenty-two tiny trinkets, shaped like little stock cars, dangled from silver links. Homicide went to work. They had already tested the hand for fingerprints, and collected nail clippings and skin cells for DNA testing. It should be easy to prove the arm was from the same body as the hand.

Back to racing, Johnny wrapped up a disappointing run at Pocono. His run at Watkins Glen saw no improvement. Tired and perturbed, he arrived home for a midweek meeting. Bryant Bright slammed his fist on the desk. The president of Daylight

Steel, Walter Rich, with blood vessels in his neck bulging, glared at Johnny. Bryant Bright issued a severe warning. "I told you before. No matter what it takes, end this bad luck streak."

Whenever Johnny's head hit a pillow, the nightmare continued.

Two schoolboys in Speedway discovered a headless torso. Reporters converged on the site. As a news helicopter hovered overhead, a cameraman on the ground panned the weeded lot. Standing in scrubby, ankle-high grass, a blond reporter forced a smile, fluffed her hair, and cleared her throat. Speaking to the camera, she described in dramatic detail the victim's smooth ivory skin, the remnants of torn scattered clothing found nearby, the slim gold chain draped around her waist.

Detective Winslow stepped into the shot. She begged for information on missing females between the ages of 19 and 25. To that end, she revealed a few identifying details: a small dark mole at the waist; the checkered flag tattoo on the corpse's left hip.

Disturbed by the super-real nightmares, Johnny traveled to Michigan International. Inside his garage, he glowered at the crew as they set up his small block, V-8 engine. He snarled as they checked each tire. He growled at everyone when they checked them again. The disgruntled team's morale began to unravel.

Johnny's dark mood gathered like a black cloud of doom. It shadowed him on every turn. In Michigan, he came in dead last. A measly 43 points was added to his dismal total.

The old man in the bar had a wicked, one-toothed smile. "It's no game for wimps and babies," he told Johnny. He spoke of the "good old days" of booze running and cheating. He remembered the day all those "girly girls" were hired to flirt with those NASCAR guys down in Daytona. "Anything went," he said. "Back when a track was red packed dirt. When guys did what they had to, to win." He counted out the money and smiled his crooked smile. "Be careful," he warned. "It's very dangerous."

Johnny saw himself reflected in the mirror behind the bar. But the old man's leering image was lost in the crackled surface as he casually unfolded his newspaper. Over his shoulder, Johnny read the headlines: *HEADLESS TORSO FOUND; OFFICIALS WON'T COMMENT*

"Let me see the sports section."

The man handed it over. Buried in the black text account of the sprint at Michigan, a sportswriter forecast Johnny's doom. "Avatar's a danger to everyone. Daylight Steel better take drastic measures before he hurts someone," the reporter warned.

"Sounds like you've got few fans," the man cackled.

"Yep," Johnny answered in a dejected voice.

"I wouldn't take any wooden nickels then," he warned.

Johnny drove home in the red Camaro gifted to him by his Daylight Steel owner. He parked in his private garage inside the Daylight Steel-leased condo. In the living room, he shrugged out of his Daylight Steel yellow-and-black jacket. With a sigh, he fingered the embroidered logo, a circle sun with rays stitched in gold thread. The heavy weight of his obligation sagged his shoulders. The encounter with the old man disturbed him.

Johnny gathered his mail and a brown-wrapped package and headed for the sliding glass door. On the patio, a quick breeze whistled past, ruffling his hair. The paper tore under his thumbs as he opened the box. Appraising the contents, Johnny cocked his left eyebrow. Inside, a crisp-folded paper rested on top of a blond hairpiece. He picked up the note and poked, with a tentative finger, at the cluster of tousled ringlets. The wayward tendrils jostled at his touch.

His forehead crinkled in a puzzled crease. He unfolded the note then picked through each word. The jagged scrawl, wild and loopy, looked like something penned by a mad man:

ANYTHING TO WIN YOU VOW
YOUR YELLOW STREAK IS SHOWING NOW.
IF I WERE YOU, I WOULD THINK TWICE.
THE COWARD PAYS A FATAL PRICE.

Johnny scratched his scalp. *Whoever wrote that was a lousy poet.* He prodded the hairy thing in the box. Pulling back in repulsion, he felt fear shoot through him. It looked like a decapitated head. Frantic, he wadded the note and tossed it inside the box, then snapped it shut.

Wrenched with disgust, the box clutched in his hand, he hustled toward a small patch of yard just beyond the patio. The soil in the flower garden was loose and damp from recent watering. Dirt clogged his fingernails as he clawed into the black earth. As water from the hose trickled through his fingers, the dirt disappeared from his skin, but he worried that he was losing his mind. The constant pressure to win, the capricious nature of fate, the meeting in the bar, and the nightmarish bad dreams had taken their toll. And now this—whatever it was. Mail from a crazed fan? He was exhausted.

Johnny's eyes snapped open. Unsure of how long he'd slept, he was relieved to find himself still sitting in his padded chaise. The bright sun hitting his face caused him to squint. Sitting up and taking a sip of his now warm soda, he felt better—even a little silly as he examined his short fingernails for remaining dirt.

Returning his attention to the stack of mail, Johnny sorted bills and shuffled through advertisements. A black-edged envelope dropped to the cement floor. Despite his early chagrin, a kernel of dread flittered through his mind as he opened it.

Two nights later, Johnny arrived at the Hilton Hotel. He checked his slicked-down, dark hair in the rearview mirror and climbed out of his red sports car. Walking toward the door, he noticed a speck of lint on the sleeve of his black-and-yellow jacket. He flicked it off then straightened the collar of his black polo shirt imprinted with the Daylight Steel logo. Before entering the crowded banquet room, he popped a breath mint into his mouth.

He was greeted by party sounds: ice tinkling against glasses, the lyrical background notes of a harp, and the communal chatter of voices all around him. Johnny accepted a long-necked, brown bottle from a passing waiter. Giving a twist to the crinkled metal cap, he surveyed the room.

After a few beers he filled his plate with race-themed appetizers. Dipping a cracker into the Pit Road Cheese Ball, he made small talk with members of his crew, people from the media and a few big-shot moneymen. He scribbled a few autographs then posed for snapshots with first a bald man and then a group of giggly women. After that, a middle-aged red-headed woman in a silver-studded cocktail dress clutched at his arm. After answering her mundane questions and giving her arm a dismissive pat, he scanned the room hoping for a quick distraction. He found it—a stunning beauty standing near the long, polished bar.

He watched her hand brush a strand of raven-colored hair from a china doll face. His eyes followed her exquisite curves and the way her satin minidress skimmed along her statuesque body. With each movement, a glitter of dancing rainbows reflected off her necklace and flickered on her throat and the underside of her chin. A multifaceted pendant dangled from a delicate gold chain. Johnny followed the chain to where the jewel seductively swayed above a low-cut neckline.

Johnny's course was set. He moved toward her and pushed against the bar, waiting for the best moment to make his move. The competition, a tall gray-haired man to her right, was making his own fast move. It didn't matter. Competition between suitors wasn't bound by gentlemen's rules. He elbowed in beside her. As if playing coy, she laughed wildly at the man's stupid joke. Johnny bided his time, waiting for the right moment to move in. It came when she reached for her glass. Johnny went for it, too.

"I believe that's mine," she told him with a friendly smile.

"Oh, sorry." His eyes connected with her pale blue irises. "I thought that was my drink."

"No, you didn't. You don't have one." She giggled and nudged his arm as if enjoying the joke.

"You don't know that."

"I know everything," she demurred, "about you, anyway." She cupped her wine goblet and leaned near. Her perfume, an exotic blend of orchids, moss and something wildly exhilarating, filled his senses, and his heart quickened its beat.

"Please tell me you aren't just a beautiful stalker. Or a crazed fan. It would break my heart if I had to run from you."

She pensively slid her finger along the glass rim, then set the goblet on the glossy, burled wood. Then, with a perfectly manicured finger, she traced the sun logo on his jacket. "Maybe you aren't all that unlucky after all. Maybe you are unsure of yourself. I think you doubt your ability and skill."

"Un huh." He pursed his lips. "I don't think so. I race. That takes a huge measure of self-assurance."

"I know you race," she told him. "That's not what I meant. Your superstitions hamper you. But do you really think a good-luck charm will do the trick? Or a dirty deal?"

He narrowed an eye in suspicion. "Are you a fortuneteller? Were you hired to be a part of the entertainment?"

She lifted her hand to cup his cheek. "Just a wise woman come to give you the answers—to help you if I can."

"OK," He warily played along. "Lay it on me, then." A patronizing smile crinkled the corners of his mouth. "Why don't you tell me how I need help? You seem to know all the answers."

Her eyes glinted with good humor. "I'm not a fortune teller. But I do know your secret." Her eyes met his. "I'd tell you, but it isn't pretty. You might not want to know the truth." She reached for his hand and motioned toward a dark corner. "Come. We can speak in private. Maybe if you're a good boy, I will change my mind and tell."

He tagged along behind her like a just-claimed pound puppy. The rear view was just as spectacular as the front. He admired the round curves as her body moved, and her pale white skin glistened against the draped fabric as it drifted dangerously low against her back. "A fine chassis," his teammates would have said of her. Then, with jocular humor, they would have playfully punched his arm and given him high fives for bagging a stunner like this one.

She settled into the depths of a plush, violet-colored booth. Johnny followed, scrunching in close. The touch of his thigh against hers sent tingles of excitement along his leg.

"You have to trust me now," she warned as her hand rested, light as a feather, on his knee.

"Just tell me. What's the big deal? What's this big, dark secret?" He smiled, softening his brusque tone.

"You are a specter," she said, her mouth curving in a secretive smile.

He let out a raucous laugh. "You must mean a spectacle?" He touched his Polo shirt collar. "I look better in a tux. But I have to wear this. To represent the team—you know—for informal and semi-formal events. I hope you won't hold it against me. I'm really more of a jeans and T-shirt kind of guy anyway." He appraised her a second. "You're not a Carl Edwards fan or something, are you?"

"No, silly." Her giggle was sweet and melodic. "Although he *is* handsome." She flashed another smile. "You do believe in ghosts, don't you?"

"Sometimes—maybe."

"You know you do. You sense and feel them, too."

He cocked his left eyebrow in a quizzical frown.

"Because, if I have to spell it out—you are a ghost, sweetie."

Johnny pinched his arm to demonstrate he was flesh and blood. Then collecting her hand in his, he gently unfolded her fingers and turned her palm, laying it flat against his chest. His heart went off the charts. "Feel that? As you can tell, I am quite human."

"No, you aren't human," she insisted with her eyes steady on his.

"So that makes you a ... what? Oh yeah. I bet I know." He cupped her chin with a thumb and forefinger. "You're an angel come to rescue me from this boring party."

"Well, maybe. But right now I am the messenger."

Johnny couldn't help but smile. "This is a joke, right?"

"No" was her solemn answer. "I'm afraid I'm dead serious."

"Gee, and I thought you liked me." He flashed a charming smile and winked. "Am I an evil ghost?" His lips pursed in a fake pout.

"Does an evil plan make an evil man?"

"It really isn't fair to judge me so harshly. After all, we've just met. Give me a chance and you'll see. I'm really one of the good guys."

Her hand flicked a dismissive wave. "Of course, you're right." A twinkle glittered in her eyes. "To clarify, a specter is not always evil."

"I'd love to believe this specter thing, but ..." *Why are the beauties always whack jobs?* "... you'll have to prove it to me, because I'm more of a skeptic. Get it? Skeptic—specter?" Johnny nudged her arm.

She rolled her eyes. "Remember that day on the backstretch? During the Brickyard? You saw something happen. Remember?" she repeated. Her eyebrow arched with knowing. "Out on the golf course?"

"How do you know about that?" A tingle of fear traced his spine. No one knew.

"I was in on it."

"Seriously, this is a joke—right? Any minute you're going to burst out laughing and tell me you're from some television show. That I've been punked."

"Nope." She winked with a sly smile.

Hours passed like seconds while she captivated him with a fantastic story worthy of Scheherazade. Although it was far-fetched, Johnny succumbed to her charm. She spoke of honor and of duels to the death, of fate versus luck, the two mirrored faces of good and evil. Eventually she revealed a dangerous plan. Johnny played along, nodding in agreement just to keep her with him. Finally, arm in arm, they left the party and walked to the parking lot.

"Tonight," she whispered, kissing him deeply beside his low-slung sports car, "you will meet your match."

"My match? Is this the spirit of—maybe an ill-fated driver?" He thought of Billy Vukovich. Although he wouldn't mind meeting the guy, he wasn't up for a ghostly encounter with bad luck. Tenderly he removed her hand from his arm. "I'm not keen about dredging up ghosts." *Racing, a sport fraught with superstition, was hard enough without capricious spirits hanging around. Plus, it would be a pain to fiddle with good luck charms; do-dads, trinkets and rituals meant to ward them off. There was enough of that going on anyway.*

"OK. It's not a ghost. Do you feel better now?"

"Not really. You're the one who said a race is a duel between danger and Lady Luck," he reminded her. "It's been a crazy night, and your proposal seems very reckless. You wouldn't want me to die doing something stupid. Would you?"

"You crack me up," she said with a playful finger poke. "You court danger every time you get into a race car. You wager with your life—for the thrill of the win."

Johnny couldn't argue that.

"Don't worry. I'm betting on you. Do as I say and you will taste the wine of victory."

"Is there a promise in that?" He nuzzled his face into the graceful curve of her neck.

"I promise." Her arm slipped around his waist.

"I don't know," he wrinkled his nose in disbelief. "I hardly know you, and to tell the truth, your story is pretty wild."

It was the thrill of the chase, he thought, *that kept him at her side. The desire to conquer. No matter what this exquisite woman asked of him, he would probably go the distance. Even if it killed him,* he thought, *he would do her bidding.*

"Come on," she teasingly tugged his sleeve. "You love life on the edge." Her bright eyes sought his. "Or maybe not. Maybe you *are* afraid."

Johnny bristled. In his huff, he missed the hint of something in her eyes. It was the same premonition of doom missed by seamen enraptured by the siren's song. It was the warning that could have saved Sampson's locks from Delilah's snipping shears.

"I'm not afraid of anything." His voice broke gruff. "I'm cautious. I can't go off half-cocked and do something stupid for the fun of it." His ego was bruised. Now, he would have to do it just to show her.

"Don't worry," she patted his shoulder. "You are exempt from pain. Remember?"

His words twisted with sardonic irony. "Oh, right. I forgot. Because I'm a—what was it you called me? I'm a ghost or something?"

"Maybe I misspoke. I shouldn't have said it. You weren't ready to hear it."

His black eyes sought hers. "OK. Then let me ask this question. If you know so much, who sent me that horrid thing in the mail?"

Her eyes darted sideways. "You ask too many questions." She paused a minute. "I'll tell you about that. But not now. Soon."

"Yeah. Sure. OK." Roughly, he plucked up her hand in his. He didn't mean to squeeze so tightly. "When?"

She slipped her fingers free. "Soon."

"Yeah, right."

"Be safe," she said, closing the car door. "Don't forget. I am on your side."

As he drove away, her exotic perfume followed. It hung in the air like smoke billowing from a burning race car.

Near home, he laughed. Nothing had happened. He had been had. Tomorrow he'd fly to his next race, and this would be nothing more than a strange encounter with a mysterious but wacky woman. His turn signal flashed on and off with a clicking sound. His taillights flashed red as he paused at the green light.

The dark car sidled up. It was sleek, black, with darkly tinted glass. The driver's side window slid down in ominous silence. Slowly a gaunt and haggard face turned out of the shadow. Their eyes met. Johnny Avatar tipped his fingers in a short salute of recognition.

"Are you ready to go racing?" the old man asked. In tandem he trounced on the brake and accelerated. Revved his engine. His car bucked against the conflicting message of opposing power. "You don't have the guts," he taunted.

Johnny clenched his jaw; set his mouth. He felt like a robot without a will of his own. "You're kidding? Me? No guts? You haven't got a chance."

"You know it's a race to the end? One winner. One loser."

"I know."

"You know the deal?"

"I know the deal," Johnny answered.

They squared up like illegal street racers; gunned their engines in tandem. The two cars barreled side by side. Together, they plummeted headlong down a steep hill through a tunnel and over a bridge. Silver moonlight streaked across the dark metal. The road twisted right and then left. It wound through a maze of trees and ramped onto a lonely highway.

Johnny led the evil apparition toward the dangerous precipice. The speedometer needle lingered at 120 then passed 130 as they sped toward the edge. Johnny saw it coming. The black sky looked like a field of pin-prick-sized holes in back-lighted paper.

Vigorously Johnny twisted the wheel. The car swerved into a hard, right-angled turn, bounced along the brim. With tires slinging dirt clumps over the edge, Johnny's car bumped safely out of the way as his opponent shot forward, went airborne, and flew through the black, empty air like a shooting star.

Heart thumping wildly, Johnny braked to a stop. In the distance, the fireball glowed. Johnny pinched his arm to see if it was actually made of flesh and bone. For the first time in his life, he felt very much alive.

"Mission accomplished," he said, slapping his hands against each other. "Good riddance."

That night he dreamed of her. *Wearing a white-and-black-checkered silk shirt and black slacks, she lounged on his couch with an amber-colored glass of beer.*

"You won," she told him. "The spell is broken."

"Cursed then un-cursed. There has got to be a price for a favor like that."

"You don't feel you got your money's worth?"

"I thought I'd have to sacrifice my life."

She laughed. "You feel alive—right?"

Johnny Avatar nodded in relief.

"Congratulations. You have finally earned your trophy."

"And that trophy? That would be ...?"

"Mortality, of course," she laughed in her musical, delightful way.

"Is that a good thing?" His tone dripped of irony. Even so, he had to admit it felt great to win.

"OK, see you at the races."

"Wait," he said, "you don't get off that easy."

She huffed in resignation. "What do you mean? You got what you wanted. What now?"

"Answers. The girl. The one that got—you know. You told me you were 'in on it'—then I got that ghastly thing in the mail. The girl? Tell me. What have you done?"

"Oh that?" Her eyes shifted guiltily away.

"Oh that?" Johnny parroted, shocked by her callous tone. "A woman got hacked to death. I think I saw at least part of what happened. That whole incident with the lights and those silhouette people ruined the race for me. It spooked me. I was distracted—lost focus. I crashed the Daylight Steel Chevrolet. I lost faith in my driving ability and disappointed my boss. I'm about to lose my entire career, and you fluff off the fact that a woman was murdered. I've been living a nightmare here. It isn't funny." His voice twisted bitter. "You shrug your shoulders. What kind of evil demon are you, anyway?"

She ignored his anger and smiled. "It started when you caught the shadow of a premonition—felt a warning. It hangs in the air waiting for someone to catch it. Some drivers, like Vuky, fail to heed such things. Some are too heavily invested. Some are just daredevils. Good luck trinkets aside, all barge ahead anyway. That's why Billy Vukovitch told his wife they should just pack up and go home. But he couldn't. Too much hung in the balance. Sometimes not paying heed to a warning results in disaster."

Johnny got the point. His own need for speed was a heady but perilous thing that had, in his life, manifested in many forms. He remembered his recklessly fearless years: skateboards, BMX, go-karts and finally NASCAR. He'd courted danger all his life.

"OK. I get it. I would have ignored the premonition too."

"So you would do anything to win a race? You would pay any price?"

Suddenly a terrible memory jolted through his mind. "But," he gulped back words, "I think I ... Did I?"

She fluttered an unconcerned wave. "Yes, you were spiraling out of control."

Johnny's jaw tightened in anger. "Why didn't someone stop me?"

"The flip side of a dream is a nightmare, isn't it?"

Despite his perplexed look, she giggled. "Gosh, it was cute. The way you made me work so hard to get your attention. I have to say, it sure wasn't easy. You were trying so darned hard. But you were virtually spinning your wheels. I just had to step in and help you out."

Johnny cocked an eyebrow. Then his face furrowed in worry.

She laughed again. "Don't take this too seriously. It's all for sport, isn't it?"

Johnny was appalled. "This isn't a joke. I'm terrified that I've done something unfathomable —something so terrible the city is gripped in terror."

"Fear is such a dynamic emotion. I don't know why people blithely play with it. But it certainly drives you."

"The fans thrive on it," Johnny offered.

"Yes. They might not want you to crash, but they sure don't want to miss the action if you do. A collision or two—a six-car pileup—that makes their day. Who would even buy a ticket to watch cars go round and round in neat rows without some element of danger?

"Besides, Johnny, it's all in fun anyway, isn't it? NASCAR is, when it gets right down to it, fairly safe. Actual fatalities are rare. And if someone does—well you know? His number is elevated to angel status, and he gets to guard all the races. Great seats, don't you think? The best in the house."

"Get back to the girl," he urged with impatience.

"Your nightmares?"

" Are you saying she didn't actually exist? No one really got hurt?"

"Well, there was that one guy. You sent him off a cliff. Remember?"

"Yeah, he looked strangely familiar. I'm positive I've raced with him before. But for the life of me, I can't recall the guy's name."

"Danger."

"Danger? His name was Danger? Johnny cocked his eyebrow.

"Yes, Johnny Danger. He's a reckless fellow. Remember, you tried to sell him your soul in that bar? The guy has no guts. Best you got him out of the way. You'll be a better driver now. You can't go into a motor sport and worry about danger all the time. It will just hold you back. He had to go."

"He was in the bar?"

"He's been around for years—many seasons of racing."

"But I ended his career. Sent him off the cliff."

"Well ... I wouldn't be too sure. He tends to pop back up. Just be careful."

He felt her arms go around him in a protective embrace. Her energy radiated like a safe, warm glow.

"I didn't get your name, did I?" He asked, not wanting her to leave.

"It's Lady Luck," she laughed. "You thought I had forsaken you. As I said before, you are a very silly man. I do have to go now."

"You're going to desert me now, when I've just learned you do exist?"

"Don't worry. I'll ride with you once in a while. However, I must warn you, I am a little fickle. You won't know for sure if I'm there. But have faith. I could be in the seat beside you."

"You can't sit there."

"Why not?"

"There's only one seat," he joked.

"Don't be silly." She blew him a kiss.

RICHARD PETTY
by Brenda Robertson Stewart

Richard Lee Petty, born July 2, 1937, is known as the greatest driver in NASCAR history. His father, Lee Petty, won the first Daytona 500 in 1959. Richard's son, Kyle, is a well-known NASCAR driver, and Richard's grandson, Adam Petty, was killed at the New Hampshire International Speedway on May 12, 2000.

Petty, who has been nicknamed King Richard, won the NASCAR championship seven times. The only other driver to accomplish that was Dale Earnhardt. Petty won a record 200 races during his career and won the Daytona 500 a record seven times. He won 27 races in the 1967 season alone. Ten of the wins were consecutive. He collected a record 127 poles, and in his 1,185 starts, 513 of them were consecutive starts.

Petty began his NASCAR career in 1958, days after his 21st birthday. He was named NASCAR Rookie of the Year in 1959. In 1964, driving a Plymouth with a new Hemi engine, he won his first Daytona 500, leading 184 of the 200 laps. In 1975 Petty won the World 600 for the first time in his career. It was one of 13 wins that led to his sixth Winston Cup. This record was tied by Jeff Gordon in 1998. Petty won his 200th race at the Firecracker 400 at Daytona International Speedway on July 4th, 1984. President Ronald Reagan attended this race and was the first sitting president to attend a NASCAR race. Richard Petty retired after the 1992 season.

In August 1993, Petty was back in a race car at the Indianapolis Motor Speedway. NASCAR was testing tires preparing for the inaugural 1994 Brickyard 400. He drove several laps around the Speedway track and donated his car to the Speedway museum. Throughout his career, Richard Petty would stand for hours signing autographs for all who asked. Despite his massive popularity, he never forgot his fans.

THE RACE IS ON
by Brenda Robertson Stewart

Brenda Robertson Stewart is a forensic artist, figurative artist, painter and author. She is the author of Power in the Blood, *a forensic mystery, and has short stories in* Derby Rotten Scoundrels, Low Down and Derby, *and* Racing Can Be Murder. *She is the co-editor of* Racing Can Be Murder *and* Bedlam at the Brickyard.

Where am I? What's this brown fur? I'm not supposed to have fur; I'm a human being. Uh-oh. This shape-shifting stuff has to be brought under control. Rabbits can't drive race cars. There are no advantages to being a rabbit. Well, actually, there are a few, but I can't talk about them in mixed company. When I get my body back, my mama would wash my mouth out with soap.

Gravel. I'm sitting on gravel. There's no gravel on the Brickyard. What's wrong with my eyes? Oh, I get it. They're not tracking like a human's. But I can still see that hound dog coming this way. Loose from his owner, that's what he is. Who's that little old lady chasing that spotted hound? She should have a lapdog. I can almost feel that dog's breath on my neck. Where to hide? Now I know where I am. I'm in the parking lot across from the race track. That's 16th Street out there. How am I ever going to cross in all that traffic without becoming a pancake? I guess that's better than being ground up by canine teeth.

Wish I could thank that woman for slowing down. That old lady has caught the spotted menace, and I'm not road kill. Whoopee!

Now, have to get into the track. Wonder what everyone's saying about me. "I always knew he was a slippery cuss," or "Where the heck is my driver? He couldn't have just vanished into thin air." Got to slip in the gate.

"Hey, rabbits aren't allowed in NASCAR practice. Git.I said, git."

Good thing that gate guard couldn't run fast.

By slipping around spectators, I worked my way over to pit row. I could see my Number 13 car on the track. It wasn't dented up too bad. Good. Now to work my way to a likely spot in the garage and hope I can change back into a human. Oh, no. I forgot. When I come out of one of these spells, I'm buck naked. Got to find some clothes. Fortunately, someone left the garage door ajar. I hopped in and tried to open my locker. It's hard to open a door when you're a rabbit. I repeatedly threw myself against the locker door, hoping it would open. After the 15th hurling, I stopped to rest and assess the situation. How could I explain what happened to my clothes? I could pretend that a head injury made me behave erratically and I peeled off my clothes. I flung my body at the locker door with all my might. It snapped open. I scrounged up some clothes off the floor of the locker. Whew. That was tough. Good thing rabbits are strong. My racing clothes must still be in the Number 13 car. My crew chief and owners are going to kill me. All the money that's been put into that car this season has been for naught. I tapped one of my front feet, trying to come up with a plan.

"Hey, there's a rabbit in the garage," I heard Rich Wayne shout. "He shouldn't be here. How the heck did a rabbit get in here with all the activity around the track? I hope he's not sick or something. Do rabbits get rabies?"

"Forget about the rabbit. How come this door wasn't locked? I smell a rat somewhere. How did our driver get away? The wreck's on film. The front fender hit the wall and the car started spinning. When it came to rest, there was no Ken Lapin. And why are these clothes on the floor? I guess we'd better concentrate on getting the car back here to see if it can be put back together for the race. I told Jim Bruner he shouldn't put a

Number 13 car in the race. It's bad luck. And who ever heard of a driver named Ken Lapin? It's all crazy." He threw up his hands.

It's OK, Stretch. Ken has to be out there somewhere. Race car drivers don't disappear into thin air. He's evidently wandered off somewhere—probably in a daze, maybe got a concussion. We'll find him. Let's get the car first. Smitty is fit to be tied."

"He's the one who wanted to be crew chief. Let him make the decisions. Where'd that rabbit go?"

"Forget the darned rabbit. Come on before both our rears get fired."

The crew finally left without picking up the clothes. Now if I can figure out how to get human again. Joe said to concentrate on what you want to be. I kept repeating "human," in my rabbit-sized brain. When I drank that stuff he gave me, he never said I could change species without rhyme or reason. It tasted awful, too. Suddenly I felt my limbs stretching. There was pain, but it was bearable. In no time, I was sitting on that ice-cold garage floor. This must be what it feels like to go out naked on the North Pole. My body began to shake like a blender on steroids. My teeth were chattering so much I bit my tongue, and I could taste the salty blood in my mouth. Just as I tied the second shoestring, I heard the tow truck outside the door.

Smitty Doyle, my crew chief, walked into the garage ahead of the truck. When he saw me, he shouted, "Ken, where the devil did you go? We've been looking everywhere for you. You're bleeding!"

I staggered around like a drunk trying to walk a straight line. I began to sweat profusely, and moisture began to drip off my brow.

"Whoa there, little buddy. You've got to go to medical to be checked out. Stretch, get the golf cart. I'm taking him over to have the doc look at him. Something's not right here."

I staggered onto the cart with Stretch's help, and Smitty whisked me over to the med building.

Smitty explained that I needed to be checked out. He told the whole story about my disappearance, bleeding out of the mouth, staggering like a drunk. The doctor said he was going to send me down to Methodist Hospital for an MRI. He couldn't find anything wrong with me, but he needed to rule out a head injury. My crew chief said he'd ride along, but I told him he needed to check out my race car to see what went wrong.

The medical staff loaded me into an ambulance and took off up 16th Street toward the hospital. I worried the entire time that I'd change back into a rabbit or some other creature. I knew I shouldn't have listened to my friend Joe and drunk that nasty-tasting stuff.

Race car drivers are treated well at the hospital. The staff knows we need to get checked out, and if nothing is amiss, our aim is to head straight back to the track. After joking with the staff about them likely finding my head empty, they wheeled me in for the MRI. It wasn't so bad. I kept focusing on the word "human" while I was in that tube. I didn't want to freak out the technician.

After the radiologist declared me fit to race, I called my garage at the track. Smitty answered and said he'd come to the hospital and give me a ride back to the garage. While I was waiting, I called my friend Joe and told him about my "haring" around. He laughed, but I was not too amused. I could have been killed getting back to the track.

"What were you thinking about when you shifted?" he asked.

"I wasn't thinking anything. I was getting dizzy from the 360s I was doing. I could hear Smitty on the radio calling out, "Lapin, hang on."

"Ah. You must have unconsciously focused on your name. You know 'lapin' means 'rabbit' in French. Don't you remember the French teacher teasing you about your name in high school?"

"Well, I've got to figure out how to control this shape-shifting or find an antidote to reverse it."

234

"That old witch who sold me that mix didn't say nothing about being able to reverse the spell. I turned into a red-tailed hawk and flew all over the hills. It was beautiful. I never felt so free."

"Wait until somebody shoots your rear for trying to catch songbirds and you may not be so glib about it. When did you change back?"

"I left my clothes under that old apple tree in the back yard. I came back, told my body to change into human form, and shazam, I was sitting on my pile of clothes. It was a wonderful experience."

"You must be better at this than me. I'll keep trying. I don't have any choice, do I?"

By the time I got off the phone, I saw Smitty parked at the curb waiting for me. "I'm good to go, according to the doctors. Did you find out what happened to my car?"

"It was sabotaged, I think, but I can't prove it. I read the boys the riot act for leaving the garage unlocked, but they swear they didn't. A good part was replaced with a defective one. I guess I'll bed down in the garage to guard the car from now on. We'll be working on the car all night tonight anyway to try to get it race ready. The back-up car isn't as fast. No one's going to try anything now. Who do you think might have done it?"

"I'd bet on those Meadows boys working for Nate King. They spend about as much time in our garage as in their own."

"I'd like to catch them doing their dirty work. They'd never work for another NASCAR team."

"We need to be more careful for sure. Those boys don't like me much anyway. Keep saying my dad bought my way into the team. He may be a sponsor, but I earned my own way."

"Yes, you did. You've worked hard to become a driver. Ignore those lowlife's."

"It's hard to ignore someone who tried to get you killed," I sputtered.

"Yeah, I know it's been a rough day. You need to get a good night's sleep. I'll take care of the car. I don't think they meant to kill you, only to put the car out of commission."

When we got back to the garage, I saw that the car repair was in full swing. I needed to find my racing suit and helmet. I could see them on the floorboard. The crew had been so busy working on the repairs that they hadn't seen them yet. They'd surely take a supper break and I'd offer to watch the car.

"Why don't you all go eat and I'll babysit the car while you're gone?" I suggested.

"I think we'd better go in shifts," Smitty said.

The crew all started to complain that they hadn't eaten since an early breakfast. Smitty threw up his hands in defeat. "OK, we'll go over to the motor home and grab some grub. The cook's probably keeping something hot for us. Shouldn't take more than 20 minutes or so. You sure you'll be OK, Ken?"

"Yeah," I said. "I'll get my gear ready for tomorrow."

As soon as they were out of sight, I grabbed my gear and stowed it in the locker. I'd sure like to know what the Meadows boys were up to. Their garage was two down from ours. I couldn't leave to check them out. I went into the bathroom and closed the door. When I started to come out, I heard voices. The crew couldn't have any more than gotten to the motor home, so it wouldn't be them. I heard one of the Meadows boys say, "It sure worked today. Look at that. Most of the damage is cosmetic. They probably won't notice if we make a few adjustments to the engine."

I knew that voice. It was Raymond Meadows. About that time, I heard Robert, his brother, say, "Even if they do, they won't know who did it." They both chuckled.

I felt my body changing. Fur again. I shook my body, ran out the door, and began to snarl at the intruders.

"What's that? Don't tell me they put a dog in here."

"No, Ray, it's not a dog. It's a huge wolf, and he looks hungry to me. Let's get out of here."

The men ran for their lives with me right behind them, snapping at their heels. They slammed their garage door down as fast as they could. I stood there snarling. Apparently they weren't bright enough to figure out I could have already had them for supper if I desired.

I went back to our garage and into the bathroom. I prayed I could become human before the crew returned. I stood on my clothes and waited. Nothing happened. I was still a wolf. I could hear the sound of the golf cart engine bringing my crew back to the garage. I managed to close the door.

"Where the heck did Ken go this time? He promised to guard the car and he isn't even here," Smitty said.

"Maybe he's in the bathroom," Rich said. "I'll check."

I could feel myself shifting. Human again, I reached over and turned the lock on the door. Whew. That was a close one.

Rich banged on the door. "You in there, Ken?"

"Yeah, I'm here. Be out in a minute."

I hurried into my clothes and walked out into the garage. "Sorry. I needed to use the john."

"We're a bit paranoid, Ken," Smitty said. "Why don't you go eat and turn in? You need your sleep for the big race."

The air felt electric when I arrived at the track for the big race. My body was tingling with anticipation even though I was starting in last place. My hands shook as I put on my racing gear. When I climbed into the Number 13 car at last, I had meditated myself into being calm and cool. I could feel the car straining to go as we waited for the green flag. Finally, we went green and I put the pedal to the metal and started passing cars. I left John Andretti and Michael Waltrip in the dust and set my sights on Tony Stewart, but it took me several laps to get around him. My heart was thumping as I swung around Dale Earnhardt, Jr. Thirty laps to go, and I was in the top 10. Smitty was on the radio telling me to take it easy. He didn't want a repeat of the practice accident. The crew had been really quick during the pit stops, and I was confident I had enough fuel to finish the race. Goodbye, Carl Edwards.

So long, Jimmie Johnson. I could see the checkered flag up ahead. Only one car in front of me. I decided to take Jeff Gordon on the outside. I had the power to win this race. I flew around Gordon and was almost to the finish line. The crowd was on its feet, and they were screaming for me.

"Wake up, Kenny. Wake up or we'll be late getting to the Brickyard." I could feel her gently shake me. "Come on, Kenny. Get your 14-year-old behind out of bed and head for the shower. Breakfast is almost ready."

"Aw, Mom, can't I sleep a couple more minutes?"

"You must have been having a great dream."

"Yeah, I was having a great dream."

ALLSTATE 400 AT THE BRICKYARD RECORDS & MILESTONES

Compiled by Andrea Smith

Most Wins

Jeff Gordon – 1994, 1998, 2001, 2004

Most Pole Positions

Jeff Gordon – 1995, 1996, 1999

Fastest Winning Time

Bobby Labonte – 2 hours, 33 minutes, 56 seconds (2000)

Slowest Winning Time

Jeff Gordon – 3 hours, 29 minutes, 56 seconds (2004)

Youngest Winner

Jeff Gordon – 23 years old (1994)

Oldest Winner

Bill Elliot – 46 years old (2002)

Youngest Pole Winner

Reed Sorensen – 21 years old (2007)

Oldest Pole Winner

Jimmy Spencer – 44 years old (2001)

Highest Career Prize Winnings

Jeff Gordon – $5.7 million

Most Career Starts (as of 2008)

15 – Jeff Burton, Jeff Gordon, Bobby Labonte, Mark Martin

Qualifying Record

Casey Mears – 186.293 mph, 48.311 seconds (2004)

Most Caution Flag Periods

13 (2004)

Most Caution Flag Laps

52 (2008)

Most Cars Running at Finish

41 of 43 starters (2008)

Fewest Cars Running at Finish

27 of 43 starters (2004)

First Driver to Win From Pole Position

Kevin Harvick (2003)

Most Lead Changes, Single Race

26 (2008)

Fewest Lead Changes in the Race

9 (2000, 2004)

Closest Margin of Victory

0.183 seconds (1997)

Largest Margin of Victory

4.229 seconds (2000)

First Driver to Host Saturday Night Live

Jeff Gordon (2003)